# SHIELD-MAIDEN: UNDER THE BLOOD MOON

## THE ROAD TO VALHALLA, BOOK 4

### MELANIE KARSAK

CLOCKPUNK PRESS

THE ROAD TO VALHALLA

# SHIELD MAIDEN
## Under The Blood Moon

# MELANIE KARSAK

*For all the moms out there…*

# GLOSSARY

## PLACES

*Bolmsö*, ruled by Jarl Hervor
*Dalr*, ruled by Jarl Leif
*Götaland*, ruled by King Gizer
*Grund*, ruled by King Gudmund
*Halmstad*, ruled by Jarl Ragal
*Hárclett*, ruled Jarl Eric
*Hreinnby*, ruled by Jarl Mjord, the Reindeer King
*Jutland*, ruled by King Harald
*Silfrheim*, ruled by Jarl Egil
*Uppsala*, ruled by King Hugleik

## HEROES OF BOLMSÖ

*Hervor*, jarl of Bolmsö
*Hofund*, prince of Grund and husband of Hervor
*Blomma*, adopted daughter of Hervor and Hofund

*Rök,* Hervor's wolf companion

*Arne* and *Ingrid,* gothar of Bolmsö

*Wodan,* ferryman of Lake Bolmen

*Svensson,* farmer near Lake Bolmen

*Skarde, Trygve Two-Hammer,* and *Einar,* elder warriors of Bolmsö

*Kára, Kit, Trygve One-Hammer, Sigrun,* and *Öd,* younger warriors of Bolmsö

*Hábrók,* Sigrun's hawk

*Asa,* servant in Bolmsö

## SONS OF ARNGRIM

*Angantyr, Hjorvard, Hervard, Seaming, Rani, Brami, Barri, Reifnir, Tind, Bui,* and the *twins, Hadding*

## HEROES OF DALR

*Yrsa,* shield-maiden of Dalr

*Leif,* jarl of Dalr

*Eydis,* völva and wife of Jarl Leif

*Eylin and Arngrimir,* children of Leif and Eydis

*Hakon and Halger,* brothers of Jarl Leif

*Frode,* housecarl of Dalr

*Eyvinder,* skald of Dalr

*Freja,* gythia of Dalr

*Birger and Ivar,* warriors from Dalr

*Oda, Hillie, Siggy,* servants in Dalr

## HEROES OF GRUND

*King Gudmund,* king of Grund, father of Hofund
*Queen Thyra,* deceased wife of King Gudmund and mother of Hofund
*Bjorn,* skald of Grund
*Frika,* sister of King Gudmund
*Rolf,* husband of Frika
*Soren, Thorolf,* sons of Frika and Rolf
*Turid* and *Toke,* mother and father of Revna
*Revna,* lady of Grund
*Norna,* junior gythia
*Ardis,* elder gythia
*Heidrek,* Hofund's great-grandfather
*Magna, Bodil,* servants in Grund
*Halvar,* housecarl in Grund

## HEROES OF HALMSTAD

*Ragal,* jarl of Halmstad
*Hella,* shield-maiden and wife of Ragal
*Ingvar,* son of Hella
*Lyngheid,* merchant in Halmstad market
*Solveig,* elder gythia of Halmstad
*Astrid,* younger gythia in Halmstad

## HEROES OF HÁRCLETT
*Eric,* jarl of Hárclett
*Bryn,* wife of Jarl Eric and daughter of Jarl Mjord
*Svanhild,* daughter of Eric
*Veigr,* housecarl of Eric

## HEROES OF HREINNBY
*Jarl Mjord*, jarl of Hreinnby

## HEROES OF SILFRHEIM
*Egil*, jarl of Silfrheim
*Asta*, wife of Egil
*Helga*, widow of Eilif
*Thyri*, eldest daughter of Helga and Eilif

## Heroes of Uppsala
*King Hugleik*, king of Uppsala
*Prince Jorund* and *Prince Eric*, sons of King Yngvi, former king of Uppsala
*Orvar-Odd*, warrior of Uppsala

## THE SEA KINGS
*Haki* and *Hagbard*

## MYTHOLOGICAL CHARACTERS AND GODS
*King Sigrlami*, the original owner of the sword Tyrfing
*Dvalin and Dulin*, dwarves who created Tyrfing
*Æsir and Vanir*, two tribes or factions of the Norse gods
*Odin (Grímnir, All-Father)*, father of the Norse gods
*Loki (Loptr)*, Norse god, adopted son of Odin, a trickster
*Balder*, Norse god associated with beauty and the sun
*Thor*, Norse god of thunder, wields the hammer Mjölnir
*Bragi*, Norse god associated with skalds and poetry
*Frigga*, Norse goddess, wife of Odin
*Sif*, Norse goddess, wife of Thor, known for her beautiful hair

*Heimdall*, Norse god of vigilance who guards the gates of Asgard

*Freyr*, Vanir god associated with sex and fertility

*Freyja*, Vanir goddess associated with love and fertility, known for her affinity for cats

*Hel*, daughter of Loki and goddess of the Hel

*Skadi*, jotun from the forest married to Njord

*Njord*, Norse god of the sea

*Huginn* and *Muninn*, Odin's ravens

*Geri* and *Freki*, Odin's wolves

*Vætt*, also referred to as a wight, a nature spirit. Can be associated with certain area of land (such as a farm), body of water, etc.

*Nøkk*, male water spirit who draws people to him by playing the violin

*Jotun*, term for giant. Not literally giants, but more likely a metaphor for strong, otherworldly supernatural creatures

*Fenrir*, wolf son of Loki

### TERMS

*Bifrost*, a rainbow bridge that connects the worlds

*Blót*, a ceremony with sacrifice, a rite

*Dísablót*, a ceremony held in honor of the dísir

*Dísarsalr*, temple of the dísir

*dísir*, female goddesses, spirits, and ancestors

*Disting*, an annual market

*Gothar*, plural

*Gothi*, male priest

*Gythia*, female priestess

*Hnefatafl*, a board game similar to chess

*Hof*, another name for a temple

*Jarl*, equivalent to earl

*Skald*, equivalent to a bard or poet

*Seidr*, a form of Norse shamanism / magic

*The Thing*, a meeting of kings and jarls and to decree law

*Úlfhéðnar*, another word for berserkers, dressed in the pelts of wolves. Possibly shape-shifting skin warriors.

*Völva*, a seeress with magical abilities

The dream was the same.

I wove through the narrow streets of Hreinnby, making my way to the Bone Tree. My heart beat so loudly that it rang in my ears. I could hear fighting in the distance; it filled me with urgency. Panic and dread washing over me, I hurried to get to the others. Overhead, the sky rumbled. Clouds rolled over the moon, casting an odd, reddish glow on the glowing orb and the world around me.

Behind me, someone started singing.

I turned to find Yrsa there. She was singing an old tavern song about a warrior and his love who died before they could wed. While the tale was filled with bawdy jokes and funny lines, including an episode where the man disguised himself as one of the woman's bond-maidens to sneak into her chamber, I'd always found the song depressing. The pair had spent their whole lives trying to be together only to be killed the night before their wedding.

"That's a jolly medley," I said with a grin. "And when did you start singing?"

"What?" Yrsa replied. "It's better than your song."

"My song?"

Yrsa opened her mouth, letting out a long, loud howl. Her head tilted back weirdly, her eyes wide and black, her mouth hanging unnaturally agape. The sound was inhuman. A shiver slipped down my spine.

Overhead, the sky cracked with lightning. I looked up, watching the clouds roll quickly across the blood-soaked moon.

"Yrsa," I whispered, looking back at her.

But Yrsa was gone.

In fact, everything was gone.

Hreinnby had burned to the ground. There was nothing. The great hall. The houses. Everything had burned. Nothing was left... except the Bone Tree.

On the hill, it stood in full bloom. Scarlet-colored blossoms covered the black limbs. I walked through the ash toward the tree. Red-tipped embers blew through the air. The red moon overhead painted everything in a crimson hue. As I stepped, branches snapped below my feet. Then I realized, they were not branches. The powder had covered the earth on which were piles of bones. I came to stand before the tree, watching blood drip from the flowers onto the earth.

Sitting on the branches, Muninn and Huginn called to me, their caws angry.

My heart pounded in my chest.

And then, I felt the presence of someone else behind me.

Expecting to find Yrsa, I turned to see the All-Father standing there.

*"Hervor.*

*"Daughter.*

*"Born of magic and blood, I shall see my will done through you."*

I opened my mouth to ask him what he meant but tasted blood on my lips. Gently touching my fingertips to my mouth, I pulled them away to find them stained red.

"All-Father," I said, turning back to him.

But he, too, was gone.

In his place, I found a woman with long, black hair. She had shining silver eyes—just like I had seen in Blomma, Solva, and Loki. She wore a fur-trimmed hat and a long robe made of a patchwork of skins. On her feet, she wore snowshoes.

"Hervor," she whispered. "They lie to you." She took another step toward me, setting her hands on my shoulders. Her silver eyes flashed brilliantly, but there was a look of desperation on her face. "They are all liars! As they lied to me, they will lie to you. Trust none of them. Trust only the woods and the trees. Hervor, daughter of wolves, believe me. Trust none of them," she said, giving me a hard shake. "Trust none of them," she screamed.

# CHAPTER 1

I woke with a gasp. It took me a moment to acclimate myself to the waking world. My chamber was dark. It was the dim, grey hour before the sun rose. Tasting blood, I sat up and touched my lips and face. I'd gotten a nosebleed, the blood running into my mouth. I wiped my mouth with my sleeve.

On one side of me, Hofund slept soundly. On the other, Rök whined in his sleep, his feet working busily as he dreamed. The pair of them had me pinned in the bed.

Rök whimpered.

"It's all right," I whispered, gently patting Rök's head. "It's just a dream."

Wind whipped across the roof of the hall of Bolmsö. Since our wedding, the winter had blown in with ferocity. The elders said they had not seen such a storm in a generation. Everyone was sheltering inside beside their fires. And the cold winter weather kept Eydis stuck here.

I sighed. Rök wasn't the only one reeling from a

dream. While my own travels left me shaken, the blood leaking from my nose was real. I slipped out of bed, wiggling free from my position wedged between Hofund and Rök.

Rök sighed then rolled onto the warm spot I had just vacated. I held back a giggle at the idea of Hofund finding Rök rather than me cozied up next to him. I went to a basin and washed my face, pressing a cloth to my nose. No doubt, the dry air had gotten to me.

I tried to push the dream aside, but it nagged at me. I didn't know the woman in my dream. She said they were all liars. Who? The All-Father? But that was not possible. Odin had always guided me, been there for me. Loki… Well, I knew enough not to trust him. Loki maneuvered us all for his own reasons. So far, those had aligned with mine. But that might not always be the case. The strange woman had warned me, but of what? And then there was Yrsa. Her howl still lingered in my ears. The dream filled me with a sense of dread. No matter how I tried to tamp down the feeling, I couldn't make the foreboding go away.

I slipped on a heavy robe. Shivering, I quietly tiptoed out of the room and went to Blomma and Yrsa's room next door.

Yrsa lay sleeping, her mouth open wide, emitting the occasional snore. Stepping silently, I went to her and pulled up her coverlets. Yrsa sighed in her sleep then rolled over, pulling the blanket with her.

I stood there a moment, eyeing her. My foster mother. All I had become was thanks to Yrsa. I adjusted her blanket, tucking her in, then left her to check on Blomma. I sat down beside the child.

When I'd taken Blomma from the field at Blomfjall, I didn't know what to expect. But somehow, this small girl had worked her way into my heart—and, I think, she'd let me into hers. Since my return from Dalr, any remaining ice between us had thawed. She'd come to accept Hofund and me as her adoptive parents. On the small table beside her bed, Blomma had lined up the herd of reindeer Hofund had carved for her—along with the wooden blossom. Hofund and Blomma were both pragmatic, contemplative creatures. And then, there was that spark of magic inside each of them. Hofund spoke only a little of his gift of foresight. At times, I saw it at work in him. But in Blomma, I saw something else. The flash in her eyes reminded me of what I guessed to be true: the girl had special parentage. One day, she would find a good use for her gifts. She would be no shield-maiden, but perhaps a greater destiny waited for her.

I pushed a stray strand of hair behind her ear, then leaned in and kissed her forehead.

She stirred in her sleep, her eyes opening a crack.

"Hervor?" she whispered.

"I'm sorry. I just came to cover you. Go back to sleep. It is early."

"All right," she said, then rolled over.

I adjusted her blankets then left her.

Heading down the hall, I stopped in Eydis's room. She was flung across her bed, taking up the whole space. In a bassinet beside the bed, the twins slept, cuddling close to one another. The room was chilly. I went to the fire, banking it up. Once the flames were burning high once more, I checked on Eylin and Arngrimir.

"Wake them, and I'll kill you," Eydis grumbled sleepily.

I laughed lightly then slipped into the bed beside Eydis.

Reluctantly, she moved aside for me.

"Your feet are cold," she whispered.

"And you complain too much. I just got done banking up your fire...you're welcome."

"Yes, yes," she said sleepily. After a moment, she asked, "Dream?"

"Yes," I said, snuggling close to her. "I saw...well, I don't know what I saw. Danger."

"For who?"

"I don't know."

"Well, we'll all die one day. We're all in danger if you really think about it."

"Eydis—"

Arngrimir sighed in his sleep.

"Be quiet, Hervor. I swear by Frigga, Freyja, and Njord, if they wake..." Eydis began but drifted off to sleep before she could threaten me more.

"I love you too, Eydis," I said, then closed my eyes. I sighed deeply, drifting back into a dreamless sleep.

## CHAPTER 2

The winter storm dragged on for weeks. As much as I pitied Eydis, I was glad to keep Hofund with me. We had spent so little time together before this, I was happy to have him at my side. Late one night, we all gathered in the hall by the fire. Svafa and Yrsa held the little ones while Blomma and Hofund were huddled over a hnefatafl board. Asa had dug out the board at Hofund's request. For the past several days, the pair had been playing late into the night. Blomma had never seen the game before, let alone played it, but she was learning quickly.

Her face scrunched up in deep concentration, Blomma set her fingertips on the top of one of the pieces.

"Hmm," Hofund mused lightly, then sat back.

Blomma paused. "What is it?"

"Look again," he told her.

She studied the board once more. Seeing that her

intended move would lead her into danger, she shifted another piece instead.

Hofund nodded. "Very good," he told her, then took one of her pieces.

"If it was very good, why am I still losing?" she asked.

"You are losing better and more slowly," Hofund replied with a grin.

Blomma smiled at him. "Who taught you to play so well?"

"My father. He is very good at this game. It is a favorite of his."

"On the board or off?" I asked.

"Both," Hofund replied with a laugh.

Blomma looked over the board and shifted another piece, taking one of Hofund's tokens.

He nodded, smiling proudly at her, then made his own move.

Svafa, who was holding Eylin, made faces at the little baby, coaxing a sweet smile from the child. Yrsa had been pacing the room with Arngrimir, showing him every shield on the wall.

"Do you play, Hervor?" Blomma asked me.

I nodded. "Not as often nor as well as I should."

"Who taught you?" Blomma asked me.

"Eyvinder, the skald of Dalr."

"You don't have a skald in Bolmsö."

"No. We have Eydis. Her stories are wild enough."

Eydis, who had been mending one of Arngrimir's little garments, laughed lightly. "Ah, but all my stories are true."

"All of them?" I asked with a grin.

"Of course! When have I ever lied to Hervor?"

"Lied? Hmm. Riddled is another matter entirely."

"We had a skald in Blomfjall," Blomma said as she studied the board. "He had terrific stories. He was well-loved until he told a tale Solva did not like."

"And then?" Eydis asked.

"And then, Solva took his head. It was a pity. He wove great tales about dragons, giants, elves, and dwarves. He knew every old song."

"Well, I'm glad I never told any of my stories in Blomf-jall," Eydis said.

At that, Blomma laughed lightly. "There is no Blomfjall anymore. Now *it* is a story."

I felt a pang of guilt at her words. "It can be rebuilt one day."

"Yes," Blomma said absently, then grinned at Hofund. "I like stories. They can be very distracting." She lifted her game piece and moved it, taking another of Hofund's tokens. "I have you now."

He laughed. Sitting back, he crossed his arms on his chest and stared at Blomma, a bemused expression on his face. "Did you get Hervor talking on purpose to distract me?"

"Maybe," she said with a little grin.

"Well, if you did, it worked. You've won. Well done."

Blomma rose. "Thank you for playing with me."

"Another round?" he asked.

Blomma shook her head. "Not tonight. I want to go to bed victorious."

He laughed. "Very well."

She stepped toward Hofund, setting a quick kiss on his cheek, then came to me. "Good night," she told me, giving me a light hug, then headed to the back.

Svafa smiled after her. "You've done well with her. She's a very bright girl, wise for her age."

"That happens when people see too much too soon," Yrsa said.

Svafa nodded. "Yes," she said, then smiled at Eylin once more. "And what about you, little one? Will you be wise, or will you be joking and jovial like your parents?"

"Are you saying I'm not wise?" Eydis protested.

Svafa grinned at her. "I would never suggest such a thing."

"She will be gentle but brave," Hofund said, his voice taking on an odd, hollow tone.

We all turned and looked at him. He was absently stroking his short beard, but his gaze was far away.

"Hofund?" Eydis asked.

Hofund shook his head. "Sorry. What?"

Eydis's gaze narrowed as she studied Hofund's face.

"See how it feels," I told Eydis with a laugh.

She rolled her eyes at me.

"Your mother got a taste of her own medicine. Serves her right," Yrsa told Arngrimir, making us all smile.

I met Hofund's gaze. He tilted his head to the side then shrugged.

"Well, Prince Hofund, if you could predict when the freeze will end, that is something I'd love to hear," Eydis told him.

"By spring," he replied with a wink.

"Very helpful," Eydis retorted.

I didn't blame Eydis's impatience. I was also anxious to know how Leif was faring. Dalr was in good hands, but the sea kings were still out there. And then there was Leif's wound. Had he recovered the use of his eye?

"Who knows, by the time you return to Dalr, perhaps Leif's new brother or sister will be born," Svafa said with a smirk.

Yrsa huffed a laugh.

"Will you go and see Asta's child?" Eydis asked Svafa.

"No. I am happy here. And I am content to let Asta live her life."

"I'll be content if she keeps her very large nose out of my business," Eydis said.

Svafa laughed. "My poor girl, you will marry her golden child. I'm afraid you will have to find a way to manage your mother-in-law."

"Give her a cat," Yrsa suggested. "That should shut her up."

"I've already given her two grandchildren."

"Probably would have been better off with a cat," Yrsa remarked with a grin.

Eydis laughed.

"It's not a bad idea," I told her.

"I'll keep it in mind," Eydis replied with a wink but held my gaze. Eydis and I had been together almost all our lives. I barely remembered a time before Eydis had been part of my world. Now, everything was changing. Soon, Eydis would be gone. Our paths would take us in different directions. But something told me, no matter how far apart we might be, our lives were forever entwined. All of us. Even Asta and her cats.

**CHAPTER 3**

I t was nearing the Dísablót when the weather finally cleared. Eydis was excited to leave for Dalr. I couldn't blame her. She loved Leif and was ready to start a life with him. As much as she enjoyed our company, she must have felt like her real life was waiting for her. I knew how painful the anticipation could be.

It took us a few days to prepare, but finally, we were ready to leave Bolmsö. I waited with Hofund and Blomma on the shore of Lake Bolmen while Wodan brought the last of our party over from the island.

"My father will be pleased if we arrive in Grund for the Dísablót and Disting market," Hofund told me. "There is a great temple in Grund for the dísir. My mother was an attendant there."

"She was a gythia?" I asked.

"Not quite. Many young women from Grund serve in the Dísarsalr, the hof of the dísir. It is a place for maidens. I suspect my mother would have stayed and become a gythia, but her family would not let her give her life to the gods. They preferred she give it to my father."

I raised an eyebrow. "But if the dísir called her, how could they be denied?"

"The elder gythia warned my grandparents that if they forced my mother to wed my father, the dísir would take revenge. And they did. But not on my mother or father. My grandparents were found dead the morning after my parents' wedding. The dísir had their vengeance."

"Then, your parents did not wed for love?"

Hofund smiled lightly. "They loved one another, that is certain, but my father was willing to give Mother up if that was what the gods wanted. He knew better than to deny the dísir. His willingness won him favor. And my mother... Even as queen, she still attended the temple. In fact, I was born there."

"It must be a truly remarkable place. I'll be happy to see it."

"I'll be happy to show you."

"Can any maiden serve at the Dísarsalr?" Blomma asked, looking up at Hofund.

He touched her chin. "Yes. Any maiden. If the dísir call them."

She smiled at him.

Eydis joined us as we waited for the last of our group to disembark the ferry. "I was beginning to think you were keeping me in Bolmsö on purpose."

"Can I control the weather now? I didn't have time to learn seidr from Jarl Mjord," I replied.

Eydis laughed.

The last party came to shore. Once more, the young warriors from Bolmsö had joined us. There was a gleam of excitement on their faces. The trip to Grund was something special. From what I could tell, most people from Bolmsö stayed on the island. The young warriors had my father's and uncles' adventurous spirits. To my surprise, after all my years yearning to leave Dalr, I was less enthusiastic about leaving Bolmsö.

I looked back toward the island. The community members had gathered to wave goodbye. Svafa's gold hair stuck out on the snowy backdrop.

I turned to Yrsa, whose eyes were on Mother. The two of them had taken a long walk along the lakeshore that morning. I could see Yrsa was torn. She didn't want to leave Svafa, but she would never be at peace until she had her vengeance on Haki.

Yrsa lifted her hand to wave goodbye to Svafa.

Across the lake, Mother returned the gesture.

Yrsa sighed heavily, then mounted her horse.

"Still don't know about taking Rök on a ship," Eydis quipped.

I glanced at the wolf, who was sniffing the snow. He pounced on a snowbank. A vole ran off, Rök chasing after it.

"I don't know how long I'll be in Grund. Seems wrong for him to miss all the fun."

"Oh, but you're fine dropping me off in Dalr like a load of cargo."

"Want to leave the children with Leif and come along?

We'll probably go raiding."

Eydis wrinkled up her nose. "Too cold."

"Princess."

She rolled her eyes at me.

"Are they arguing?" Hofund asked Yrsa, gesturing to Eydis and me.

"Don't know. Trained myself to ignore them when they prattle on like that."

"Prattle? Who is prattling?" Eydis protested.

"You see, such nice weather today," Yrsa said, looking around at the natural landscape, an expression of mock wonder on her face.

Hofund laughed. "I see very well," he told Yrsa, then turned to me. "Well, my wife, are you ready?"

I nodded.

Hofund, Eydis, and I mounted. Hofund motioned to the others, and we rode out. Sigrun loosened Hábrók. With a sharp cry, the bird lifted off into the sky and flew in the direction of Halmstad. The time for rest was over. With spring on her way, the work of war was about to begin again.

WE ARRIVED IN HALMSTAD LATER THAT DAY. RAGAL AND Hella met us, journeying with us to the dock. There, preparations were already underway. We'd sent a messenger the day before with the news that we would be leaving.

"Your ships are supplied and ready to go," Ragal told

Hofund. He turned to Eydis. "Now, let me have one last look at those little ones before you're off."

"You know," Eydis said, "since they were born, it seems everyone has forgotten to pay attention to me."

Ragal chuckled. "The wife of Hervarth served Bolmsö admirably. You will be much missed, Eydis."

At that, Eydis smiled.

Ragal took Arngrimir from her. "Come here, boy. Now, let me look at you. We expect you to live up to that name."

Arngrimir, whose dark eyes were sparkling, laughed in reply, and reached out to pull Ragal's beard.

Ragal laughed then kissed the child's hand. "That a boy," he said, then handed Arngrimir back.

Siggy, who had chosen to come with Eydis to Dalr to help her attend the children, moved closer to Ragal. Eylin lay sleeping in her arms.

"Pretty thing," Ragal said, gently touching the child's brow. "I wish you well, little one."

"We're sorry to see you go," Hella told Eydis. "But a new future waits for you. I wish you all the best."

Eydis gave the shield-maiden a hug. "Thank you, Hella."

"Has there been any news of Haki and Hagbard?" Hofund asked Ragal.

Ragal shook his head. "Not that we've heard."

Hofund frowned. "Then they've found somewhere to hide."

Ragal nodded. "We'll send word if we learn anything," he said, then turned to me. Looking over my shoulder, he spotted my warriors from Bolmsö. "So, taking them with you again?"

I nodded.

"Trygve," Ragal called. "You've got your mother's pestle on your belt. Where is your hammer?"

"What?" Trygve asked, confused.

*Don't look at your belt.*

Trygve looked down at his belt, where his hammer was clearly displayed. He frowned at Ragal. "I'll leave the pestle to you. You'll need it for cooking while you sit getting fat by your fire, *Jarl* Ragal. Best let the young men go off and fight."

"Keep Rök close to you, in case you can't handle the battle."

Trygve shook his head, then boarded the boat.

"You shouldn't tease him so," I chided Ragal.

"How could you deny me such pleasure?" Ragal replied with a laugh. "But I have no doubt, you'll harden them up yet. And you," he said, giving Rök's ear a scratch. "You will give them something to talk about in Grund. Keep an eye on our jarl," he told Rök, who wagged his tail in reply. Ragal turned to me. "Be safe, Hervor."

"And you, my friend," I said, setting my hand on his shoulder.

"Hervor," Hella said, giving me a quick hug. "Good luck in Grund."

"Thank you."

"Watch over them," Ragal told Yrsa.

She nodded. "Be well, both of you," Yrsa told Hella

and Ragal. "May the gods keep you safe."

"And you," Ragal told her.

With that, we began boarding the ships.

"It doesn't seem possible that I'm heading back to Dalr and under such different circumstances," Eydis said.

"Life was not always kind to you, my friend, but the Norns are weaving you the fate you deserve."

"Life was not always kind to me, but my mistress was."

We exchanged a warm smile. Eydis was a free woman now. Like me, the moment she stepped on the boat to journey to Samso, her life changed. She had left Dalr a slave, but would return the beloved—and soon to be wife —of the jarl. We didn't know anything about Eydis's past. She had missed the life she'd been born into, but the life before her was a golden one.

Leaving Eydis, I went to check on my warriors.

Trygve was frowning.

"Don't let his teasing bother you," I told him.

Trygve huffed with annoyance.

"Perhaps if you come home with a bag of gold and a princess over your shoulder, they'll keep quiet," Kára suggested.

"Now, if I can find a princess," Trygve replied with a grin.

"Or gold," Kit added.

Everyone laughed.

"We're going to see the king. That is reward enough," Öd said.

Kára sighed. "There goes Öd. Always trying to keep

us humble."

A light flicker of a smile crossed Öd's somber expression.

Rök was standing in the middle of the boat, swaying with the waves, a confused expression on his face.

"Best lie down," I told him. "It's a long ride."

Hofund called to the others, and soon, we pushed off.

I turned, waving farewell to Ragal and Hella. Halmstad was in good hands. Already, the city was changed. I looked forward to seeing what future Ragal and Hella would shape for the port city—and themselves.

We maneuvered the ship out of port and headed across the sea. Once more, we would return to Dalr. But a new Dalr awaited us.

I settled onto the bench across from Yrsa, both of us rowing.

"We're headed back again," she said.

I nodded. "But not to the same Dalr."

"No."

"Thank the gods."

Yrsa nodded solemnly. A strange quiet had fallen over Yrsa in the past months. While she was glad to be with Svafa in Bolmsö, I could see her mind was preoccupied. What had happened with Haki had wounded Yrsa. Until that wound was healed, she would not be the same again.

I reached out and set my hand on her shoulder.

"We'll find him," I told her.

She nodded. "I know. Now row," she said, motioning, a wisp of a smile on her lips.

I smiled at her, then got to work once more.

## CHAPTER 4

When the boats turned toward the harbor in Dalr, a strange feeling washed over me. I reminded myself that Grandfather was gone. I reminded myself that things would be new now. The darkness had passed Dalr, just as it had passed Halmstad.

Eydis turned and looked back at me, a smile on her face.

*Odin.*

*All-Father.*

*Thank you for your many gifts.*

A horn sounded from the dock. We saw a flurry of activity in the village as they gathered to see who had come. Not long thereafter, I spotted Leif, Hakon, and Halger at the end of the pier. The boys were jumping up and down, waving.

Lining the dock, green-and-white banners fluttered in

the breeze. The sun shone brightly. I could feel spring on its way. And with it, change for all of us.

Hofund called to the crew, maneuvering the ship into port.

As we docked, I got a good look at Leif. An angry red scar crossed his face from his brow to his cheek. He wore a leather patch over his eye. I turned and looked at Eydis, watching as she took it in. I had warned her that he'd been injured. A flicker of emotion crossed her face, but as fleeting as it had come, it went.

"Hail Jarl Leif," I called playfully.

"Happy returns," Leif called with a smile. "All of you!"

"Hervor!" Hakon called.

"Hervor!" Halger echoed.

I smiled at them then turned to Yrsa. She was looking farther down the dock. I followed her gaze, spotting the gythia Freja in the crowd.

When we tied up, Leif came to the side of the ship. He reached out for Eydis, who was holding Arngrimir. Taking her free hand, he helped her from the boat. The pair stole a quick kiss. Eydis set her hand on Leif's broken cheek then whispered something to him, making Leif smile. Siggy, who was holding Eylin, joined the pair.

The rest of us debarked. I lifted Blomma out of the boat, setting her gently onto the dock. Rök leaped out behind us but did not go far. He sniffed the wind, taking in every scent.

"It is good to see you," Leif told us all. "Svafa didn't come?"

I shook my head. "She's content in Bolmsö."

Understanding, Leif nodded.

I wrapped my arms around Hakon and Halger. "Every time I see you, you are nearly twice the size you were before," I told them, kissing each of them on the top of their heads.

"Hervor, is that a wolf?" Hakon asked.

"This is Rök," I told them, motioning for Rök to come. "He is my companion."

"Is he… Is it safe?" Halger asked.

I gave Rök a scratch on his ears. "It is. But he is new here," I said, then set Halger's hand on Rök's head. It occurred to me that Rök and Halger were practically the same height.

Rök gave Halger's hand a lick.

The boy laughed.

"You see," I said, patting Rök once more.

Hakon looked around the wolf to the figure hiding behind me: Blomma.

"Hakon, Halger, this is Blomma, my adopted daughter. Blomma, these are my cousins."

Hakon and Halger looked at one another, excitement in their eyes.

Without a care for her shyness, the boys left Rök and went to Blomma. Snatching her hand, Halger said, "Come on. We'll show you everything in Dalr. Let's go." He turned, pulling Blomma behind him.

"Hervor?" she called. To my surprise, she was smiling.

"It's all right," I told her.

She gave me a grin then ran off with the boys.

Rök whined.

"Not you. You'll have half the women in Dalr screaming if they see you lumbering through the streets. Stay with me for now."

We turned and headed to the hall. As we went, the townspeople called out to us, greeting us with cheers and smiles. Yrsa and Freja fell into step together. We made our way through Dalr to the hall. As we went, I saw construction on two new boats underway. Men were working on felled timber, cutting boards. A new building was being constructed along the shore. As we passed the center square, I saw many had come for the market. They cheered and called to us.

But most of all, the heavy pall that had hung over the place was gone.

Dalr was taking her first steps toward a new beginning. You could feel it in the air.

Inside the hall, my eyes went to the hearth. The faintest of stains of the jarl's blood still marred the stones. Otherwise, the room had been rearranged, Leif's green-and-white banners with the image of Grímnir's eye at the center hung from the timbers. The servants worked busily, bringing food and drink, occasionally stopping to fawn over Arngrimir and Eylin.

"Hervor," a sweet voice called.

I turned to find Hillie. Lifting her, I kissed the child on her cheeks then set her back down. "How are you, Hillie?"

"I am excellent. I'm so excited to see Eydis's babies."

I took Hillie's hand, and the pair of us joined the

others. Lifting the girl, I brought her in close. "That is Eylin," I told her, motioning to the girl Siggy was holding. "And that is Arngrimir."

"They are very little!"

"So they are. But in no time, they'll be chasing you all around this place."

"Is that your big dog?"

"That is Rök," I said, setting her down so she could see.

Rök, it seemed, was getting everyone's attention. But he didn't mind. As curious as ever, Rök stepped forward and gave Hillie's hair a sniff, making her laugh.

After everyone had greeted one another, food was served. I asked Oda to bring in a plate for Rök as well. She didn't disappoint. A massive heap of meaty bones was set before Rök, who thumped his tail in appreciation.

"Rök got the best meal," Trygve said.

"He's not one for sharing," I replied. "But you could try."

"I'd rather keep my hand."

I laughed. "What, the sea air made you hungry, Trygve?"

"Every time."

"Oda, this young warrior is starving," I told her.

"All young warriors are starving," she said, but she also set an extra bowl of mutton before him.

"How was your journey?" Leif asked.

"It was fair," Hofund replied. "With three children, a hawk, and one wolf aboard, it couldn't have gone better. May Thor be praised."

"They've grown so big," Leif told Eydis. He had traded off Arngrimir for Eylin. "I wondered if the fierce winter would ever pass. I missed you all," he told her.

"Finally, spring is upon us again," Hofund said. "But if we are moving, we are surely not the only ones."

Leif nodded. "I've had no word, no sign of them. Nor has Egil."

"How are Egil and Asta?" I asked.

"Faring well. Awaiting their child," he said with a roll of his eyes.

"You hear that?" Eydis asked Arngrimir. "Your aunt or uncle shall soon be born."

Leif chuckled. "What a funny thought. Otherwise, the only other news I've heard is that Eric and Bryn will wed in Hreinnby on the Dísablót."

I was not surprised. The couple was well-suited to one another. "Is it the marrying season?"

Leif looked from me to Eydis. "I hope so, if Eydis will still have me."

"I suppose. If I must," she replied with feigned exasperation.

"Now, we must see what the gods have to say. Where is Freja, anyway?" Leif said.

"She disappeared with Yrsa," I replied.

"Are you here for long?" Leif asked Hofund and me.

"I would like to be in Grund by the Dísablót," Hofund told him.

Leif nodded. "Well then, my bride. If we can get the gods to agree, shall we see to it?"

"Nothing would make me happier."

At that, we all let out a cheer. Leif wrapped his arms around her, planting a kiss on her cheek.

"Oda, let's have the good mead. Today, we celebrate," I called.

Grinning, I turned to Hofund. He took my hand then and gave it a kiss. May the gods be praised. The world was turning to right again.

*"For now, shield-maiden. For now."*

## CHAPTER 5

Later that afternoon, I was standing on the steps outside the hall when Hakon and Halger returned with a red-cheeked Blomma.

"We've shown her everything," Hakon informed me.

"Yes, we took her everywhere," Halger agreed.

I looked at Blomma. "Is that so?"

"I have seen Grímnir's Eye and the effigies of the gods," she told me. "There was never a bigger tree in Midgard."

"None that I have seen," I replied.

"Is it bigger than Jarl Mjord's tree?"

The brothers looked at Blomma.

"It is. But Jarl Mjord's tree is...different."

Blomma looked back toward Grímnir's Eye. "Wondrous."

I ruffled Hakon's and Halger's hair. "Now, eat something, all three of you."

Hakon took Blomma's hand. "Come on," he said, pulling her away.

Yrsa joined me, her arms crossed on her chest, a bemused expression on her face. "So, she is a child after all."

"So it seems."

Yrsa had returned earlier with Freja, who was now in the hall speaking to Eydis and Leif.

"I will go to the cave, collect the rest of my things," Yrsa told me.

"Leif and Eydis hope to wed soon."

Yrsa nodded. "I'll go now."

"Yrsa..." I began. I knew it would be painful for her to go, to feel the sting of Gobi's and Bo's absence. "I can go with you."

"I will be back soon enough."

"Eydis won't be happy if you miss her wedding."

"I would not miss a thrall becoming the lady of Dalr for all the gold in Niðavellir," she replied. Her gaze went to Rök. "He looks like he could use a stretch."

I set my hand on Rök's head. "Want to go with Yrsa?" I asked the wolf.

He cocked his head at me.

"Go on, then."

"Come on, Rök," Yrsa said, then the pair of them headed off.

I returned to the hall, taking a seat by the fire. Hakon, Halger, and Blomma were all sitting together at a table in the corner. The boys were laughing wildly. Blomma wore a little smile on her lips, her eyes laughing. I liked the lightness that had come over her. Here, in this place, she was only mine and Hofund's daughter. There were no memories of Solva to contend with. Hakon and Halger had accepted her as family without a second thought. Had Bjartmar been here...but he wasn't. He was gone. He was nothing more than a memory now.

Hofund joined me. He slipped his hand into mine. "Shall we walk, shield-maiden?" he asked. "My legs are crooked from the long boat ride."

I nodded, and the two of us strolled toward the exit. At the end of the hall, the warriors from Bolmsö sat drinking. Trygve was still eating. I stopped and set a hand on Kára's shoulder. "I'll be back in a bit. Keep an eye on Blomma?"

"Yes, jarl."

I nodded to her, and we went outside.

Hofund and I walked across the field toward the grove. The path to the grove was worn, the field covered with a light dusting of melting snow.

"Hervor," Hofund said, a note of caution in his voice. "I think we should talk about Grund. My father is a jovial and honest man, but in Grund, things are not always easy. Some maneuver and manipulate everyone close to the throne for their own gain. I grew up in such a place and have learned the game and know the players. You are an outsider. Some will test you."

I let Hofund's words sink in. "Then, I shall do as always. Watch."

"Watch. And keep your people close to you."

I grinned. "And if that fails, there is always Tyrfing."

Hofund chuckled. We stopped at the edge of the forest near the effigy of Odin. "My mother knew you were the right wife for me. She saw you in a vision. But I knew you were right for me by what I saw of your nature, your heart. You are a good person, and because of that, you may find Grund challenging."

"I'll rely on your guidance and that of the gods. I've always managed to escape people's attention. Perhaps it will be no different in Grund."

Hofund set his arm on my shoulder. "Hervor, you are my wife. One day, you will be their queen. Expect attention in excess."

"Then I'm glad I brought Rök. He's a great dissuader."

Hofund laughed lightly. "There are wolves in Grund as well. They just hide in sheep's clothing—usually, finely woven and expensively trimmed."

"I'll keep that in mind," I said. We headed into the forest. When we did so, I felt the magic in the air. It gathered around, almost touchable. When we approached Grímnir's Eye, I could feel the presence of the gods. They watched Hofund and me.

We knelt before the pool, both of us closing our eyes and offering a prayer.

I dipped into my pocket, pulling out a small ingot of silver. I dropped it into the water. The surface of the pool wavered. After a moment, an image formed on the water. A massive tree—neither Grímnir's Eye nor the Bone Tree —was framed by the moon. In the distance, fires burned on hilltops. Like crowns of flame, they leaped into the air, burning atop three great mounds.

I shuddered hard.

The vision faded.

"Hervor?" Hofund asked.

I shook my head. "It's nothing. Nothing."

*Please, Odin. Let it be nothing.*

# CHAPTER 6

The night passed with great merrymaking and joy. I watched my dearest friend and my cousin smile at one another all evening. The sweetness of their love touched me. For so many years, they had hidden their genuine affection for one another. Now, it was on full display. With their two little ones, they were the image of perfect happiness. One day, perhaps, Hofund and I would have our own children, joining Blomma. The idea filled me with joy, a feeling at odds with being in the great hall of Dalr. But nothing was the same here. In one corner, Eyvinder sat with Blomma, Hakon, Halger, and Hillie. Siggy with Eylin, Oda holding Arngrmir, they also listened. Gesturing wildly, the skald recanted some magical tale. The childrens' eyes grew wide. Eyvinder threw his hands toward the sky, making Hillie gasp. Then, Eyvinder toppled off his seat, making everyone laugh. No. Things were not the same in Dalr, and I was glad.

The following morning, I went to the docks to see the

boats under construction. Hofund had joined the men of Dalr working on the nearby building. Blomma and the twins had disappeared after the morning meal. I knew there was an excellent chance that Hakon and Halger would lead Blomma into mischief. For her sake, I hoped they did.

I was eyeing over the work when Leif joined me.

"What do you think?" Leif asked, gesturing to the boat.

I set my hand on the prow. It was a finely carved piece of wood, shaped like a stag with a massive set of horns.

"It's beautiful," I said, stroking the timber. "So, what did Freja decide?"

"The runes are in our favor. We will wed tomorrow night. We must make sacrifices to the dísir and keep the festivities going from the time of our wedding to the Dísablót."

"That's good," I said with a nod. In previous years, Dalr held a market ahead of the blót. But with everything that had happened, Dalr was quiet. "The dísir will see you honor them."

"Next year will be different. Next year, Dalr will hold a great market and blót."

"I'll look forward to that."

"I've sent a rider to Silfrheim, inviting my mother to come for the nuptials."

"What did Eydis say?"

"She doesn't think Asta will come. That was the only reason Eydis agreed to send word."

I chuckled. "Eydis may be a völva, but she underestimates Asta's love for you."

"For now."

"For now?"

"Let's see what happens when another of Egil's children are born. I may find myself in second place to my brother or sister."

"I knew you secretly liked being Asta's favorite," I said with a laugh.

Leif chuckled.

"How is your eye, cousin?"

"Still healing. Freja said it was Jarl Mjord's fast work that saved it. It will take time to recover, but I can see color and light. The images are not yet sharp. I may never recover them. We don't know yet."

"May Odin take pity on you. He knows the difficulty of life with one eye."

"I gave my eye to win Dalr. Perhaps Odin thinks it a fair trade. I am content with whatever he thinks is best for me."

"Cousin, you almost sound wise."

Leif laughed. "*Almost*. You are not the only one who can spread wisdom from time to time," he said then elbowed me.

I returned the gesture.

"Will you and Hofund stay for the wedding?"

"I wouldn't miss it for all the world."

"May the gods continue to shine their favor on us," Leif said, setting his hand on the ship.

My mind went back to the image I saw in the grove last night. "Indeed, cousin. Indeed."

LATER THAT DAY, WE FEASTED WELL IN THE HALL. THE NEWS of the upcoming wedding spread across Dalr. In the center square, women worked tying and hanging garlands. The thralls prepared the hall for the nuptial feast. Excitement filled the air.

Eydis, who was standing at the entryway to the family quarters, motioned for me to join her.

"Is everything all right?"

She nodded. "The children are asleep. Since I have no trove of gowns from a long-lost grandmother to get sentimental about, I find myself in a conundrum. I have no wedding gown."

"What about Svafa's things? Has she left anything? Or, perhaps, Gudrun's dresses?"

"I can't bring myself to touch Gudrun's gowns."

I nodded. "Let's see what Svafa left."

While the hall felt different, being in my old room alongside Eydis brought back memories.

"There are still shadows in every corner," Eydis said when we entered the chamber. "It will take time before they recede." She lifted the lid on Svafa's trunk. To our luck, mother had left behind half of her belongings.

"You know, if nothing fits here, you can always look through Asta's things," I said with a wicked grin.

"Can you imagine her reaction if she found me marrying her golden boy wearing her gown?"

We laughed.

"I suspect Eylin and Arngrimir will smooth things over between the two of you."

"Let's hope."

Eydis pulled out a dark purple gown. I recognized the dress. It was one Mother rarely wore, but it was beautiful. "This?" Eydis asked.

We looked the gown over. It was in good condition, and Eydis and Svafa were similar in size.

"Do you think Svafa would mind?" Eydis asked, swishing the purple gown in front of her.

I shook my head. "She loves you, Eydis."

Eydis slipped out of the simple dress she was wearing. With my help, she pulled on the purple gown.

I stepped back to look at her. "You look beautiful."

"I feel... No. Never mind."

"What?"

"I feel like a pretender."

"What do you mean?"

"I grew up in this place as your thrall. And now I am here, in Svafa's gown, about to marry the jarl of Dalr."

I set my hands on Eydis's shoulders. "The gods have their own plans. Loki moved you to a place of importance and power. You always have been his favorite."

Eydis grinned.

There was a knock on the door.

"Eydis?" It was Siggy.

"Come," Eydis called.

Siggy entered carrying Eylin, who was red-faced and fussy. "Oh!" Siggy exclaimed, seeing Eydis in the dress. "How lovely. Eydis, I'm so sorry, but this little one will have no one, not even her father. I think she's hungry."

Eydis sighed. "Yes, my dear, yes, yes. You're the real princess here. Help me out of this thing," Eydis told me.

Siggy bounced a fussy and increasingly loud Eylin while I hurried Eydis out of the gown.

"Enjoy your time before you start having little ones of your own," Eydis warned me. "After that, there is no peace."

"Keeping that in mind," I said, pulling the dress over Eydis's head, "I think I'll go hunting. Let me see if I can find a stag for your wedding table."

"You're going after Yrsa. Don't lie."

"Lie to you? Never."

Eydis laughed. "It's not me you have to convince. Go tell your husband."

"I shall," I said, then laid the dress down on the bed. I crossed the room to Eylin, kissing the angry baby on the hand. "Be easy on your mother, little one," I told her. "It's nearly her wedding day."

I headed to the door, giving my friend one last look as she settled in with her baby.

"Well, go on," Eydis said. "Just make sure the two of you are back on time. I'm not getting married without you."

Grinning, I passed Eydis a wink then left.

Despite her protests, I had a feeling Yrsa should not be

alone. Grabbing my gear, I found Hofund and let him know where I was going, then started up the mountain.

I KNEW EVERY JAGGED STONE, EVERY ROOT, EVERY LEDGE. As I made my way, I spotted wolf prints in the snow. I could see they had come this way but had not yet returned. Soon, I caught the light scent of wood smoke.

When I reached the ledge outside of Yrsa's cave, I saw the glow of orange light within. Expecting Rök to bounce out any moment, I braced myself, so the wolf didn't send me flying off the ledge. But he never came. I entered the cave slowly. Yrsa sat beside the center fire pit. The place was a mess, and aside from Yrsa, decidedly absent. The sense of loss, the feeling that Gobi and Bo were missing, permeated the room.

Yrsa didn't look up when I entered.

I righted a stool then sat down beside her.

Yrsa was staring into the fire. Her cheeks were wet with tears. She was holding the bears' claws tied on their leather string in her hand.

"When my father died, I was lost. Svafa's mind was gone. The jarl and I were embattled. You were just a squalling, wrinkled little thing. I was alone here for years. From time to time, I would go to town to see Freja, to try to talk to Svafa, to see you. The servants always brought you out to me. I'd hold you a bit then move on, not wanting the jarl to have any reason to look my way. It was just me until

Gobi and Bo came. Funny how such great creatures became family to me. I raised them. Trained them. Taught them how to be bears. With them, I wasn't alone anymore."

"Yrsa," I whispered, my voice choked.

"Then you started coming around," she said, patting my shoulder. "Couldn't shake you once your curiosity was piqued. Then, it was the two of us...and those bears." She looked down at the claws in her hand. "He killed them like they were nothing, like wild hogs, beasts of sport." She shook her head. "They may have just been animals, but to me, they were the only family I had. I took their mother from them, so I had to take her place. I know...it's probably hard to understand."

"No. It's not. I loved them too. And if anything happened to Rök, I would feel the same."

"Just some damned marauder. Killed them. Hurt Svafa. Hurt me," Yrsa shook her head. "When are we leaving for Grund?"

"Eydis and Leif will marry tomorrow night. We'll leave the next day."

She nodded. After a long time, she said, "Your wolf ran off. He smelled something interesting."

"He'll be back."

"It's getting late. Better if we go back down in the morning after the sun comes out."

"All right."

Yrsa sighed then rose. "I need to tidy up anyway. Got enough firewood covered up outside to keep us warm for the night."

I nodded then stood. "I'll go bring some in."

"You eat?"

"Not yet."

"I'll make us something."

I inclined my head to her, then headed outside. I stood on the ledge, looking down over the valley. From here, I could see the ships in the harbor. The water in the fjord sparkling in the dying light. I inhaled deeply. In the cool, twilight breeze, my breath made a billowing cloud. A lot about Dalr had been wrong. But this place had always been good. With Yrsa, I'd always had a home...even if it was in the side of a mountain.

"Mushrooms and barley?" Yrsa called. "Don't have much else."

"Sounds good."

I smiled. One last night with Yrsa before everything started anew. Turning, I removed the pine boughs covering the woodpile, loaded up my arms, then returned to the cave.

## CHAPTER 7

Yrsa and I returned to the hall the following morning just as a boat arrived at the dock. A horn sounded, announcing the arrival of visitors.

Leif and Hofund exited the hall to find Yrsa and me on the steps.

Hofund smiled at me. "My wife returns from the wild."

"Tried to tell her not to come. She was never a good listener," Yrsa said.

"You didn't even leave Rök to keep me warm," Hofund chided me, greeting me with a quick kiss.

I laughed.

"And you missed my sumbel," Leif told me. "My head still aches. Your warriors drink very well, Hervor."

I laughed. "I *am* sorry I missed that."

The horn blew again.

Leif winced. "My head."

Yrsa looked toward the water. "It's Egil...and Asta."

I laughed. "You think your head hurts now."

Eydis appeared at the door. "Who has come?"

"Asta," Yrsa replied.

"Right. I'll be inside."

Leif grabbed her hand. "You most certainly will not. Now, where are our little ones? Siggy?"

"Yes, jarl?" Siggy called from within.

"Bring the children."

"Leif," Eydis whispered.

"Come on," Yrsa told Eydis. "Don't let that lump of a girl intimidate you. We'll all go together."

I grinned at Yrsa. Somehow, she'd managed to adopt Eydis along with me.

Leif held Eylin while I took Arngrimir. Rök trotting along beside us, we went to the pier.

When we got to the dock, Egil was helping Asta from the boat. She was heavy with child. When she saw Leif and Eydis, a flash of mixed emotion crossed her face. An odd mix of love and smothered rage contorted her features.

Eydis slowed her step, but Leif pulled her along.

"Egil, Mother," Leif called. "Welcome returns."

The last I'd seen Egil, he was covered from head to foot in blood. Now, he was neatly dressed, his hair braided. He even had a bit of a paunchy stomach. Marriage suited him well.

Egil smiled at Leif. "We were pleased to hear your news," he said, then turned to Asta.

I saw him give his wife a knowing look.

"Leif," she said, stepping toward her son. But her eyes were on the little girl in his hands. "Who is this?"

"This is my daughter, Eylin," he said. "Hervor is holding my son, Arngrimir. They are my children...with Eydis."

"Your children?"

He nodded. "Born in the autumn. They've been in Bolmsö. I had Eydis and the little ones stay there until things were settled here."

"I..." Asta began.

Yrsa chuckled under her breath.

Looking stunned, Asta scanned the crowd. "Where is Svafa?"

"Bolmsö," I answered.

Asta's eyes went to Rök. "Oh," she said. "How big he is."

Eydis left Leif and lifted Arngrimir from my arms. Holding the baby, she approached Asta. "Come to your granny, my boy," she said, then handed Arngrimir to Asta.

Asta paused for a brief moment, then took the baby.

"Twins?" she asked, looking at Eydis.

Eydis nodded. "You should have seen me. Twice as big as you are now."

Asta looked from Eydis to Arngrimir. "What lovely curls you have," she said, stroking the boy's ebony-colored locks. "Your hair curled like that when you were little too," Asta told Leif. "But his hair is far darker than Leif's was, more like yours," she told Eydis. "What a handsome boy."

Arngrimir laughed, blowing bubbles in the process. He reached out for the cat pendant Asta always wore.

Stunned, Asta kissed his hand.

"Come along, Eylin," Leif said, bringing the baby closer to Asta.

Asta looked from Eylin to Arngrimir. The thunder that had been brewing inside her calmed to nothing. Now, there was only raw emotion. "How lovely she is. Oh, Leif, they are such beautiful children."

"You didn't tell us," Egil said.

Leif bobbed his head from side to side. "No, I didn't."

Asta handed Arngrimir to Egil then took Eylin from Leif. "A beauty. Just like your mother."

Eydis flicked her eyes at me for just a moment, a flash of disbelief on her face.

"Come, let's go to the hall," Leif said, then motioned for the others to follow.

Asta went alongside her son, carrying Eylin.

"Prince Hofund," Egil said, inclining his head to Hofund.

Hofund smiled lightly. "It is good to see you again, Jarl Egil."

Egil joined Leif and Asta.

The three of us held back for a moment, letting the others go ahead.

"Well, that went better than I expected," Yrsa remarked.

"What can she say? All of Asta's secrets are out now. She cannot pretend to be righteous anymore," I replied.

"Never stopped her before," Yrsa said with a chuckle.

Hofund laughed. "Children have a way of smoothing things over."

"Let's hope so."

## CHAPTER 8

Back in the hall, preparations for the wedding were well underway. Garlands hung from every beam. The smells of roasting meat and baking bread filled the air. The servants worked busily, bringing barrels of ale from storage. Everywhere I looked, I saw a commotion. While the actual wedding ceremony would take place in the grove, the hall was ready for the wedding feast that came afterward.

After a quick morning meal, Leif, Hofund, Egil, and the other men left with the gothar for the grove. There, Leif would undergo his rites.

When Freja arrived, we would begin preparing Eydis.

As we waited, Asta got acquainted with her grandchildren. I was surprised by the change that came over Asta. I had expected her to rage at Leif for marrying Eydis. Instead, she said little, merely played with the little ones. Asta, it seemed, had softened. Love could do that. Maybe, in some ways, she understood Leif better now.

But as much as she understood Leif, she still did not understand Hakon and Halger—nor what she needed to do to make amends with them. Like wild things, they'd come tumbling into the hall, dragging Blomma along with them. When they spotted Asta, they froze.

"Halger? Hakon?" Asta called to them.

After a long moment, Hakon looked to Halger. "Let's go," he whispered. "Blomma, come on."

"I...I should stay here and help Eydis," Blomma told them. She had detected the tension but hadn't understood the source.

"Okay. We'll find you later," Hakon told her, then the twins fled the hall.

"Boys," Asta called after them, but they were already gone.

Blomma, feeling uncertain, came to me.

Asta stared after the twins for a long moment but did not follow them. Choking back her emotions, she turned to Blomma and me.

"Who is this?" she asked me.

"Blomma, this is my aunt Asta," I explained. "Asta, this is Blomma, mine and Hofund's adopted daughter."

"Daughter? Is she Hofund's child—"

"No. She is not. But she is our daughter," I said sharply.

"Oh," Asta said, catching my tone. "I see." But she did not see. A million questions formed in Asta's eyes. Thankfully, Freja arrived in time to save me from them.

"Freja," I said, standing.

She smiled at me then turned to Asta. "Asta, welcome returns."

Asta gave her a half-smile then turned back to Eylin, who was sleeping in her arms. A tangle of emotions worked on Asta's face, but she asked nothing more. Asta was busy fighting her own battles. In the end, my adopted daughter and I meant little to her.

Catching Yrsa's—who had been lingering across the hall with Kára and Sigrun—attention, I motioned to her, then Yrsa, Blomma, and I joined Freja and headed to the back.

"Your aunt is Svafa's sister?" Blomma asked.

"She is. She is Hakon, Halger, and Leif's mother."

"She is very unlike Svafa."

I chuckled. "Yes."

"Don't Hakon and Halger like their mother?"

I paused. "It can be difficult. I think you can understand that."

"Yes," she said, but added, "but it is a shame. They are merry boys." Blomma smiled.

"Yes, that they are," I said, pulling her close and kissing her on the head.

We entered the bedchamber to find Eydis half-dressed and looking panicked.

"What's wrong?" I asked her.

"I've just remembered. What am I going to do about a sword? No one led me off to a magical burial mound of dubious existence to get some ancestral iron," Eydis lamented. "I have nothing for Leif."

Jokes aside, Eydis was right. While I had nothing to

share, perhaps Eyvinder could think of something. I turned to leave, but Yrsa motioned for me to stay.

"I prepared something for you," Yrsa told Eydis. She went to the bundle she'd returned with from the cave. From within, she pulled a fine sword. It was freshly oiled and polished.

"What's this?" Eydis asked.

"It belonged to my father," Yrsa told Eydis, handing her the blade.

"Oh. But, Yrsa," Eydis began. "I can't accept—"

"Don't ruin it by getting sentimental."

"Wouldn't dream of it. Thank you, Yrsa." Eydis cleared her throat, choking back tears.

Yrsa inclined her head to Eydis.

"Best get started," Freja said.

"Blomma and I can fix her hair," Siggy offered.

"And I must begin with the markings. Hervor, please bank up the fire. Yrsa, a pot of fresh water, please," Freja instructed us.

I nodded, then all of us got to work. Tonight, my dearest friend would marry my beloved cousin. And I couldn't have been happier.

WITH HER LONG, DARK HAIR BEAUTIFULLY BRAIDED AND adorned with leaves and small flowers, and dressed in the purple gown, Eydis was the picture of beauty. She shined like a bride should. Once Freja had finished her work, she led us from the hall.

Asta was waiting outside the hall with the other women. She smiled when she saw Eydis. Yrsa, Blomma, and I walked behind Eydis as we made our way from the hall to the grove, bringing Eylin and Arngrimir along with us. As the women of Bolmsö had done at my own wedding, the ladies of Dalr accompanied us, singing the bridal song. Even Asta joined in.

How strange the whole world had become. How had Eydis and I ended up here?

We made our way across the field and into the grove. Rök, who had been busy exploring Dalr, appeared out of the darkness. He was wet and smelled feral.

"Rök," Eydis hissed at him. "If you shake yourself on me, I'll turn you into a coat."

Rather than tempting fate, Rök ran ahead of us and into the trees.

I chuckled. Even Rök knew when Eydis was serious.

Once we reached Grímnir's Eye, we found Leif and the others. My cousin was neatly dressed, his hair unbound. He wore a dark green shirt and tan leather trousers. He'd removed his eye patch. This was the first time I'd seen the extent of his injury. Part of his eye was moon white, but the eye was open. With time, perhaps, he would see normally again.

My eyes went to Hofund, who met my gaze. Not long ago, we were in this same place.

My husband smiled softly at me.

*My* husband.

May the All-Father be praised.

The gothar called the gods, and Freja led the ceremony. But unlike on Bolmsö, a cow had been brought for sacrifice. The eyes of the gods on us, the gothar bled the cow into the pool before Grímnir's eye.

Eydis and Leif exchanged their swords and rings.

"Eydis, I give you this sword, which belonged to Jarl Njal, to keep for our children," he said, handing his grandfather's sword to Eydis. Had Egil brought it for him?

"Leif, I give you this sword, the weapon of Halfdan, father of Yrsa, to keep for our children." My gaze shifted to Yrsa for just a moment. Despite all the petty grumbling between the two of them, Yrsa and Eydis loved one another.

Eydis and Leif exchanged their weapons then donned their rings.

"Under the eyes of the All-Father, with the people of Dalr as witness, you are now married. Kiss and celebrate the beginning of your new life together," Freja intoned.

We let out a great cheer.

Eydis and Leif had married.

The world was all new.

# CHAPTER 9

The wedding celebration was raucous. All of Darl had come to celebrate. These were strange times for the people of Dalr. Jarl Bjartmar had been despised. War and death had come to Dalr. They had not seen such conditions since my great-grandfather's time. But with Leif in control of the village, peace reigned once more.

The community linked arms with Eydis and Leif, dancing in a circle around the central fire with the others while the musicians played. My warriors from Bolmsö joined them, Kára's booming laugh echoing across the square. Hakon, Halger, and the other children from Dalr were running wild amongst the crowd, chasing one another, Blomma following along with their merriment.

"You are never one to join the dance," Hofund said, then put his arm around me.

"I danced at our wedding."

He laughed. "Barely. You are like Yrsa, too serious to dance."

Yrsa was on the other side of the square, speaking to Freja. She had a horn of ale in her hand and was ignoring the music entirely.

"The gods didn't make me for dancing," I replied with a grin. "But I think you were. Go on, if you like."

Hofund grinned. "Not without you. So, if the gods did not make you for dancing, what did they make you for?"

I leaned toward him. "For you."

He kissed the top of my head. "And I for you," he said, then kissed me again. "And I for you."

THE NIGHT PASSED ALONG HAPPILY. WHEN WE FINALLY retired to the hall, I found Asta sitting by the fire, her boots off, and her very swollen feet resting by the flames.

"Asta," I said, noticing how very uncomfortable she looked. "Can I bring you anything?"

She shook her head. With a wince, she shifted. "This one digs in worse than Hakon and Halger did. It is the way of things, Hervor. One day, you will learn."

I sat down beside my aunt. She looked exhausted. Empathy bubbled up in me. She, too, must have felt very strange being back in the hall. And with the tension between her and her twins still lingering, no doubt she was troubled.

"How is your mother?" Asta asked.

"She is adjusting to her new life in Bolmsö."

"She will not return?"

"No."

Asta scanned around the hall. "I don't blame her. I would not be here either if not for Leif."

I bit my tongue, wanting to say something about Hakon and Halger, but I held back. Asta had already grown beyond her former self to come here. I had to credit her for that.

"And in Silfrheim? Are you well there?" I asked.

"Well enough. The repairs to the hall are done, so we are comfortable there once more. If I can find someone to wed Helga and her girls off to, I'll have peace."

"Have they...recovered?"

Asta looked at me, a knowing expression on her face. "Helga, yes. The younger girls are coming around. But Thyri, Helga's eldest daughter, is with child."

"Hagbard's?"

Asta nodded, then winced, shifting her weight again.

A sick feeling made my stomach knot. My heart ached for Thyri.

Asta groaned tiredly.

"Why don't you rest?" I asked. "I can call a servant to help you."

"I cannot bring myself to go back," she said, eyeing the family wing.

"Take my old room. It is not large, but it is big enough for you and Egil."

"All right. I will," Asta said, then tried to rise.

I reached out, helping her up.

At that same moment, the door banged open, and Hakon, Halger, and Blomma rushed in.

"Boys," Asta said, smiling at them.

The twins looked at one another then crossed the hall quickly, not giving their mother a second glance.

Blomma composed herself, smoothing down her skirt, then joined me.

Asta's eyes followed her sons, but she said nothing more. She turned her attention to Blomma, assessing the child, then looked at me. "So, where did you find her?"

"The All-Father brought us together," I replied, setting my hand on Blomma's head.

Asta sighed. With exasperation in her voice, she retorted, "Must you be so obscure?"

Irritation flashed in me, burning away the empathy I'd felt toward Asta. The fact that Blomma was my enemy's daughter was not Asta's business. "It doesn't matter. She is my daughter now."

Asta shook her head. "All right, Hervor. Keep your secrets. As if anyone truly cares anyway." Without another word, she turned and headed toward the back.

I looked down at Blomma. "Don't mind her. She was never nice."

Blomma chucked lightly then heaved an exhausted sigh. "I'm tired. I think I'll go to bed now."

"Very well," I said, pulling her close. "Good night, my dear."

"Good night," she said, then headed to the back.

I, too, had had enough for the night. Finding my way to my own chamber, I discovered Rök stretched out by the fire. He was damp and smelled like some strange mix of meat and algae. "Where have you been?" I asked.

He thumped his tail but didn't lift his head.

"I guess Blomma wasn't the only one running wild tonight."

I sat down beside Rök, patting him gently on the head. "Tomorrow, we're for Grund. Are you ready?"

Rök rolled onto his back, his tongue hanging from his mouth, a goofy expression on his face.

"I brought you with me to show them the might of Bolmsö, and this is what you give me?"

Rök gave a soft bark.

I laughed then pressed my head against his. "Let's hope we both don't have to stand on our heads to please the people of Grund." Hofund and I had started our lives together in my world. Now, I would join his world, and I had no idea what that even looked like. More than anything, I had wanted Hofund. Soon I would see what I had agreed to along with him.

For better or worse.

THE FOLLOWING MORNING, EYDIS AND LEIF JOINED US AT THE dock as we prepared to depart for Grund.

"I wish you well, cousin," Leif told me.

"And you. Of course, now that you have stolen Eydis from me, I'll have to make my way without the help of a völva."

Eydis grinned at me. "As if anything I ever told you made a difference."

"I did put on a blue dress on your advice."

"Is that so?" Hofund asked.

I nodded.

"Then it is you I should thank," Hofund told Eydis.

She smiled at him.

I took Eydis's hand. "I will miss you."

"Then, don't be gone long."

Leaving Eydis, I went to Siggy and Oda, who were holding the little ones.

"Siggy, will you be all right here in Dalr?"

She nodded to me. "Yes, jarl. I will miss Bolmsö, but these two little ones are too dear to me. I cannot let them go."

I set my hand on her shoulder then leaned forward to tickle Eylin's chin. "Don't grow too quickly, little one."

Eylin laughed.

Taking Arngrimir from Oda's arms, I said, "And you, my fine boy, don't let that berserker name get you into mischief." I kissed him on the cheek then handed him back to Oda.

I glanced back at the boat. Yrsa was getting Rök settled while the others waited. I reached down for Blomma's hand. "Ready?"

She nodded.

Behind Eydis and Leif, Egil and Asta waited.

"Jarl Egil," Hofund said, "please let us know how you fare. We'll see Silfrheim fully recovered. Whatever I can do to help…"

"Thank you, Prince Hofund."

I set my free hand on Asta's stomach. "I wish you well, Aunt. May Frigga and Freyja watch over you. May your little one be born healthy and safe."

"Thank you, Hervor. And you...off to Grund. One day you will be our queen," she said. From the tone of her voice, I could see she was struggling with the idea. "I..." she began, her voice pinched and sharp, but her words faltered. "Let us all have the future the gods have decreed for us. May the gods guide you and keep you safe, Hervor."

"And you."

"Send my...my love to your mother."

"I will."

With that, I turned to Eydis one last time. Our eyes met, but we said nothing more. After a lifetime of being together, our ways were parting. I didn't know how many months would pass until I saw her again.

Eydis smiled gently at me then nodded for me to go on.

I turned to Leif. "Cousin."

Leif kissed me on the cheek then leaned into my ear. "Watch yourself in Grund. Lots of adders lying about."

I nodded to him.

Leif turned to Hofund. "Be well, Grund."

"And you, Dalr."

Hofund clapped Leif on the shoulder one last time, then we boarded the boat. Blomma picked her way to the front of the ship, taking up a spot by the masthead.

Sigrun whistled. A moment later, a black speck swept

down from the mountain. Sigrun held out her arm. Rök, his eyes flashing with curiosity, watched as Hábrók rejoined us.

At that, Hofund motioned to one of the men who sounded his horn.

Working the oars, we maneuvered the ship back out to sea.

"Blomma! Blomma!" a pair of voices called from the dock. Hakon and Halger ran to the end of the pier to wave goodbye to us.

Blomma waved to Hakon and Halger. She was smiling, an honest and happy expression on her face. Who would have thought that Dalr could open someone up, bring them joy? But there it was. And I was glad of it.

I glanced back at Hofund.

His eyes were on the sea.

He was going home.

And I, wife of the prince, was going to Grund.

Who was this new Hervor?

*"Hervor.*

*"Daughter.*

*"You are right where I want you."*

# CHAPTER 10

We sailed along a peninsula, a strip of land protecting Grund from the sea. Grund sat in a valley between two high mountains, one of which had a waterfall that fell from its highest point into a river below. The sight was breathtaking. At the center of the town, sitting at the highest point between the mountains, was the king's hall. It was bigger than any building I had ever seen. Its massive peaked roof was trimmed with ornate carvings. It was a wonder to behold. At the water's edge, piers jutted into the water, the docks loaded with boats, the wharf busy with a flurry of activity.

I turned and looked at Yrsa, who raised and lowered her eyebrows.

I had faced armies, but something about this place's magnificence made an uneasiness splash up in me. Once, long ago, Svafa had made the trip to Uppsala, home of the late King Yngvi, and her life had changed forever. What would Grund do to me?

Rök sat up, his ears twitching as he took in the sight, his eyes flashing with excitement.

I glanced back at my warriors. They, like me, looked on with awe.

Hofund sounded his horn, alerting the dock of our arrival.

Someone at the pier answered.

And then another horn, and another, and another, sounded through the city until the sound reached the king's high hall.

"It's so grand," Blomma whispered.

I looked down at the girl, seeing a mix of wonder and terror in her eyes. It occurred to me that her feelings were very likely a reflection of my own. But it was my job to ease her mind.

"Just houses and people," I said.

She looked at me, then frowned. "A lot of houses and people."

I chuckled lightly. "Yes."

"Have you met the king?"

I nodded.

"How is he?"

"Merry and kind."

Blomma, looking only slightly more reassured, looked back at the city.

She was right to be hesitant. We both were. This place was full of people we did not know whose motives we would not be able to guess. But still, I came here as a jarl. I had my people to think of and my daughter. I would rely on Hofund to guide me. Marriage was truly a partnership in vulnerability. Like it or not, in Grund, I was exposed in a way I had not been before. Let's hope that the combination of Tyrfing and Rök dissuaded any possible would-be meddlers.

There was a flurry of excitement as we approached the dock.

In the center of it all, I spotted the burly form of King Gudmund. He headed toward the dock with an entourage of warriors and servants following him.

Hofund directed the others, moving the ship to the dock.

"My prince," a man at the dock called, smiling when Hofund tossed him a line.

"Argus," Hofund replied with a smile.

"Welcome returns."

The sailors and fishermen cleared the path for the king to make his way through the crowd.

Hofund debarked the ship. He motioned for me to hand Blomma to him. Once she was on the dock, Hofund took my hand and helped me out, Rök leaping out behind me. Yrsa and the other warriors from Bolmsö followed.

"Son," King Gudmund called, coming down the ramp to meet us, his arms outstretched.

The king looked far heavier than he had when I'd last seen him, his face pudgy and reddish, his gait stiff.

King Gudmund pulled Hofund into an embrace.

"Finally. And in time for the Disting. Very good. Very good," he said, then turned from Hofund to me. "By the gods, I am pleased to see you again, Hervor." He turned to Hofund. "Now…my daughter?"

"Yes, Father. Hervor and I were wed in Bolmsö."

Gudmund laughed. "Couldn't wait for me, eh? I don't blame you after the run-about we got from Jarl Bjartmar. Hervor," King Gudmund said, pulling me close. "You are welcome to Grund."

"Thank you, King Gudmund."

"You will call me Father."

"Very well, Father," I said with a smile, then turned to Yrsa. "May I present Yrsa, my foster-mother."

Yrsa stepped forward. "King Gudmund."

"Well met, shield-maiden," King Gudmund said, but I could see a look of confusion on his face.

"It was Yrsa who looked after me, given my mother's condition," I told the king.

"Ah, I see. Yes," he said with a nod. "And who is this?" King Gudmund asked, looking at Blomma, who was hiding behind Hofund. She was holding on tightly to his belt.

"This is Blomma, our adopted daughter," Hofund told his father.

"So you return with a wife and child? Hofund, you never do anything in halves," he said with a laugh, then turned to Blomma. "I'm too old to bend and look at you properly. Come here, girl," King Gudmund said, motioning to Blomma.

Gently guiding her, Hofund moved Blomma in front of him.

"Your Majesty," Blomma said, then curtseyed lightly.

King Gudmund raised his bushy eyebrows. "Nicely mannered. Where are you from?"

"I am from Blomfjall, but I live in Bolmsö now."

King Gudmund nodded. "Very good, little princess. Come, take my hand," he said, reaching out for her. "Let's go back to the hall. Do you like sweets? A ship came to Grund selling a strange new dessert made in squares. I was about to try them when the horn blew. Will you help me eat them?"

"If you allow it, king."

"I allow it," he said with a laugh, then he eyed Rök. "Fine beast," he told me, then eyed the warriors behind me. "Come. All of you. It has been a long trip. Come and take your rest."

We followed behind the king as we made our way back to the hall.

Blomma looked over her shoulder at me.

I gave her a reassuring glance.

As we headed up the pier, I eyed the waterfall that tumbled over the mountain into the river below.

"Skadi's Tears," Hofund said, motioning to the waterfall. "This is the land of Njord. Do you know the story of Skadi and Njord?"

"Vaguely."

"When the giantess Skadi's father was killed by the Æsir, she demanded compensation from Odin. In recompense, the All-Father told Skadi that she could marry any of the gods she wished. The only trick was that she had to choose them by their feet. Skadi, thinking she had chosen Balder, the most beautiful of the gods, actually selected Njord as her husband. Njord was the god of the rivers, oceans, and seas. These lands were once the home to Njord. After they wed, he brought the giantess Skadi to live here with him alongside the water. But Skadi grew unhappy. Her own lands were deep in an ancient forest. She became homesick for the mountains and the sound of wolves howling in the woods," he said with a knowing grin.

I winked at him.

"Skadi, in her sadness, would sit on the high cliff and cry for her home. That is how the waterfall and river were born. Eventually, Skadi and Njord divorced. Skadi returned to the forest, and Njord stayed here by the sea."

"Let's hope we have better luck than them," I replied.

"Well, you didn't choose me by my feet, so I'd say we're off to a good start," Hofund answered with a laugh.

As we went, I saw fishermen bringing in their catches, traders moving merchandise on and off their ships, and boat builders pounding timbers. Once we reached the shore, we passed many drinking houses and shops on our way up the hill toward the hall. There was row upon row of houses and establishments. Many people stopped to watch us pass. They called to Hofund.

Rök brought out a few shrieks from children and demure ladies who stepped away from him. Unsettled, he stayed close to me, his eyes watching everything, ears twitching.

Overhead, Sigrun's bird soared. The hawk called to its master, circling above the city, then headed toward the river. Sigrun smiled, her face tipped toward the sky, as she watched her creature fly. Hofund's tale of Skadi came to mind. I had brought the forest with me. I hoped for all our sakes that Skadi would watch over us here.

Soon, we came to the market. The place was bustling with vendors. The sellers stretched up and down the adjoining streets.

"They are here for the Disting," Hofund told me. "It's not usually this busy. The market will go strong for a week. If there is anything in the world you ever hoped to buy, you will find it here."

I scanned the many vendors, seeing everything from leather goods to steel to jewels to food to thralls. A horse auction was underway in one pen. In the pen beside it, slaves were being sold. I frowned at the sight. While taking people as prizes from raids was a common practice, I didn't like it. A human's heart and mind were worth far more than a bit of silver.

As we made our way to the hall, I noticed a narrow path that led away from the main square toward the mountain. The path was lined with torches. I saw flickering flames near a jumble of rocks outside a crevice in the mountainside in the distance.

"What is that?" I asked, gesturing.

"The Dísarsalr, the temple of the dísir," Hofund told me.

"It's in the mountain?"

Hofund nodded. "We will go there."

I eyed the distant temple. The dísir were a somewhat elusive combination of female spirits. From personal, family ancestors to spirits who had ties to the land—much like a vætt—to the Norns, Frigga, Freyja, and Skadi, the feminine divine made up the dísir. Truth be told, they had never much spoken to me. I had always heard the voice of the All-Father. Or, when things were getting very peculiar, there was Loki. Only the Valkyries, sometimes called Odin's dísir, whispered to me. They were a secret sisterhood I longed to be part of. One day, if the All-Father willed it, I would ride with them on their starlight steeds. But otherwise, the dísir's mysteries were something I knew nothing of and didn't understand. Except for one strange dream...

"Ah, that is the temple of the dísir," King Gudmund said, seemingly answering Blomma's question.

The girl's eyes flashed silver as she stared at the place.

We walked up a bending path that led to the hall. King Gudmund led us inside.

I tried not to gawk like a girl who'd come fresh from my farmstead when I entered, but the tall ceiling hung over me as high as a canopy of trees. The hall even had rooms on the second floor. A vast, round fire pit burned at the center of the hall. King Gudmund's warriors, well-dressed ladies, servants, and others filled the space.

A hush fell over the company when we entered.

The king led us to the front of the room.

"Come, Hervor," he said, motioning for me to take a seat alongside his on the dais at the front of the room. "They will want to meet you. Son," he said, motioning for Hofund to take his place on the other side of his father.

For a brief moment, panic flickered across my heart.

I turned and looked at Yrsa.

She motioned for me to go on.

I took my seat, Rök coming to sit protectively beside me.

"People of Grund," King Gudmund called, gathering everyone's attention.

Blomma fidgeted awkwardly beside him.

"Blomma, come to me," Hofund whispered.

Relieved, Blomma joined Hofund, who wrapped his arm protectively around her.

The king continued. "Let's drink mead and rejoice. I come before you with great news. Not only has Hofund returned, but he does so with his new bride, Jarl Hervor of Bolmsö!"

There was a momentary pause, as if everyone in the room was struck dumb, then Gudmund's men let out a loud cheer. The others joined in, clapping and calling happily.

"A toast to Hofund and Hervor!" King Gudmund said, lifting a cup sitting on the table beside his throne. "May Thor bless their union and bless Grund. Skol!"

"Skol!" the assembly called.

I scanned the room, feeling almost every eye on me. And while many looked on with joy, others had less pleasant emotions in their eyes.

Behind me, I felt the presence of another person.

I looked over my shoulder, finding no one, but a

familiar voice whispered in my ear. He was so close, I could feel his breath on my skin.

*"Now, shield-maiden, the real battle begins."*

Loki.

Something told me he was right.

## CHAPTER 11

The flurry of people in a hurry to meet me was dizzying. Hofund introduced me to the many warriors, families, and leaders of Grund. Blomma shrank back until Yrsa took her aside, saving her from the crush of people and noise. At that moment, I wanted to escape with them.

"Hervor, this is Grund's housecarl, Halvar," Hofund said, introducing me to a grizzled looking warrior with curly, steel-grey hair and sharp eyes. He had scars on his chin and neck, telling of his days spent on the field.

"I'm pleased to meet you," I told him.

"Jarl, welcome to Grund. Please let me know if you need anything."

"I will."

With that, he nodded to me, then departed.

Hofund chuckled. "A man of few words, but a loyal companion to my father. They've been friends since they were young and even fought together."

I nodded.

Another man approached us, a smile on his face.

"Jarl Hervor, I am Bjorn, skald to great King Gudmund," a man in a long black robe said, bowing to me. He was far younger than Eyvinder, the skald of Dalr. He had yellow hair, which he'd braided from a knot on top of his head, and flashing blue eyes.

"I'm pleased to meet you."

"So, you are the jarl of Bolmsö?"

"I am."

"Then, you are the blood of Arngrim?"

"I am his granddaughter, daughter of his son, Angantyr."

He tipped his head to the side, considering. "Interesting." His eyes went to Rök. "What a ferocious creature. Is it dangerous?"

"Only when provoked."

Bjorn raised an eyebrow at me, a playful sparkle in his eyes.

"Are you harassing my bride, old friend?" Hofund asked the skald good-naturedly, setting his hand on the man's shoulder.

"Certainly not. You've married the blood of a berserker who brought her pet Fenrir to Grund. And then there is Tyrfing, the sword of legend, on your wife's hip. I wouldn't dare."

Hofund chuckled.

"You know the blade?" I asked.

He nodded. "It is my duty to know all the best stories.

But tell me, how did you get it? Orvar-Odd left it on Samso in the burial mound of the sons of Arngrim."

I leaned toward the man. "I walked through the fires of Hel to snatch it back."

"No doubt you did, shield-maiden," he said with a friendly grin.

"Bjorn is full of stories and mischief. Pay him no mind."

"But you love my stories."

"I do."

"That's why I leave all the fighting to you," Bjorn told Hofund. "I cannot sing or compose new tales if I am dead."

Hofund chuckled.

Bjorn looked over his shoulder. "The unenlightened await," he said, looking back at some finely dressed men and women who seemed eager to speak with Hofund and me. "Don't let them dissuade you, Jarl Hervor. Not everyone in Grund is bad," he told me with a wink.

"I'll speak to you again soon, my friend," Hofund told Bjorn.

"Bring your wife. She's far prettier and more interesting to talk to."

Hofund laughed. "Get your own wife, skald."

"My lady in white," he said mysteriously, lifting a finger as if considering, then winked at me and walked away.

I looked at Hofund.

"Bjorn is one of my oldest friends. His mother was a

völva at the temple. Bragi whispers to him. You will be surprised when you hear him sing."

"I'll look forward to that."

"Prince Hofund," a rich, feminine voice called. I turned to see a well-dressed older couple approach us.

"Thurid," Hofund said, inclining his head to the lady. "And Toke," he added, acknowledging the older man.

"We are so pleased to see you returned," she said, but then her gaze went to me. It turned icy. "And with a bride. That is quite a surprise."

Ignoring the look, Hofund said, "May I introduce my wife, Jarl Hervor of Bolmsö?"

"Bolmsö. Where is that?" the woman asked.

"In Lake Bolmen, near Halmstad," I replied.

"I've never heard of it," the woman said scornfully.

"Bolmsö is the home of the berserker Arngrim," a young woman standing behind Thurid said.

The couple parted to reveal a woman of striking beauty. She had long, dark hair and dark eyes. She was richly dressed and adorned with long earrings and a beaded necklace.

Thurid smiled at the girl. "Always so bright, my dear." She turned to me, "*Princess* Hervor, this is my daughter, Revna."

*Princess?*

"I am pleased to meet you, Jarl Hervor," the girl told me, bowing deeply.

"And I, you," I said, with more warmth than I felt.

When the girl rose, her eyes fell on Hofund.

To my surprise, he was smiling at her.

"I'm pleased to see you home safely," she said, batting her long lashes at my husband. "We prayed to Thor to keep you safe."

"Thank you, Revna."

"And here you are. With...a wife?"

Hofund nodded. "I have been working to win Hervor's heart for many months now."

"Oh," the girl replied, her eyebrows rising. "That's a surprise." She turned back to me. "Bolmsö, the home of Úlfhéðnar."

"So it is."

"Berserkers," Thurid said, sounding scandalized.

Revna looked back at my warriors. "They are from Bolmsö as well?"

"Yes, they came with me."

"And your dog?"

"This is Rök. He is a wolf."

"A wild beast," Thurid said, pulling her skirt away from Rök.

Rök tilted his head at her, emitting a low whine.

I chuckled then set my hand on his head. "He is only fierce when he needs to be."

Revna, ignoring her mother, nodded. "The warriors appear to be fine fighters," she said, then turned to Hofund. "I'm so glad to see you returned."

"Thank you."

The pair exchanged a meaningful glance, then Hofund turned from her and cleared his throat.

"Returned, yes. But with a wife," Thurid whispered to her husband.

The man ignored her. "We must not keep the prince," Toke, the woman's husband, said, motioning to his wife that it was time to leave. "There are others who will wish to meet the princess."

The woman waved at her husband to be silent. "Just a moment longer. Who is that young girl with you?" Thurid asked Hofund, motioning to Blomma.

"That is Blomma, my adopted daughter," he replied.

The woman gasped then turned to me. "Yours? You already have a child?"

Something mean snapped. Rök, sensing my tension, rose to his feet, his manner stiff.

Revna, noticing Rök's posture and the look on my face, whispered, "Mother..."

"Blomma is under my care," I said stiffly.

"And she is our daughter," Hofund added.

"Oh. I see," Thurid said. "Well."

Revna shook her pretty head. "Look, Mother. There is Urla. Surely, she wants to talk to you."

"Yes. Yes, you're right," Thurid said, then turned to Hofund. "Welcome returns," she told him, then turned to me, giving me the weakest of smiles. With that, she moved away, her husband following her. Before she was out of earshot, however, she turned to her husband and asked, "So, is that child hers or not?"

Her husband shrugged. "Can't say."

Revna sighed heavily, then set her hand on Hofund's arm. "Welcome home," she told him, her eyes soft. She held his gaze far longer than she should have before she turned to me. "I'm pleased to meet you, Jarl Hervor."

I nodded to her.

With that, the girl rejoined her parents.

I looked at Hofund out of the corner of my eye.

"That is a long story with a short ending," he said. "I will tell you later."

I watched the trio go. Thurid was still grumbling in her husband's ear. I couldn't hear what she was saying, but I did catch her husband's reply.

"It's not uncommon for a man to take a second wife," he told her, then the couple and their daughter retreated, Revna casting one last look at Hofund.

I looked away. I didn't like the jealous, angry feeling bubbling up in me. I especially didn't like how such petty people could evoke the fire in my blood. Nonetheless, I could hear my heart beating in my ears. I inhaled slowly and deeply, calming my nerves.

"Hofund, Hofund, my boy?" an extremely elderly man walking with a tall staff called as he slowly crossed the room. He was accompanied by a young woman dressed in an off-white tunic, a veil draped over her head.

"Hervor, please come," Hofund said. "Great-grandfather, stay where you are. We're coming," Hofund called.

"Very good. Very good. I hear you," the old man said, smiling wide. He was an ancient thing with short white hair. He had deep wrinkles which etched his face. His eyes were white with blindness. Holding onto a staff with one hand, he held out the other for Hofund.

Hofund wrapped his hand in the old man's, kissing his fingers. When Hofund let him go, the old man patted Hofund's face.

"Yes, there you are. The rumors are true. You have the beard of a married man," he said with a laugh.

"Great-grandfather," Hofund said, chuckling softly. He turned to the veiled woman. "Norna," he said, inclining his head to her.

She returned the gesture.

Hofund turned back to the old man. "Great-grandfather, I am pleased to introduce you to my wife, Hervor. Hervor, this is Heidrek, my mother's grandfather."

Smiling, the ancient man turned his white eyes toward me, then reached out for me.

I took his hand.

"Ah, here she is," he said, touching my fingers. "My goodness, this is no soft maid. She has a warrior's callouses."

"Hervor is a shield-maiden, Great-grandfather."

"Yes, yes, of course, she is. Thor would not have you marry a pampered pet. May I touch your face?" the old man asked me.

"Of course."

His soft hand gently felt my features. "But a beauty all the same. And your hair. What color?"

"Yellow."

The old man laughed. "And the eyes are blue, no doubt."

"No, Great-grandfather, Hervor's eyes are the color of pine sap in spring."

"I hear them whispering the names of Angantyr and Arngrim in this hall. Are you the daughter of the berserkers?" he asked me.

"I am."

"A wolf-skin," the man said in awe.

I signaled for Rök to come forward. "You don't know how right you are, sir," I said, then set Heidrek's hand on Rök's head.

The man stilled then gently stroked Rök's ear, which Rök rewarded with a lick.

The man laughed. "Have you brought the wolves to Grund, Hervor?"

"I have."

He grinned. "Good. Good. They deserve a little growling at here."

"Heidrek," King Gudmund called, joining us.

"And here is the king," Heidrek said with a smile.

"I am glad to see you about."

"I was out walking when I heard the horn. The ravens told me you would be home soon, Hofund. Norna was passing and offered to help me to the hall."

"Our thanks to you, Norna," the king told the veiled girl.

"Ardis asked me to come and see if it was Hofund who had returned. We are pleased to see you here for the Dísablót," the gythia told Hofund. "And to see you have brought the shield-maiden of Bolmsö with you. Have I heard right that you have a daughter?"

"Yes," Hofund said. He turned to Blomma and Yrsa, motioning for both of them to come forward. "Blomma," Hofund said, reaching to her. "Please, come and meet my great-grandfather Heidrek. Great-grandfather, Hervor and I have taken this young lady into our care," Hofund said, placing Blomma's small hand into the old man's grasp.

"I am blind, little one, but I can feel the gentleness of your spirit. Welcome to our family."

"Thank you," Blomma said politely.

Norna, the priestess, knelt to look at Blomma. "Blomma, is it?"

"Yes."

"Hofund and Hervor should bring you to the temple so you may make your offerings to your dísir upon the hörgor," Norna told Blomma. "Will you see to it?" Norna asked Hofund.

He inclined his head to her, then turned to Yrsa. "Great-grandfather, I also wish you to meet Yrsa. She is the foster-mother of Hervor."

Yrsa stepped forward and took the man's outstretched hand.

"Ah, yes. And here I feel the hand of a fighter," Heidrek said. He let go of Yrsa's hand then touched her face, his fingers gingerly brushing the scar thereon. "Seen your share of battles."

"I have."

"And won them all, or you wouldn't be standing here," he said with a chuckle.

"So far," Yrsa replied with a laugh.

"Well done, my boy," Heidrek told Hofund. "None of the girls they tried to throw at you were ever suitable matches."

King Gudmund laughed. "Your granddaughter always said the same, that Hofund would find his own path. No amount of coaxing from me could make it work."

"Well, my granddaughter was always smarter than you, Gudmund."

"That she was. And better looking too."

Heidrek chuckled. "Now, Norna, my legs are tired. Find me a place to sit. Go on, Hofund, go on. I am sure they are all eager to meet your bride." Heidrek clapped Hofund on the shoulder one last time before the gythia led him to a seat nearby.

Yrsa looked down at Blomma. "Come on. Let's find something to eat," she told her, the pair escaping once more. I felt jealous.

Hofund and I left his great-grandfather. From what I could discern, there were many prominent families in Grund. War or trade—I didn't know which—had given them enough wealth to make them bold.

It was growing late when a richly dressed woman and her husband approached.

"My aunt, uncle, and their sons," Hofund whispered.

"Hofund," the man called. He wore a fistful of impressive silver rings. "We are pleased to see you in Grund once more."

"Uncle. I am glad to be back."

"I think you spend more time away from Grund than here," the woman, who looked around the room like she disliked everything she saw, said with half a yawn.

"I go where I am needed, Aunt," Hofund told her.

Behind the pair, two young men about my age exchanged a glance.

"Hervor, may I introduce my aunt Frika—my father's sister—and her husband, Rolf. And these are my cousins, Soren and Thorolf."

"I am pleased to meet you," I told them.

"They say you are a jarl," Rolf told me.

"I am jarl of Bolmsö."

"What will Bolmsö do now that you are the princess of Grund?" Frika asked.

"Bolmsö is well in hand," I replied. Something told me that this woman didn't need to know the details of my business.

"Cousins," Hofund said, motioning to the men behind his aunt and uncle.

"Welcome returns, Hofund," the taller of the pair, a man with long, dark brown hair and a trim beard, said. "I'm Thorolf, Jarl Hervor," he said, introducing himself.

I inclined my head to him. To my surprise, Thorolf looked more like Hofund's brother than his cousin; their hair and eye color were the same. As well, I saw a similarity in their brows and square jaws.

The other cousin, however, took after his father. He had honey-colored hair that was cropped at the neck and brow. His pinched face, with his pointed nose and squinting eyes, matched the feel of contempt oozing from him. He smirked knowingly at Hofund. "So, you have returned for the Disting. We wondered if you'd come at all. I certainly hoped so, considering King Harald and King Gizer are expected. Hated to think you would shame your father by wasting your time wandering about while you were needed here," he told Hofund.

"Ah, Soren," Hofund said with a smile. "It is good to see you too. This is my wife, Hervor."

The man turned to me. He opened his mouth to speak, but the flame inside me ignited first.

"Hofund has been at war," I said. "Not exactly wandering unless that's how you define defending your kingdom." The moment the words slipped from my lips, I *almost* regretted them.

They all looked at me. Even Frika snapped out of her either feigned or real boredom—I wasn't sure which—to give me a shocked look.

"Yes, well, war is something Hofund does well," Soren said. "It is unfortunate we are not strong enough to keep things peaceful."

I opened my mouth to speak when Hofund said, "I shall forever endeavor to keep things peaceful in Grund so you may lounge in your hall and sleep comfortably at night, cousin."

Rolf cleared his throat and gave Soren a stern look. He turned back to Hofund. "Ever the son of Thor," he said with a nod to Hofund. "And a shield-maiden as your bride. May the gods be praised. Right, my love?"

"What is it?" Frika asked.

"May the gods be praised."

"Oh, yes. May the gods be praised," she said with a sigh, then looked at Rök. "What a fine animal. Its fur looks so soft. You must be sure to have a cloak made of it when it dies. Come, dear. I will have mead now," Frika said, then turned away.

Rolf nodded to Hofund then followed his wife, Soren trailing along with them.

"It is good to see you, cousin," Thorolf told Hofund, then turned to me. "You are welcome in Grund, Jarl Hervor."

"Thank you."

After they left, I turned to Hofund. "Did she really just suggest I turn Rök into a coat?"

"She did. And with that, you have learned everything you need to know about my aunt."

Hofund motioned to a servant to come to refill my mead cup.

"Drink," Hofund told me. "It's going to be a long night."

## CHAPTER 12

By the time the night had ended, I had seen more faces and learned more names than I could possibly remember. It was late when the hall finally quieted.

"I should take Blomma to sleep," I told Hofund.

He nodded. "You and I will stay in my old room. Blomma and Yrsa can lodge in a chamber close to ours. Father arranged for a maid for you, and we also have someone to tend to Blomma and Yrsa."

"Yrsa will love that," I said with a knowing laugh, which Hofund shared. "And them?" I asked, motioning to my warriors from Bolmsö.

"They'll be housed here in the hall as well."

"Thank you."

"You get Blomma, and I'll meet you upstairs?"

I nodded.

Hofund left me.

I joined Yrsa. She'd been nursing a mug of ale while

watching everything happening in the hall with varying shades of bemusement, disgust, and suspicion.

"You're still on your feet, and you didn't have to kill anyone," she told me. "Well done." She clicked her mug against mine.

"I didn't have to kill anyone *yet*," I corrected her.

Yrsa laughed.

"I might be on my feet, but Blomma is not," I said, looking back at the little girl who was leaning heavily against Rök, her eyes drowsy. "Hofund has put the pair of you in the same chamber. I was going to take her up. Want to come along?"

Yrsa nodded. "Ale got warm anyway," she said, sloshing the last of her drink into the fire.

Yrsa and I crossed the room to collect Blomma.

"Blomma, why don't you come to bed? You look tired," I told her.

"No, I'm only watching. Rök is the tired one."

She didn't want to miss anything. "Yes, you're right, but Rök needs his rest. Hofund's servants have prepared a chamber for you. Yrsa will stay with you. Although, I'm not sure you'll get much sleep between Yrsa's and Rök's snoring."

"I snore less than you," Yrsa told me.

I laughed at the absurdity of her joke.

Yrsa winked at me.

"All right," Blomma said tiredly.

The three of us went upstairs, Rök padding along behind us.

The family wing of the house was located on the

second floor. Guards stood at the entry to the family quarters and at the top of the stairs. Of course, the king and his family would be well-protected. The hall below was filled with warriors. If anyone wanted to get to Gudmund, they'd need to kill two dozen men first.

I marveled at the superb workmanship of the hall. Every beam, every rail, every timber was carved with ornate designs. Even the walls had been engraved to show images of the gods, Thor fighting with Jörmunganer, Thor beating his hammer on an anvil, Odin's eight-legged horse Sleipner, Frigga being pulled by a chariot yoked to a team of cats, and others. Impressive sets of antlers, shields, spears, and furs hung on the walls.

Outside one of the rooms, Hofund was speaking to a silver-haired woman. They both turned to look at us.

Hofund smiled. "Ladies, this is Magna," Hofund said, introducing the woman. "She watched over me when I was a boy. She will look after Blomma and see to anything you might need, Yrsa."

Yrsa nodded. "All right."

"I will see to your girl, Jarl Hervor," Magna told me, then knelt to look at Blomma. "Let me see you, young lady. My, what a beauty. I've got everything ready for you inside. Would you like to come have a look?" She reached out for Blomma's hand.

Blomma paused. Uncertain, Blomma took Yrsa's hand instead. "Shall we go see?" she asked Yrsa.

"I suppose. Come on, Rök," Yrsa said.

Magna, nonplussed by Blomma's rejection, simply

smiled benevolently at her, then they headed into the chamber.

After they had gone, Hofund turned to me. "I told her Blomma was skittish. Magna was a second mother to me. They will get along well in no time. Now, come and meet Bodil."

"Bodil?"

"Your maid."

"Ahh," I replied, feeling very unsure about the idea of a maid. Eydis had been more my friend than a servant. And while she took care of me, I felt very uncertain about letting a stranger get so close. Maybe Blomma wasn't the only one who was skittish.

Hofund opened the door to the chamber next to Blomma's.

I forced myself not to gasp at the beauty of the engraved poster bed covered with rich blankets and furs. A window looked out on the stars overhead. A standing metal brazier kept the cold away. Bear skins covered the wooden floor. Two chairs sat before the fire. There was a table on the other side of the room. Behind it, scrolls filled the shelves.

In the center of the room was a young woman with a wild tangle of curly, red hair.

"Bodil," Hofund said kindly.

She smiled from him to me. "Ah, this must be Jarl Hervor."

"I am."

"I'm so happy to meet you. I was so excited when King Gudmund asked me to attend you," the girl told me.

"Anything you need, I'm here to help you. My room is just on the other side of yours," she said, pointing down the hall. "Can I assist with anything tonight? I have the fire prepared. Do you want me to help with your hair…" she asked, giving my hair a dubious look, one I'd seen Eydis make many times before.

"No, I'm fine for now. Thank you."

"All right. I'll be next door if you need me." With a smile, she exited the room.

I raised an eyebrow at Hofund.

He chuckled. "Father asked her. She's Revna's cousin. Revna's aunt has many daughters. Bodil is the eldest."

"Revna's cousin?"

Hofund nodded absently, not sensing my hesitation, then turned and looked around the room. "So, I am home," he said with a heavy sigh. Hofund crossed the room and touched the corner of the table. "I used to hide here. Frequently."

"Hide from whom?"

"That depends on who is below."

"And which of the people I met tonight did you hide from?"

Hofund motioned to the chairs before the fire. We sat. "Can you guess?"

"Your cousin Soren…"

Hofund laughed. "I never hide from Soren. That would make him too comfortable, which is the opposite of what I want. Soren hopes I will be killed on one of these raids so he can become king."

"Is he your aunt's eldest?"

Hofund nodded.

I rolled my eyes. "He dresses more finely than Asta."

"He's never been in a battle. He thinks he fights here," Hofund said, tapping the side of his head. "But even there, his armor is new."

I chuckled. "And his brother? Thor—"

"Thorolf," Hofund said. "Thorolf is different, but he does as his parents dictate. Most of the time, they dictate poorly. He has a warrior's heart, but he either cannot or chooses not to find a way to join me."

"As followers of Thor, how can they stand in his way? If he was determined to fight..."

"Which says everything you need to know about his determination."

"Ahh," I said with a nod. "While they were all very polite, the wealthy families treated you...warily."

"You are not the only one who knows how to skulk quietly, observing what people whisper. I have learned not to trust them, and they know it. Given I will be their next king, they should be wary."

"Is there danger here?"

Hofund shrugged lightly. "It is more a dance than danger. Now that you are here—and Blomma, along with you—you have reshuffled the game board. None of them know how to move. And they will all try to see if they can move you."

"They'll find I'm quite unmovable."

"I know. Why do you think I married you?"

Laughing, I rose and sat in Hofund's lap. "And Revna?"

"You see. You miss nothing."

"Oh, do elaborate."

"She was the favorite to be my wife."

"A favorite of whom?"

"Her mother and my aunt."

"And your father?"

"My father listened but dictated nothing. After all, he married a völva from the Dísarsalr. He was not inclined to force me into anything."

"What about Revna herself?"

"Revna didn't want me as a husband any more than I wanted her as a wife. In that, we were simpatico."

While my husband was a wise man, a great strategist, and a warrior, at that moment, I saw his weakness. Revna most certainly *did* want to be his wife. Knowing Hofund, pretending the opposite was likely Revna's best course to stay close to him. If he didn't feel pressured by her, he wouldn't avoid her. Cunning.

"Jealous, Hervor?" Hofund asked, a surprised look on his face.

"Of course. I will not let someone have what is mine, not even in their thoughts."

Hofund laughed. "Revna has her charms, but they are not for me. She is no Hervor." Hofund shook his head. "I never saw anything in Grund, or anywhere else in the world, that I wanted as much as you...you in your blue dress. Just as my mother foresaw."

"That's a good answer."

"I'm glad you like it, shield-maiden," he said then rose, lifting me along with him.

I laughed. "What are you doing?"

"Taking my wife to my bed," he replied, carrying me across the room and lying me down.

Hofund helped me unbuckle my weapons, setting them on the chair nearby, then slid onto the bed with me. His hands drifted up my chest and neck, where he gently grabbed a handful of my hair, his fingers stroking my long braid. He leaned forward and set a kiss on my lips. I breathed in deeply. The bed, the linens, everything smelled of the man I loved. I reached up as I slipped my hands under his shirt, feeling the skin on his back.

"Hervor," he whispered. "I love you. Never fear Grund. For you, I am Grund," he said, then kissed me again and again and again.

And there, in the king's great hall, I gave my heart to my love once more.

## CHAPTER 13

The next morning, Hofund and I set out along with Yrsa and Blomma to explore the great Disting market. Rök, his nose busy as he sniffed all the strange smells, trotted along beside us. Hofund put Blomma on his shoulders as we made our way through the crowd.

"Too many people," Yrsa grumbled.

She was right. It felt like the entire population of Bolmsö, Halmstad, and Dalr were here all together. The market was brimming with food, clothes, jewels, smith work, and supplies like I had never seen before. Farmers were auctioning horses, pigs, and sheep. Slavers sold their thralls. We meandered down the lanes, Hofund stopping to purchase a honey cake for Blomma.

"Please, my prince. No charge," the woman told him.

Hofund smiled genteelly at her. "I will remember your offer with gratitude. But I insist you return it by taking my payment."

The old woman laughed. "Very well."

Hofund handed the cake to Blomma.

"Thank you," she told him nicely. Pinching off a piece, she dropped a bite into Rök's anxious jaws.

The wolf swallowed the first bite, then looked to Blomma for another.

"Now, now," I told Rök. "Don't get too used to such comforts."

"I'll have a look there," Yrsa said, motioning to a man selling an assortment of daggers. "Go on. I'll find you."

"You're just planning to escape," I told her.

"Am not."

I laughed. "Fine. We'll see you soon."

Hofund and I moved on.

"And what can I find for Hervor?" Hofund asked, kissing my hand.

I shrugged. "I don't need trinkets."

"No. Nor weapons either. But I did spot something," Hofund said and moved me in the direction of a woman who had bolts of fine fabric on display. From deep emerald green to twilight blue, she had a wide assortment of fabrics, yarns, and threads.

"Prince Hofund," the vendor said, inclining her head to him.

"Such a fine color," Hofund said, touching a bolt of indigo-colored material. "How do you get it so blue?"

The vendor, who had an unusual pattern of tattoos that crossed her face from her forehead to her chin, smiled proudly at the cloth. "In the sea, there are creatures that produce a liquid that can be used to color the fabric. It is not easy to coax the color, but it comes to those who are patient."

Hofund nodded. "It's magnificent. We'll have it. And the red. Will you have them sent to the hall?"

"Of course, my prince."

Hofund turned and looked at me. "Anything else you fancy?"

I chuckled. *He* was the one doing the shopping. Regardless, I looked over the beautiful cloths hanging there, spying a pale green fabric. "And that. For Eydis," I said.

The woman nodded. "Very well."

Hofund left the vendor with an obscene amount of silver then we went on our way.

I scanned behind me, looking for Yrsa, but she was no longer at the weapons dealer. As I suspected, she'd escaped.

"What do you need besides cake?" Hofund asked Blomma.

Blomma paused as if unsure what to say. "I need nothing." But I could see from the look on her face that she wasn't telling the truth.

"Blomma?" I asked.

She frowned. "I would not ask, but my boots are tight."

Hofund turned and looked at me. "A growing child."

I nodded.

We wound our way through the market until we came upon a cobbler. The man measured Blomma's feet, promising to have a pair of boots for her before the end of the market. We left him then stopped by a vendor selling jewels and other trinkets. There, I picked up a hairpin for Mother and, after some deliberation, another for Asta. Remembering the cat amulet she always wore, I found a hairpin to match.

We had walked the length of one row of the market when Yrsa appeared once more, a round of bread in one hand, an ale horn in the other.

"I knew you were making excuses," I told her with a laugh.

"Was not," Yrsa said, her mouth full of bread. "I ordered myself a new shield. And then, I found the crew from Bolmsö. Joined them for a horn of ale."

I rolled my eyes at Yrsa then snatched a piece of her bread.

We walked the rest of the market, past the smelly fish vendors and a woman selling cheese. We paused at the horse fair, watching an auction underway.

"Can you ride?" Hofund asked Blomma.

"Not well."

"Then we must make sure you have a chance to learn."

From the dock, far on the other side of the city, a horn sounded. And then another. And another.

Hofund's brow flexed. "An important visitor has come."

"Should we go?" I asked.

Hofund nodded.

"Not us," Yrsa said, taking Blomma from Hofund's shoulders. "We have our own matters to attend to."

I raised an eyebrow at her.

"Mind your own business. This is between Blomma and me."

"Very well. We'll see you in the hall."

Hofund and I departed, Rök joining us.

We headed toward the docks. Three ships with deep red sails, an emblem of the sun thereon, were coming to port.

"King Harald," Hofund said.

"You know him well?"

Hofund bobbed his head. "Well enough. His father died two years back. He was a good man. Harald is ambitious and fierce. He has launched many raids to the east and south. His forces grow in spades."

"Ally or enemy?" I whispered.

"Ally...for now."

We arrived at the dock just as the king debarked. There was no doubting his status amongst his men. He was finely dressed in black and silver, his weapons gleaming. He was a tall man with a long, dark braid. His head and cheeks were tattooed. Again, I saw images of the sun. The crowd cleared to let Hofund and me through.

"Hofund?" he called. "This is a surprise."

"King Harald," Hofund said. "We are pleased to have you in Grund."

"I heard you were chasing Haki and Hagbard," the king told him.

"So, I was. Come, I want you to meet Hervor," Hofund said, turning to me. "Hervor, may I introduce King Harald. Harald, this is my wife, Jarl Hervor of Bolmsö."

The man raised an eyebrow at Hofund. "Married?"

Hofund chuckled. "Yes."

He turned to me. "I can see why. Well met, Jarl Hervor."

"I am pleased to meet you, King Harald."

"And who is this fine beast?" he asked, turning to Rök.

"This is Rök," I said, setting my hand on Rök's head.

"I've never seen a wolf of this size."

"He is from Bolmsö."

"Bolmsö," Harald said, considering. "The home of Arngrim?"

I nodded. "He was my grandfather."

Harald laughed then clapped Hofund's back. "Left all the pretty maids of Grund and went off and married a berserker. Of course, you did." Harald turned to me. "Best watch those pretty maids, berserker. Now that you've stolen their prize, they'll have daggers for your back."

"Why do you think I brought Rök?"

King Harald laughed.

"Come, my father will be anxious to see you," Hofund said. Turning, we made our way to the hall.

"Who else has come?" Harald asked.

"We expect King Gizer today. Princes Jorund and Eric are also expected."

Rök and I followed along behind Hofund and King Harald. One of King Harald's men joined me.

"Jarl Hervor," he said, nodding to me. "I'm Rudolf, chief man to King Harald."

Rudolf was about the same age as the king and myself.

He had curly red hair, pale blue eyes, and a face full of freckles.

"I'm pleased to meet you. I trust your journey went well."

"May the All-Father be praised. My mother is from Halmstad. Do you know how things are there?"

"Halmstad had a tumultuous year, but now she is under a peaceful jarl."

"Asmund?"

"No. He died in battle."

"Then...Asger?"

"Also died in battle. Jarl Ragal is the ruler of Halmstad now."

"Ragal. I don't know him," he said then sighed. "I do not see Halmstad often, but I am sorry to hear of such chaos."

"As was I, Rudolf. As was I. But all is well now."

When we finally arrived at the hall, King Gudmund met us at the door. His face was looking very red and swollen. It seemed to me he was walking with a limp.

"Too slow for you young men," he said. "Welcome, King Harald. Come, my friend. Let's drink and talk."

"Father," Hofund said, a tinge of worry in his voice. Apparently, he also noticed the king's condition.

Gudmund motioned to Hofund to say nothing.

We went inside.

The place was as busy as it had been the day before. The wealthy families of Grund had gathered once more. I spotted Revna talking with Soren and Thorolf. Revna's and Soren's eyes followed Hofund and Harald. I met

Thorolf's gaze. He lifted his ale horn to me. I nodded to him then turned away.

"Have your men make themselves comfortable. Eat and drink," Gudmund told King Harald with a good-natured smile.

King Harald nodded to his men, motioning for them to go on.

"Jarl Hervor," Rudolf said, leaving me.

Beyond the great hall was a meeting room. King Gudmund led us there. I followed the others inside.

When King Gudmund finally turned, a look of surprise crossed his face when he saw me there.

"Hervor," he said, then paused. "You don't have to stay for talks. Perhaps, Blomma..."

"Hervor will stay," Hofund said simply.

King Gudmund looked from his son to me. He nodded then smiled. "Very well. Very well, indeed. Please, sit."

"Hofund tells me you expect Gizer," King Harald told King Gudmund.

King Gudmund poured Harald a glass of mead. "We do."

"Hugleik?"

"No. In fact, a ship has come from Uppsala with a message from King Hugleik."

"When?" Hofund asked.

"While you were out. It seems the sea kings Haki and Hagbard are amassing forces outside of Uppsala. King Hugleik has asked for our help."

King Harald drank his mead then asked, "What,

Hugliek's jugglers and courtesans cannot fight his battle for him?"

I furrowed my brow. "Jugglers?"

"King Hugleik is no warrior. He is a man of ease and comfort. He prefers the entertainment of the court life to the actual ruling," Hofund explained to me.

*Much like half the people in King Gudmund's hall.*

"Now we see the folly of not having Eric or Jorund on the throne in Uppsala," King Harald said, referring to the sons of the late King Yngvi.

"And why aren't they on the throne?" I asked.

"When Alf took the throne from his brother, King Yngvi's young bride fled with her sons to her father's jarldom. There was no doubt Alf would kill the boys—who were children at the time. But the jarl protected his grandsons, and Alf let them live so as not to start a civil war. For all the good it did him...Alf was, in turn, murdered by his own son, Hugleik. Of course, being the coward he is, Hugleik used poison. Now Hugleik sits on the throne, and King Yngvi's rightful heirs wait," King Harald explained.

I nodded thoughtfully. In the story Loki had told in the hall of Dalr, he had said that Jarl Bjartmar had wanted Svafa to marry Prince Alf. What a wretched fate would have awaited her. While the gods had stolen Svafa's memories, they had also saved her from misery.

King Gudmund sat down with a heavy sigh. "These sea kings have become a menace."

King Harald nodded. "There was word they'd taken Dalr and Silfrheim."

"They tried," Hofund replied.

"Routed them, did you?" King Harald asked with a grin.

Hofund turned to me. "I had help."

Harald lifted his cup, toasting me. "I fended them off from Jutland. They must be dealt with once and for all. What say you, Gudmund?"

"In my younger days, I would have painted my horses and met them on the open field," he said, then turned to me. "They used to call me Gudmund One-Mane, leader of the Wild Hunt. I would paint my horses to look like skeletons, and we would mark our own faces to match, making the enemy believe they were fighting the dead. But those days are behind me. It is for younger men—and women—to take up the sword and fight."

Hofund sat back and crossed his arms on his chest. "Uppsala," he considered.

"Accessible by land and river, is it not? If they attack the city by river, it would be easy to pinch them, trap them in port. If they travel by land, leaving their boats behind, we could burn their boats, cutting off their retreat. Then, all you have to do is kill them," I offered.

Harald laughed. "By the gods, she truly is the blood of old Arngrim," he told Hofund. "You'd scare my wife to death, Hervor. But she's a timid thing. Even loud noises make her jump."

"I hear you have a child," King Gudmund said. "Born in the winter. Your first child, was it not?"

He nodded. "It was. A daughter. Helga. Small but

healthy babe. Her birth took quite a lot from her mother. My wife is still abed from the effort."

"Congratulations on your first child," I said, then lifted my drink.

"To little Helga," Gudmund agreed. "May the All-Father grant her wisdom, Thor grant her strength, and Freyja give her beauty."

"And may the Norns weave for her a fate that a gentle maid deserves," Hofund said, his voice sounding hollow.

Harald lifted his cup. "To Helga," he said, accepting the toast and drinking to his daughter.

My gaze shifted to Hofund. I knew that sound in his voice and the faraway look in his eyes. He had seen something about Harald's daughter, but what?

Hofund turned and looked at me.

The expression on his face was one of terror.

He quickly hid it behind his cup.

*Odin.*

*All-Father.*

*What are you gods plotting?*

## CHAPTER 14

After some time, we rejoined the company in the hall. The kings would make no decisions about the problem in Uppsala until King Gizer and Princes Jorund and Eric arrived. I took Rök out for some air. The wolf was exploring a grassy field not far from the river when his ears perked up, and he gazed into the crowd. A moment later, he shot off after something.

"Rök?"

Confused, I went after him. Once I got closer to the crowd, I spotted a pair I knew. Yrsa was leading a pony upon which Blomma was mounted. When Blomma caught sight of me, she waved. Rök jumped happily along beside them.

The pony, undeterred by the wolf's presence, dawdled along.

Grinning, I joined them.

"What's this?" I asked.

"Blomma said she hadn't had a chance to ride much," Yrsa said. "Thought we'd better start somewhere. Plus, I got this sturdy little beast for a good price."

"At the horse fair?"

Yrsa nodded.

"Look at him," Blomma said, leaning down to hug the neck of the pony. He was a strong little horse with chestnut-brown hair and a golden mane.

"You'll have to think of a name for him," I told her, petting the horse.

"We'll start lessons tomorrow," Yrsa told Blomma. "For now, let's take him to the stables."

We turned back toward the city, Yrsa leading the pony.

"Who came?" Yrsa asked me.

"King Harald."

"Never heard of him."

"From Jutland."

"Still never heard of him."

Blomma giggled.

I shook my head. "Well, that's what happens when you live in a cave."

Yrsa huffed a laugh.

When we arrived at the stables, Yrsa lifted Blomma off the pony then took him to the stablemaster. They exchanged a few words, then Yrsa returned.

"They'll see to him," she reassured Blomma. "Now, let's find something to eat," Yrsa said, and we all headed back inside.

Yrsa and Blomma went to grab a bite while I scanned

for my warriors from Bolmsö. Kit, Trygve, and Öd had made friends with Grund's warriors who'd fought with us at Dalr. They sat drinking together. Sigrun had joined a small band of shield-maidens from Grund. And Kára... Kára had somehow found herself under the attentions of Soren.

"He's trying to get information about you," a voice said from behind me.

I turned to find Bjorn, Hofund's old friend and skald, standing there. "He's been asking around all day."

"And what has he discovered?"

"From your own people, nothing," Bjorn said with a laugh. "They are smart enough not to play such games. But that one," he said, motioning to Kára, "that one is filling his head with tales of such horror, Soren will see you in his nightmares tonight."

I chuckled.

"That said, there are rumors enough to be had."

"What do they say?"

"Many things. But mostly, they're wondering about that sword on your hip. Does it really make its wielder invincible?"

"So to speak. As long as you keep your hand."

Bjorn grinned. "Good."

"Good? That's all?"

"Yes. Good."

I laughed. "I thought skalds were always loquacious."

"We are. But sometimes, simple is enough. And other times," he said, motioning again to Kára, "the more detail the better."

Kára set her finger on the top of her head then drew it down her face and chest to her waist, her hands going wide.

But not as wide as Soren's eyes.

As Kára continued, Soren grew pale.

"See how white he is," Bjorn said with a chuckle.

"He asked."

"It is better if they fear you. Otherwise, they will seek to maneuver you."

I turned and looked at him. "And what about you? Will you seek to maneuver me?"

"I already am, isn't it obvious? I am pointing out your enemies. That paints me as your friend."

"What if I'm suspicious of everyone?"

"Then you are already smarter than most of the men in this room."

"What about the women?" I asked, hearing the echo of Eydis in my words.

"And *all* of the women."

"Maybe not one," I said, my gaze going to Yrsa.

He laughed. "Frika tried her. Your shield-maiden foster-mother grunted a reply and walked away. They've learned she will not share anything."

I shrugged. "There is nothing to share."

"Nothing? No hidden secrets, Jarl Hervor?"

Grinning, I looked at him. "If I say no, you will not believe me. And if I say yes, you will dog me to learn them. So what if I say nothing…like Yrsa."

"Then, she has taught you well."

"Bjorn," Hofund said, joining us. "Are you harassing

my bride?"

"He's trying to pry all my secrets from me."

"Do you have secrets?" Hofund asked.

I winked at him.

"I was giving your wife advice," Bjorn told Hofund.

Hofund nodded slowly, thoughtfully. "I am sure there are many whispers afoot. What have you heard, old friend?"

"Aside from the fact that Soren is disappointed you're still alive?"

"That comes as no surprise."

"No. I'm sorry to deflate your ego, my prince, but they aren't interested in you anymore. It is Hervor they are seeking to unravel," Bjorn told him.

Hofund grinned at me.

"I'm mysterious," I told Hofund.

"And alluring…especially in blue."

"In blue?" Bjorn asked, looking at Hofund. "And did she wear blue? As your mother foresaw?"

Hofund nodded.

"Ah. Well. Perhaps there is hope for me yet."

"How so? I asked.

"Hofund's mother saw a bride for me as well. She rode a pale-colored horse, the woman and horse all white."

I furrowed my brow, trying to make sense out of the riddle.

"It's no use, Jarl Hervor. I could not find an answer in all these years. But I shall be sure to keep an eye on every woman who rides into Grund."

"I shall pray that Frigga rewards your diligence."

"May the gods let it be so," Bjorn replied.

## CHAPTER 15

L ate in the afternoon, the horn sounded once more. King Gudmund, who was deep in talks with King Harald, waved to Hofund. "Go and see who it is, my son."

Hofund nodded to his father, then the two of us returned to the docks.

"Hofund," I said gently. "Your father... he does not look altogether well to me. Did you notice anything amiss?"

Hofund's brow furrowed. "He always overeats during the blots. When he does, it bothers him. His body swells, and he gets red-faced. He is over-fond of sweet things."

"Should you say something?"

"I have. He agrees with me then carries on anyway."

I frowned but said nothing more.

We arrived at the dock to find three ships with black sails, white eagles designed thereon.

"King Gizer," Hofund told me.

Rök bounded off the pier and went for a swim while Hofund and I approached the boats. At the end of the dock, I spotted a grinning man with yellow hair, his body heavily tattooed. He laughed and joked with his men, his hands on his hips as he watched his other ships making port. He wore a circlet around his head. His booming laugh echoed down the pier.

I looked up at Hofund, who was smirking.

"Don't let Gizer's impish nature fool you," Hofund whispered. "He is probably the deadliest man I know. He murdered at least a dozen jarls and the last king of Göta-land to get that circlet on his head."

"At least I've found someone to look up to."

Hofund laughed. "So says the second-deadliest person I know."

I chuckled.

"King Gizer," Hofund called loudly.

The king turned. "Hofund," he called, his arms outstretched. "Look at you," he said, eyeing Hofund over. "I hear you took out old Bjartmar. Not a scratch on you, though," he said, slapping Hofund on the cheek. "In blood and honor."

Hofund grinned, clapping Gizer on the shoulder. "In blood and honor."

"And who is this shield-maiden? Introduce me," Gizer said, pushing Hofund aside.

"King Gizer, may I introduce Jarl Hervor of Bolmsö," Hofund said.

"Well, well," King Gizer began, stepping close toward me. "I am pleased to meet you, shield-maiden." He took my hand and set a kiss thereon, lifting his eyes to meet mine in the most shameless of flirtations.

"Jarl of Bolmsö...and my wife," Hofund added.

Gizer paused, then laughed. He kissed my hand one last time, then let me go. He turned to Hofund. "Of course you would find the prettiest jarl," he said, then turned back to me. "Well, wife of Hofund, I am happy to make your acquaintance all the same."

"Likewise, King Gizer," I replied.

"Enough flirting with Hervor," Hofund said. "Come, let's get you to the hall. King Harald has been here since this morning, maneuvering father into this and that. You're missing all the fun."

"I am late with good reason," Gizer told Hofund.

"News?"

He nodded. "A plea from King Hugleik."

"We've received word as well. Come, old friend, let's talk."

"Drink first. Then flirt more with your pretty wife. Then talk."

Hofund laughed then turned back to me. "I told you life in Grund would be challenging."

"Oh, I think I can manage," I replied to Hofund with a wink.

Gizer laughed then elbowed Hofund in the ribs. "She's got wit too."

"Thank the gods," Hofund said.

THE EXCITEMENT IN THE HALL WAS PALPABLE THAT NIGHT. Troupes of musicians played, and a man entertained the crowd by spinning fire. Blomma marveled at the sight. Yrsa watched the scene warily, her eyes more on the crowd than the entertainers. I could see why. With the kings here, many were calculating their next moves. Soren worked his way from Harald to Gizer and back again, always whispering. But his kind of trouble was the obvious kind. It was the less obvious ones you had to worry about.

Late in the night, King Gudmund called for Bjorn to sing. "Come, skald. Let us hear the rich voice with which Bragi gifted you. Sing for us."

"What would you like to hear?" Bjorn asked.

"Something to stir the imagination," Gudmund said.

Bjorn nodded. Motioning to the musicians, they went to the front of the room.

"This Dísablót, we are honored to be in the presence of three wise kings. But new to Grund is a shield-maiden who has become our princess, wife of our prince, and one day, our queen. Tonight, I shall sing of the dwarven sword Tyrfing," he said, then began. His deep, rich voice echoed around the room, silencing the hall. When he sang, he wove the tale of King Sigrlami, the dwarves Dvalin and Dulin, and of the sword Tyrfing. Bjorn told Arngrim's tale, how he won the blade from Sigrlami and the princess Eyfura. He sang of the isle of wolves. He sang of the sons of Arngrim and of my father's death by the hands of the hero Hjalmar of Uppsala. And then he sang parts of the tale I had never heard before. He sang about me, Angantyr's daughter, and Svafa's suffering caused by the gods. He sang of Yrsa, a grizzled shield-maiden who mothered and mentored me. He told the tale of the waking of Angantyr on Samso and how I went to Hel to retrieve Tyrfing, returning with the blade to slay old Arngrim's enemies.

As he sang, all eyes went to me.

Part of me wanted to crawl under a table. But the other part of me felt pride hearing how I fit into the tale of my family. In the end, I forced myself to ignore the pangs the attention caused me and smiled lightly.

"He left out the part about Hervarth," Yrsa whispered in my ear.

"Thank the gods."

Bjorn told of my wars in Blomfjall and Halmstad. He sang of how I was a wolf-skin, shifting form on the battle-field as I fought against the giantess Solva. Flattering, all in all. And while I was not a fan of the attention, a quick glance at the crowd told me that Bjorn had been purposeful in his choice of song. Since I'd arrived, they had all gossiped and whispered about me. Bjorn ended the conversation for them. Now, there was no need for rumors. My whole life had been recanted in the ballad—with some embellishments on the truth.

When the last note left his lips, the audience fell to silence for a moment then cheered.

"All hail Jarl Hervor," Bjorn called.

"Hail Jarl Hervor," the crowd called, cheering me.

I smiled then rose. "You flatter me, Bjorn, but I am

indebted for your remembrances of family. Skol," I said, lifting my cup to toast him.

The skald bowed to me.

"Skol," they called to Bjorn.

"Very good!" King Gudmund called. "Now, music," he said, motioning to the musicians.

Once more, the hall was filled with music and laughter.

My eyes shifted to Blomma. While the retelling had painted my family in a favorable light, it had not been kind to Solva and the people of Blomfjall. Blomma looked upset.

I took a seat beside her. "Blomma," I whispered, unsure what to say.

Her eyes met mine. "I know what my mother was, but..."

I nodded then gently set my hand on the back of her head, pressing her forehead against mine. "Your mother was a great warrior. Perhaps she was not a good mother, but she was fierce. We should honor her for that."

"Yes," Blomma whispered.

I kissed her on the forehead, then pulled back.

A moment later, Hofund joined us. He took Blomma's hand, meeting her eyes. Reading the situation, he said, "I will speak to Bjorn. That part of the tale will not be repeated," Hofund assured Blomma.

Blomma paused for a moment. "No. Let them sing of her. That way, her name will be remembered."

Hofund smiled gently at Blomma, then touched her chin. "As you wish."

Blomma sighed tiredly. "May I go to bed now?"

"Of course," I said, turning to find Magna. I waved to the woman who crossed the room to join us. "Magna is coming. Shall I come up with you?"

Blomma shook her head. "I'm all right. Good night," she told me, kissing me on the cheek, doing the same to Hofund.

"Ready for bed, little princess?" Magna asked, holding out her hand to the child.

Blomma nodded.

Leaving us, she went to Magna, pausing only to stop beside Yrsa.

"Good night," she told Yrsa shyly, then kissed her on the cheek as well.

Yrsa chuckled then ruffled Blomma's hair.

With that, the pair retired.

King Gizer refilled his tankard then came and sat down beside me, pushing in between Yrsa and me.

"That got them talking," he told me, motioning to the room. His attention then went to Yrsa. He eyed her over with such intensity that she frowned.

"So, you are Yrsa then?" he asked her. "Jarl Hervor's fierce protector."

She shrugged.

He tapped his cup against hers. "Skol, shield-maiden."

"Yrsa, this is King Gizer," I introduced.

"King Gizer," Yrsa replied with a nod of the head.

Gizer laughed. "I always preferred shield-maidens to such refined ladies," he said, motioning to a clutch of women—including Revna, Thurid, and Frika—gathered in hushed conference across the room. "But they aren't without weapons. You see, they work their tongues to sharp points—too much maneuvering for my taste. Shield-maidens are more honest. They see the beauty in bashing things into compliance."

Yrsa laughed.

Gizer turned to me. "Is it true that is the dwarven sword you wear, Jarl Hervor?"

"It is."

"Let's have a look."

I shook my head. "As Bjorn said, it is a cursed blade. If I unsheathe it, it will not sleep until it has tasted blood."

Gizer shrugged. "It needs your hand to kill. Just don't kill anyone."

I laughed. "And any cut from the blade is lethal. Have you heard that part as well? I may not try to kill anyone, but Tyrfing has a mind of its own and will have its blood. I will not tempt the Norns. But, no doubt, thanks to Haki and Hagbard, soon, you will see the blade in action."

"Oh, I greatly look forward to that," he said with a laugh.

The rest of the night passed along with much merriment, song, and food. It was late when I decided to retire.

"I'll check on Blomma," I told Hofund.

"They will have me up half the night," Hofund told me, motioning to Gizer and Harald. "I'll join you when I can. You should expect to be woken in the morning before the sun rises. We will journey with my father to the Dísarsalr to make our prayers to the dísir."

"Very well," I said.

We kissed, and I left the hall. Rök coming with me, I went to Blomma's chamber. There, I found Magna asleep on her cot. Blomma was tucked into her bed. I went to pull up her covers. When I did, I spotted a timber just above her head. On it, she had lined up the small herd of reindeer Hofund had created for her.

"Hervor," she whispered.

"I'm sorry. I didn't mean to wake you."

"No. I wasn't asleep. I was thinking."

"About your mother?"

"Yes. Tomorrow, we will go to the hof to worship the dísir. I will honor her memory, if that is all right with you."

"Of course."

"I'm not sorry Solva is gone," Blomma said. "I don't feel sad about it. Is that wrong?"

"Sometimes there are people in our lives who are supposed to love us, but for whatever reason, they don't love us as they should. We are not duty-bound to love those who mistreat us. You are generous to remember your mother's spirit."

"I will remember Solva," Blomma said, "but you are my mother now."

Touched by her words, I kissed her forehead. "I love Svafa very much, but when I was young, she was not there for me. She left me on my own. Yrsa was my mother. I love her as such, and there is nothing wrong with that."

Blomma smiled lightly. "I like it here," she whispered.

I was surprised. "You do? It's not too loud for you?"

"The grand hall is very loud, but it is easy to drown out all the loud rumblings when they clang all together like that. No, it's not the hall I like, it's the whispers."

"What whispers?"

"Coming from the Dísarsalr."

"I have heard nothing."

"A soft wind blows down the mountain. It smells like spring flowers. And with it, I heard them singing, whispering."

"Tomorrow, I will listen closely and see if I can hear them too."

Blomma nodded.

"Now, get your rest. Hofund says we will wake before the dawn."

Blomma nodded. "Rök," she called, patting the bed.

The wolf hopped up, joining her.

"Good night, my love," I whispered, kissing her forehead.

"Good night."

I left her and went to my chamber. I sat down by the fire and pulled off my boots. My head ached. I was glad Blomma was able to shut out all the noise and crush of people in the hall, but I was not so lucky. The truth of the matter was plain to me. One day, I would be queen here. If I wanted to protect my future—and Blomma's and any children Hofund and I might have—I'd better start figuring this place out...soon.

# CHAPTER 16

In the grey hour before dawn, the servants woke Hofund and me to give us time to prepare for the blót.

"Ugh," he whispered, holding his head. "I will be glad when the Thing is done. I just came to bed."

I chuckled. "The dísir wait for no one."

"Nor am I so sorry to wake early to greet them. This is Gizer's fault."

"I can see Leif thriving very well here."

"Leif had the luxury of taking no one seriously. Grund was far more entertaining for him."

I rose and splashed water on my face. "Will the gothar come to prepare us?"

Hofund shook his head. "No. The morning ritual is private. The sunrise prayers are for the family of the king only. When we are finished, the other families and towns-people can attend the shrine. Father will lead the ceremony tonight." Hofund looked me over. "You must unbind your hair and wear a simple white shift. No belts, no bindings at all. No adornments. No weapons. No boots."

"I cannot leave Tyrfing."

Hofund frowned, puzzling at the problem.

"The Valkyrie are dísir. They will understand."

"Let's hope you can convince Ardis. She is chief amongst the gothar here, and she is very particular."

I said nothing more. When I took the sword from the barrow, I did so with the promise that I would be its keeper. Angantyr warned me that the sword would cause harm to any man who touched it. As long as Tyrfing was with me, it would be safe.

I dressed as Hofund suggested, then we went next door to find Blomma and Yrsa already similarly prepared.

"Ready?" I asked Blomma, who nodded.

My gaze went to Yrsa, who simply shrugged, giving me a half-smile.

The four of us headed downstairs where we found King Gudmund. Like us, he was wearing a simple shift, his torc and coronet gone. Norna, the young woman who had accompanied Hofund's grandfather to the hall, waited with the king. Gudmund nodded when he saw us.

"Very well, Norna," he told her. "We are ready."

"Yes, my king," she said. Her eyes danced over all of us, her gaze briefly falling on Tyrfing. She paused but said nothing.

A contingent of armed guards with us, we headed outside, the gythia carrying a torch before her.

When we exited the hall, I was surprised to find Frika,

Rolf, Soren, and Thorolf waiting for us outside. While Frika had rid herself of her jewels and other adornments, her eyes were still heavily painted. Her long hair was unbound, revealing streaks of white in her auburn locks.

I shifted my gaze just for a moment to Thorolf, who returned the look with a welcoming smile. I didn't need to look to Soren to guess he looked as though he'd eaten a bitter apple. I could feel his attitude emanating from him.

King Gudmund smiled at Frika. "Fair Dísablót to you, sister."

Her gaze warmed for a moment. I saw the glimmer of genuine affection between the siblings. "Thank you, brother."

"Come along," Norna called to us.

Following the gythia, we headed to the temple.

It was silent that morning. The little houses were quiet, the animals just stirring. From the docks, I heard a few voices on the wind. Early risers were already at work. We passed through the square. Many of the vendors were sleeping on mats by a fire or on the back of their wagons. A few lifted their heads when we came through.

We made our way away from the village to the mountain and the jumble of rocks at its base.

The torch the gythia held flickered and crackled in the morning air.

Rök, who was trotting along beside us, shifted his ears to the left and right, listening for any sound. I set my hand on his head. My wild creature was faring well in the city. He was more curious than anything about the new life in which he'd found himself thrown.

The air was chilly that morning, the winter not far behind us, and spring still coming slowly. My feet ached with cold, but I forced myself to ignore the feeling. I took Blomma's hand. Her small fingers were frigid. I set a kiss thereon then rubbed her cold digits.

We wound through a narrow passage of rocks leading to the mountain. On them, runes and other wards had been carved. We finally reached the opening in the mountain. The stones all around the entryway were carved with images of eagles, serpents, cats, and horses. Runes were interspersed between the images. Torches burned, illuminating the cave opening.

Ancient Heidrek, Hofund's great-grandfather, waited for us at the entrance. Dressed like us, he leaned on a tall staff, a young priestess holding onto his other arm.

"Heidrek," Gudmund called, greeting him.

"Ah, here you are. Let us go in and send our prayers to my sweet granddaughter."

Gudmund set a gentle hand on the old man's shoulder.

From inside, three veiled gythia appeared. One stepped forward.

"King Gudmund," the chief gythia said, greeting the king. The woman had a deep, rich voice. Like Norna, she wore a plain, cream-colored robe. I could see that her hair was dark, but I couldn't make out her features. Her eyes turned to Hofund. "My prince. You have brought your new family."

"Ardis, this is my wife, Hervor, my adopted daughter, Blomma, and Hervor's foster-mother, Yrsa."

Ardis smiled first at Blomma. "Hello, little one," she told her. "What beautiful eyes you have."

"Thank you," Blomma replied politely, but she gripped my hand tighter and stepped back.

The gythia turned her attention to Yrsa, giving her a polite nod. Then, she turned to me.

"Princess Hervor, you are a stranger to our customs here. Please, remove your sword. It is forbidden to bring a weapon into the temple."

"I must beg your forgiveness and that of the dísir. I cannot let Tyrfing from my sight. The blade has a mind of its own and the will to carry out the curse upon it. I have sworn an oath to protect the weapon. Surely, Odin's dísir will understand."

Ardis stared at me. I could just make out her eyes through her veil. They were marked heavily with kohl. A long, uncomfortable moment passed. She stepped toward me, her voice low so Frika and the others could not hear.

"I see the All-Father all around you, shield-maiden, but this place belongs to the dísir. This is a place of female spirits to whom you have grown deaf. Now, battle-maid, lay down your sword if you wish to please the Norns this Dísablót."

King Gudmund was staring at me.

I debated what to do. I didn't want to offend the dísir, but I would not relent on my promise to my father.

"I can wait with the blade," Yrsa offered.

I shook my head. "Rök," I called, motioning for the wolf to join me. I knelt and looked in his eyes. "I trust you with my life, and I trust you with this sword," I whispered to him. Unlatching the scabbard, I motioned for Rök to sit. Then, I placed the sword under his front feet. "Stay here." The wolf licked my face then lay down, the dwarven blade under him.

King Gudmund laughed lightly.

I patted Rök on the head then joined the others once more. I turned to the gythia Ardis. "I'm ready."

Behind her veil, she smiled. "Very well," she said. "Follow me."

Taking a torch, she turned and headed into the temple.

King Gudmund followed behind her.

Hofund stopped by his great-grandfather. "May I help you?"

"I remember every rock, every turn, but it is more difficult to navigate these days," he assented, giving Hofund his free hand. He held on tightly to his staff with the other.

Hofund smiled lightly, then led him inside.

When we entered, Frika and her family followed along behind us.

I looked down at Blomma. She looked at the temple entrance, her eyes wide. And for a moment, I saw that flash of silver.

I turned my attention back to the shrine.

Whatever called to Blomma was silent for me here.

No ravens shrieked.

No gods whispered.

Instead, there was only silence.

## CHAPTER 17

The rich smell of earth and the tang of minerals filled my nose. The priestesses led us into a cave. Torches lit the place. We passed through a narrow passage to emerge into a large chamber. At the center was an altar. Around the altar were effigies carved in stone. Water ran from somewhere deeper in the cavern, rushing as a babbling brook that split as it traveled around the center altar then rejoined once more to disappear under the cave wall. My eyes went to the idols. Freyja, Frigga, and the giantess Skadi watched over the place. Freyja's idol was carved with cats at her feet, Frigga held a spear, and Skadi was dressed in furs, wearing snowshoes, and carrying a bow.

I stilled when I saw her.

I knew this image.

I had seen her before.

In my dream.

I exhaled slowly, then turned and looked around the

room. The domed space was carved with runes and swirling designs. The ceiling had been painted with images of the heavens. On a background of stars, Freyja flew in her chariot, pulled by her giant cats. The Norns stood amongst the heavens, the middle sister at the loom as the others wove and cut the strands of life. Then, there were my sisters, the Valkyries, on their starlight steeds racing across the skies. Everywhere I looked, I saw and sensed the dísir.

The All-Father was missing from this place.

This was a place for the feminine divine.

Along the cave walls were small alcoves, wide enough to fit two people. Inside were small shrines. Idols sat on shelves carved into the cave walls. Candles were lit beside each.

Ardis placed her torch in a holder at the foot of the altar then came before us, the other priestesses alongside her. As I looked around, I saw there were no men amongst the holy people here. Only the veiled priestesses attended this place.

Hofund and Gudmund turned their attention to Ardis.

The priestess raised her hands.

Everyone grew silent. All that could be heard was the sound of the water rushing through the chamber and the flicker of flames.

Ardis spoke. "Dísir, on this Dísablót, the house of King Gudmund has come to honor their ancestors and seek your blessings. Spirits of our divine female ancestors, listen to their words, hear their prayers. Watch over and bless those gathered here.

"Norns. Great ones. The house of King Gudmund honors you. Weave a golden future for its sons and daughters. Shine your favor upon Gudmund, Hofund, and his new family.

"Skadi, whose tears flow in this place, may you bless all maidens who find their way to this shore. Fill them with the contentment that eluded you here in Njord's lands.

"May all women be remembered and honored in this place. Go now, each of you, and pray to your ancestors. Honor their memories," Ardis said. With that, she turned to the altar.

Leaving us, King Gudmund went to her side.

Hofund turned to me. "There is a shrine for my mother," he whispered. "I would like you and Blomma to see it. Great-grandfather?"

Heidrek gave Hofund a soft smile then turned to the room. "Where is Norna?"

"I'm here, Heidrek," the girl said, coming forward.

"Norna, my girl, take me to my shrine. I shall offer prayers to my ancient mother first," he told her, then turned to Hofund. "Go see to your own mother, my boy. I'll be along shortly."

"Very well," Hofund said, then motioned for Blomma and me to follow.

I looked at Yrsa.

One of the priestesses had joined her, handing her a small, clay effigy of a woman. "You may place the idol at one of the shrines," the priestess told Yrsa. "That way, you may honor your ancestors here."

Yrsa was staring at the small idol in her hand. After a long moment, she nodded. The priestess motioned for Yrsa to follow her. She led Yrsa off to one of the small shrines just off the center room.

Yrsa had never spoken of her own mother. I realized then that I didn't even know the woman's name.

Frika's family went with her to the other side of the temple. They gathered before another family shrine.

Hofund led Blomma and me to a small alcove. There, we found a small statue of a woman carved in stone. Candles were lit all around her. As well, small trinkets had been placed at her feet: feathers, shells, holed stones, and a wooden carving of a boy and a man.

"Since my mother, Thyra, was a priestess in this temple, they honored her here when she died. This shrine was made in her memory," he said, then touched the face of the idol.

"What was she like?" I asked.

"Her hair always smelled good," he said with a light chuckle. "Like flowers. It was dark, like mine, as were her eyes. I was Hakon and Halger's age when she grew ill and passed." Hofund put his arm around me, pulling me close. He moved Blomma before us.

"Mother," Hofund whispered. "I bring my wife and daughter to you. From the land of the dead, I want you to see that your prophecy was true. A girl in blue has become my bride, and with her, I gained a child. Mother, grant us your blessings. Offer Blomma your protection. On this Dísablót, I honor all you gave me."

A soft breeze blew through the cavern, and for a brief

moment, the flames on the candles around her feet flickered blue.

"Did you see that?" Blomma whispered.

"Yes," Hofund said, patting Blomma's shoulder. "She has heard our prayer."

"I don't think I should honor my mother in this place," Blomma said.

"Why not?" Hofund asked her.

"My mother was a jotun. It will make the gods angry."

I knelt to look at Blomma. "Look there," I said, pointing behind us to the idol of Skadi. "Do you know who that is?"

"Skadi?"

I nodded. "She, too, was a jotun. The gods accepted her as one of their own. She was the bride of Njord for a time. Skadi will understand you. Pray to her. Honor your mother under Skadi's eyes. In this place, Skadi will protect you."

"All right," she said, then left us, going to the statue of Skadi.

Hofund's eyes followed Blomma. "Is it true?"

"There were rumors that both her mother and father were, at least in part, jotun."

"Then you are right. Skadi will watch over her, especially here in Grund." Turning, Hofund set his fingers on his mother's foot. "My mother would have liked you. She liked people who do not fit the mold of what is expected."

"Like herself?"

With a smile, Hofund nodded.

I touched the idol. "Thyra, I am sorry I was not able to meet you."

King Gudmund joined us. He smiled at the effigy. "Your mother would be proud to see you here with your wife," Gudmund told Hofund. "She always told me you would marry well."

"She always knew the important things," Hofund said.

Gudmund nodded. "So, she did."

I motioned to Hofund that we should step aside to let King Gudmund have a moment alone.

"Father," Hofund said, setting his hand on Gudmund's shoulder, then we left him, returning to the center altar.

"Prince Hofund," the gythia Ardis said, joining us. "It is good you returned in time for the Dísablót. I am pleased to see you here with a wife...and a daughter," a hint of surprise in her voice. Her gaze shifted to Blomma, who was kneeling before the image of Skadi.

"I am pleased to be back in Grund," he said.

"I have heard much about you, shield-maiden," the priestess said, inclining her head to me.

Unsure what to say, I simply nodded.

"Come," she told me. She motioned for Hofund to stay behind, then waved for me to follow her. "This is the public chamber," she said, gesturing to the room. "A stranger to this place, and one who listens to the voice of the All-Father, I am sure it is silent to you. But, perhaps, there is another place in our temple that will speak."

Taking a torch, she led me down a narrow corridor

that led away from the central chamber. The space was barely wide enough for the two of us to pass. But at the end of it, there was a small alcove.

The moment Ardis's torch illuminated the room, the whole space glowed brilliantly, metal reflecting the torch-light. A relief had been engraved onto the wall, showing Odin's dísir, the Valkyries, their swords lifted as they raced across the sky. At the base of the altar and on the walls were shields, their metal trimmings shimmering brightly.

"Grund has had her share of heroic shield-maidens but never as our queen. One day, the red-and-black of Bolmsö will hang in this place in your honor. I will leave you," Ardis said. Setting the torch in a holder on the wall, she turned and headed back to the main chamber.

The Valkyries' shrine felt neglected, overshadowed by the presence of the Norns, Skadi, Frigga, and Freyja and the many ancestors of Grund who watched over this place. But here, in this tiny corner, I felt a presence that had thus far eluded me. Here, I felt the eyes of the dísir on me.

Not Odin.

Not Loki.

I felt something different. Sisterhood. Camaraderie.

I reached out and touched the image on the wall. A vision took hold of me. I felt myself riding a horse, galloping quickly. Ahead of me, many other women also rode, their hair flying in the breeze. Their weapons raised, their shields at the ready. I felt the thundering steed under me and heard the pounding of the other horses. I felt breathless with excitement. I looked down to see, not the solid earth, but stars. We were galloping across the night's sky.

"*Hervor.*

"*Sister.*

"*One day, you will ride a midnight steed along with us.*

"*One day, you will lead us.*"

I shuddered a little, then startled when I heard someone behind me.

Surprised, I looked back to find Yrsa there.

"Yrsa?" I whispered.

"You called my name. I followed your voice."

I took my hand away from the wall. "Ardis brought me here. This is the shrine of the Valkyries."

Yrsa stared at the relief on the wall. After a long pause, she said, "Almost as far as I can go back, it was just my father and me. I was a small girl, younger than Blomma, when my mother died."

"Your mother… What was her name?"

"Olga," Yrsa said with a light smile. "I barely remember her. She had yellow hair, like mine. I remember the long tangle of it, how it would tickle my face when she leaned down to hug me." Yrsa was silent for a long time. "Most of my memories of her come from my father. Truth be told, I hardly remember to think of her. She's like a ghost in my memory. But when I do think of her, the recollection is a good one." Yrsa shook her head, a twist of emotions on her face.

I wrapped my arm around her waist, leaning my head on her shoulder. "You will see her again one day."

"Yes."

We stayed there, both of us still, for a long while.

"My ugly boy," Yrsa finally whispered, then kissed the top of my head.

*Dísir.*

*Sisters.*

*I stand before you with my mother. Give us your blessings.*

A soft wind blew once more.

*"Hervor.*

*"We see you. Both of you.*

*"Mother. Daughter. Sisters."*

## CHAPTER 18

Ysa and I returned to the main chamber. There, King Gudmund and his sister stood together before another family effigy. Hofund waited with Heidrek, Soren, Thorolf, and Rolf. Norna, the young priestess who'd led us from the hall, was kneeling beside Blomma before the idol of Skadi.

"Can you imagine picking your husband by his feet?" Norna was saying to Blomma.

Blomma giggled then looked up at the effigy. "I honor Skadi, and I hope she will forgive me for saying so, but she should have picked a man who had callouses on his feet."

"Why?" Norna asked.

"Because then she would have known he knew how to do hard work."

Norna laughed lightly. "You make an excellent point."

"Did Skadi ever have another husband?" Blomma asked.

Norna nodded. "After she returned to the forest, she had a mortal husband named Ull and gave him a daughter whom they called the princess of winter. Other legends tell that after Ull's death, Skadi became the beloved of Odin and gave him sons."

At that, Blomma cocked an eyebrow.

I smothered a laugh.

Blomma looked up at the effigy once more.

Norna rose. "Princess Hervor," she said, bowing to me. "And Yrsa, isn't it?"

Yrsa nodded.

"Your daughter has an affinity for Skadi," Norna told me.

"We have all come from the forest to these shores," I said, giving her a simple explanation.

"You are welcome to come to pray to Skadi and the dísir whenever you like," Norna told Blomma.

King Gudmund and Frika joined us. The king turned to Ardis. "Ardis, I believe we are done here."

Ardis nodded. "Very well. We shall see you at the rites tonight. And thank you, King Gudmund, for the white calf you sent to us. We will see it bled in private."

King Gudmund nodded then motioned to Hofund.

"I will return with you," Norna told us then turned to Heidrek. "May I help you to the hall, ancient one?" she asked, setting her hand on his arm.

"No, sweet girl, I will go home and find my boots. My feet are freezing."

Norna laughed. "Very well. I shall see you there first."

Another priestess, torch in hand, motioned for King Gudmund to follow her, and we all exited the temple.

Yrsa took Blomma's hand, and we followed along behind the others. Frika, Soren, and Rolf left along with King Gudmund. Thorolf fell into step with me.

"The dísir are whispering this morning," Thorolf said, surprising me. I gave him a sidelong glance. He truly could have been Hofund's brother. They had the same color hair, and both wore it long. Thorolf's beard was longer than Hofund's, and he wore his hair loose, whereas Hofund braided his from the temples. Their eyes were also similar in color. Thorolf was taller than Hofund and broader built. There was a softness to his eyes, but still, I felt wary.

"It is their day. If they want to whisper, this is the time," I replied.

Thorolf laughed lightly. "So it is. Did they whisper to you?"

"Perhaps."

"What did they whisper?"

"It's not wise to reveal the dísir's secrets."

"No. You're right. I only hoped the gods were doing their part to make you feel welcome here. I think we are not doing our best on that score. I know Grund can be…intimidating."

"I will tell you a secret," I said, leaning toward him.

Thorolf grinned. "What's that?"

"I'm hard to intimidate."

At that, he laughed, causing his mother to cast an annoyed glance at him over her shoulder.

"I heard Bjorn's song. The woman in that story would not be daunted. But as a friend, I caution you. Foes often come as friends, especially in Grund."

"But you come as a friend, do you not?"

"I do. See how tricky it can be to weed out honest intent from trickery? Tyrfing cannot solve that riddle for you, shield-maiden. But...but if you have a friend who wanted to look out for you, a friend who admired you, a friend who could guide you, that would be a good thing."

"Where do you suppose I could find a friend like that?"

"Ah, that's where the whispers come in. I'd hoped the Norns had made a suggestion."

I grinned. "Well, I shall listen to all the whispers I hear today and see if the dísir can find such a friend for me."

"Any who are lucky enough to be called your friend are amongst the fortunate." Thorolf smiled at me, then moved ahead, joining his parents.

I paused to wait for Yrsa.

She eyed Thorolf, then leaned toward me and said, "A sickly calf, a willful thrall, witches' flattery, a walking corpse, a brother's killer, a half-burned house, a horse too fast, a friend too keen...never be so trustful as to trust these."

Odin's words from the *Hávámal*. I looked from her to Thorolf. One thing about Yrsa, her suspicions about everyone had gone a long way to keep her alive.

"There is only one element there to disagree with," I told Yrsa.

"Oh?"

"Where would we be without our willful thrall?"

At that, Yrsa chuckled.

When we emerged from the cave, I saw that a long line of villagers waited to enter the shrine. Rök sat staring at the crowd, his haunches raised, Tyrfing safely under his feet.

Frika stepped wide around Rök, a look of terror in her eyes, hanging on to Soren as she went.

"A vicious, wild beast. It has no place in Grund," Soren told his mother, who nodded.

"Rök," I called to the wolf.

His head snapped to attention. When he saw me, he wagged his tail and relaxed his stance.

I went to him, giving him a scratch on the ears. "Good boy," I whispered, kissing his forehead. I picked up the sword, belting it around me once more.

When I rose, I found Soren's eyes on me. I met his gaze and held it. Fury flickered to life in me. If he wanted to play, he would find that more than one vicious, wild beast had come to Grund.

Soren turned away.

Behind me, Yrsa chuckled under her breath. "And they called Hervarth *ergi*."

I chuckled.

Hofund looked over his shoulder at us, a look of mild distress in his eyes.

I composed myself once more. For his sake, I would cage the wolf. But Soren was playing a dangerous game. One he would lose.

## CHAPTER 19

We returned to the hall to change our clothes, then joined the festivities.

"Don't let Soren work your nerves," Hofund told me as he pulled on his doublet. "He will press to see where you are weak. Don't give him the satisfaction of finding a soft spot. Their games are beneath you, Hervor."

"Be that as it may, I will not stand by and allow anyone I care about to be insulted. Including Rök."

Hofund nodded. "Fair enough. Though, in so doing, you show them what you care about. They will seek to pull you into their web. You must be wary and not allow yourself to be snared in their games," he said, then came behind me. "Bodil went to the hof. Let me help with your dress." Pushing my hair aside, he worked on the laces on my gown.

I inhaled sharply when he gave them a tug.

Hofund laughed lightly. "Sorry. My hands are not as gentle as Bodil's."

I chuckled. "It's not that. I think the food in Grund is far richer than my table in Bolmsö. Loosen them a bit?"

"Of course," Hofund said. I could hear the smile in his voice.

"Thank you for your counsel. I have too much of my father in me. I can't abide fools."

"There are plenty of them here. Pay them no mind."

I nodded.

"Where did Ardis take you?" Hofund asked.

"To the shrine of the Valkyries."

Hofund nodded. "Good."

"Good? Why?"

"I want you to have a place here."

I nodded but said nothing. It was hard to explain that the voice of Odin was with me everywhere. I didn't need a temple for the All-Father to hear me nor for me to hear him.

Hofund stepped back, admiring me. "Blue," he said, looking at the dress. He played with the raven brooch I wore, the gift Svafa had given me on my wedding day. "You look beautiful, my love."

"Thank you."

"Come, let's go see what the spiders are weaving now."

"Is there anyone in the hall you trust?"

Hofund looked thoughtful. "Several people, actually. You. My father. Yrsa. Blomma. Your pack. My warriors. Bjorn. King Gizer...and Rök."

I grinned. "King Gizer?"

Hofund nodded. "Of all of us, perhaps he is the most honest. He says exactly what he thinks. That is what makes him so dangerous. But also, trustworthy."

I chuckled. "I shall keep that in mind. And I'm glad Rök made the list. Perhaps you won't let Frika turn him into a cloak after all."

Hofund shook his head. "Frika is a jealous, petty thing. Soren more so."

"And Thorolf?"

Hofund sighed. "My cousin..." Hofund shook his head. "He could be a great man. All his life, he has been torn between what Frika wanted him to become and the thundering in his own heart. He has never been able to free himself."

"Perhaps he needs a little help."

"Father has suggested, more than once, that he raid with me, but Frika never allows it. Thorolf capitulates to her will."

"Suggest it again. When we face Haki and Hagbard, perhaps Thorolf should come."

Hofund cocked an eyebrow at me. "Why an interest in him?"

"He presents himself as a friend. So either he is, or he is playing. Let's bloody him up and find out."

Hofund laughed then held my shoulders. "By the gods, what fine sons you will produce."

"Could be daughters. Twelve shield-maidens, remember?"

"Then fine daughters," Hofund said, then kissed my

forehead. "Come, shield-maiden. Let's see who you can bloody up with your words today."

WE RETURNED TO THE HALL TO FIND THE REVELRY FULLY underway. Musicians were playing, a feast was heaped on the tables, and everyone was drinking. Already, the expected parties were making the rounds.

"Everyone will gather here today," Hofund told me. "There will be a great ceremony tonight."

"Hofund," King Harald called, waving for Hofund to join him.

"Go on," I said. "I'll join you soon," I replied, then left Hofund to meet the warriors from Bolmsö. Rök trotted along beside me.

"Jarl," Trygve said, rising when I joined them.

I motioned for him to be at ease. I took a seat beside them and grabbed a plate. "Will you go to the hof?" I asked them.

"Line is too long," Kára said.

I chuckled. "You risk offending the Norns because the line is too long?"

"Not at all. Someone said there will be a rite tonight. I'll be there."

I shook my head. "How are you all faring?" I asked.

"The warriors from Grund with whom we fought have shown us the way around," Kit said.

"For better or worse," Kára commented.

"Meaning?" I asked, raising an eyebrow.

"Trygve's only been in one tavern brawl so far. And only one fool tried to kiss Sigrun. We haven't been in too many fights yet," Kára replied.

I laughed.

"They are curious about you, jarl," Sigrun told me.

"What have you heard?" I asked.

"The people of Grund are pleased with you. They like that Prince Hofund picked a strong bride. But these people," she said, motioning to the room. "All questions."

"Oh, and I've answered," Kára replied. "Nearly made that Soren shite himself."

We all laughed.

"Have you heard anything about the sea kings?" I asked as Yrsa joined us, filling her plate as she sat.

Trygve nodded. "They say they are making moves to sack Uppsala."

"We cannot let them," Öd stated.

"Obviously," Trygve replied.

"If they take Uppsala, they will be strengthened and emboldened," Öd clarified.

"Those kings," Kára said, gesturing with her chin at Harald and Gizer. "Will they help King Hugleik?"

"I don't know. They are waiting for the princes Eric and Jorund, sons of old King Yngvi, to come. When they arrive, there will be talks."

"Join them," Yrsa told me.

I raised an eyebrow at her.

"It is good if they come to see you as equal to them now. It will make it easier later," she added.

I nodded.

Kára clapped crumbs from her hands then sat back, setting her hand on her belly. "I feel like I could burst. They eat well here."

"That they do," Trygve said, jabbing a morsel in his already over-full mouth.

"Too well," Sigrun said. "It makes them soft. Half the men here look like women," she said, her eyes drifting to Rolf, Soren, and the group of well-dressed men standing in one corner.

The others chuckled.

"Wealthy merchants and the like," Yrsa said. "There is a lot of money in Grund."

Sigrun shrugged. "A lot of good it will do them when someone tries to put an axe through their head."

Yrsa huffed a laugh then lifted her ale horn. "Skol."

"Skol," we answered, clicking our cups.

"May the All-Father protect them, because those fancy clothes certainly won't," I said with a grin.

*"Hervor.*

*"Daughter.*

*"That's what I have you for."*

## CHAPTER 20

The pack from Bolmsö left to explore the market, taking Yrsa and Rök along with them. I went to check in on Blomma. She and Magna were in Blomma's chamber looking at a skin covered in runes.

"Blomma," I said, smiling at her. "Everything all right?"

"She didn't want to come to the hall," Magna told me, "but I made sure she had something to eat."

"Thank you," I told her, then turned to Blomma. "What are you looking at?"

"I asked Magna to teach me the runes," Blomma replied.

In Dalr, only the gothar and Eyvinder could read the runes. I was surprised to discover Magna could read them.

"I only know a little," Magna told me. "I know the symbols but not how to divine the future with them. Like many girls in Grund, I spent time in the Dísarsalr. I can show Blomma what I know, but if you approve, once the Dísablót has passed, I can ask the gythia Norna to teach her."

I looked at Blomma. Eydis had seen a different future for my foster daughter. Perhaps, this could be a start. "Very well. Are you comfortable here, Blomma? Do you need anything?"

"I'm pleased to stay here with Magna," she told me. "The hall is crowded, and I'm tired."

"Get some rest today before the rite tonight."

Blomma nodded.

"I'll be sure to find you if she needs anything, princess," Magna told me.

"Very well," I said. I gave Blomma a quick kiss on the cheek then left the pair to their silence. In a way, I was jealous. I used to be able to escape the hall too. Now, there was work to be done there. Yrsa was right. One day, Hofund and I would rule Grund. I needed to stake my place alongside the kings.

Returning to the hall, I scanned the room. Hofund and King Gudmund were missing, but King Gizer and King Harald were drinking together. I grabbed a mug of ale then turned to join them when I found myself waylaid by Revna.

"Jarl Hervor," she said. "I'm sorry we haven't had a chance to talk."

I wasn't sorry.

"Revna," I said with a smile. "Your cup is empty."

She laughed. "My cup is always empty. No one ever noticed before."

I chuckled.

"How do you find Grund?" she asked.

"Busy."

"Hmm," she said, then gazed around the room. "Yes, I suppose that you would find it so. You are from Dalr, are you not?"

"I grew up in Dalr. My home is Bolmsö."

"That is an island, isn't it?"

I nodded.

"I often think that a simple village life would be more congenial. Far less to worry about."

"Only starvation, illness, and war."

At that, Revna laughed. "Ahh, so you have all the same comforts we have here. What is this I hear about King Hugleik? Is he besieged?"

"Threatened."

"Should we expect to be threatened?"

"Not if I have anything to say about it."

Revna laughed. From the tone, it felt like she was laughing at me.

I frowned.

"Oh, don't get me wrong," she said, setting her hand on my arm. "It's only...I am acquainted with your cousin Leif from Dalr. I expected you to be like him. Leif *never* took anything seriously. You, I see, take *everything* seriously."

I didn't reply.

Revna sighed then leaned against a table. "It is good to be serious about matters of importance. It's funny, though, that your cousin Leif never mentioned his cousin was Jarl of Bolmsö and the daughter of a hero. In fact, I didn't remember him mentioning you at all."

"Perhaps he didn't think it would interest you."

"Perhaps not. He was a fun one though," she said, then lifted her cup, hiding her smile behind her lips.

I wanted to slap her. Hard. Leif was devoted to Eydis. It was apparent what Revna was implying, but I had no time nor patience for it.

"Have I heard right that Leif is jarl in Dalr now?" she asked.

Ahh, that was why she was interested in Leif. He was someone of importance now.

"Yes. In fact, Hofund and I have just come from Dalr, where we attended Leif's wedding."

"Wedding?" she asked, surprise and disappointment in her voice.

"Yes." *By the gods...*

Revna sighed. "All the best men are taken. You know, everyone expected Hofund and I to wed—don't be jealous —but it seems you got there first. Though, it is common for kings to take a second wife. Many have reminded me of such, including Hofund's aunt."

With a smile, I patted her on the shoulder, probably a little harder than I should have, but definitely less hard than I wanted. "I'm sure you'll find someone worthy of you. Excuse me, I need to have a word with King Gizer and King Harald," I said, then left, not waiting for her reply.

Maybe Hofund found some admirable quality in Revna, but she annoyed me to the point of making my eye twitch. A second wife? Never. Hofund would not think of it. But Hofund was right. They were testing me. I would not fall into Revna's web. Thinking on her no more, I headed to the other side of the room and joined the kings.

"Jarl Hervor," King Gizer said, smiling up at me. He slid to the side so I could sit.

I joined the pair.

"You look agitated," King Gizer said, refilling my cup.

"Do I? I guess I haven't found my court face yet. Is this better?" I asked, then tried to smile placidly.

They both laughed.

"Decidedly, no," King Harald told me.

"In a flock of sheep," King Gizer said, motioning to the room. "It is far better to be a wolf."

I chuckled.

"Speaking of sheep, we were talking of King Hugleik. Two important visitors arrived while you were gone," King Harald told me. "Gudmund and Hofund went to meet them at the dock. They are just returning now," he said, motioning behind me.

I turned to see Hofund and King Gudmund entering with two fierce-looking warriors.

"Those don't look like sheep to me," I said.

"No. They are not. They are Eric and Jorund, sons of the late King Yngvi."

I stared at the young men. My mother had met Princess Ingeborg, King Yngvi's only child—at the time— when she'd gone to Uppsala. But after the princess's death, King Yngvi remarried and had two fine sons...in time for the king to die and leave them without protection. But the boys had prospered under their mother's father. While the throne of Uppsala eluded them, they had still made a name for themselves. "I heard they killed King Gudlög of Hålogaland," I said.

King Gizer nodded. "Gudlög got what he deserved. We were all glad to hear he was dead."

"Will they ask our help retaking Uppsala?" I asked.

"That is certainly what they want," King Harald replied.

"But what they ask for could be an entirely different thing altogether," Gizer added, drinking his ale as he eyed the pair. "There is more than one way to retake a city."

I raised an eyebrow at Gizer.

"You are leading Hofund's new wife into intrigue," Harald chided Gizer.

"Not at all," Gizer said. "Can't lead someone to where they already are. Isn't that right, daughter of Angantyr?"

"So it is. Skol," I said, tapping my cup against his.

Gizer chuckled merrily, Harald joining him.

"Skol," they both answered, tapping their cups against mine.

## CHAPTER 21

King Gudmund motioned for us to join him. The three of us followed the king into the meeting room.

"King Harald, King Gizer," one of the brothers said, greeting the men. Both brothers bowed to the kings. They were very similar in looks, with long, curling blond hair. One brother wore his pulled back at the temples, the other letting his long locks hang loose. They were tall and had warriors' builds. One brother had twin axes on his belt. The other carried a sword.

The man with the twin axes turned to me. "I am sorry. I do not know your name, shield-maiden."

"Prince Jorund, this is Jarl Hervor of Bolmsö. My wife," Hofund said, introducing me.

Both men turned to Hofund.

"Your wife?" asked the other, presumably Prince Eric. Hofund nodded.

"Felicitations on your wedding, Jarl Hervor," Jorund told me, then turned to Hofund. "When did you find time to wed? We were told you've been busy fighting."

"So I was, at Jarl Hervor's side. We wed between blows, so to speak," Hofund replied.

At that, the men chuckled.

"Come," King Gudmund said. "Let's drink and talk. There is much to discuss."

Gudmund waved his thralls away. We sat at the table, Hofund pouring drinks for the others. When he handed me a cup, he winked knowingly at me, then took a seat beside me.

"Well, what is the news?" King Gizer asked the brothers.

"As expected, King Gizer," Prince Eric said.

"Things are turning dire in Uppsala," Prince Jorund elaborated. "Haki's and Hagbard's attack is imminent."

"How are King Hugleik's numbers?" King Gudmund asked.

Prince Eric shook his head. "Sadly, our cousin would rather play dice and carouse with fools than make allies, though there are a few who stay loyal to the throne. But not enough."

"Hugleik's sons?" King Harald asked.

"Echoes of their father. They have already fled."

King Gudmund frowned.

"Has your cousin asked for your help?" King Gizer asked as he tapped his finger on the side of his cup. He leaned forward in his seat and eyed the brothers carefully.

Prince Jorund nodded. "He has."

"And?"

Jorund and Eric looked at one another.

Jorund cleared his throat. "We will not go to Uppsala. Yet."

Chuckling, King Gizer sat back. He met King Harald's gaze, giving him a knowing look.

"You will not go?" King Gudmund asked.

"Hugleik is a murderer and son of a murderer. Let him fall. When it is done, we will remove the sea kings from Uppsala," Prince Jorund said.

"And place yourselves on the throne," King Harald said, more stating than asking.

"We are the lawful sons of King Yngvi, the true king of Uppsala. Eric is my elder brother. By right of blood, Uppsala is his," Prince Jorund said.

There was a long pause before King Gudmund asked, "You would ask our aid in this?"

The brothers looked at one another.

"Yes," Prince Eric told him. "We ask all of your help. Once Hugleik has fallen, we ask all three of you to support our bid to retake Uppsala."

King Gizer grinned then sipped his drink.

King Harald, on the other hand, looked pensive. He stroked his thumb across his lips as he considered.

King Gudmund rose. "I fought many times at the side of King Yngvi. It was a sad day when that great warrior fell," he told them. "But we must consider your request," he said, his eyes flicking toward the door.

Understanding, Prince Jorund and Prince Eric rose.

"Of course, King Gudmund," Prince Eric said.

"Eat. Drink. The hall is merry, and there are many pretty maids here for the blót. We shall join you again soon."

The princes bowed to the kings, and without another word, left us.

King Gudmund sighed heavily, then sat once more.

"Conflicted, Gudmund?" Gizer asked. "Do you prefer raiders to jugglers?"

King Gudmund frowned at Gizer.

"If any of us were in danger, would Hugleik's courtesans and skalds come to defend us?" King Harald remarked then sighed. "I did not know King Yngvi, but you did," King Harald told King Gudmund.

"Yes," the king said with a sad nod. "His death was a great loss. Alf, his brother, was always the vicious one."

"And Alf's son is both weak and vicious," Gizer said. "Eric and Jorund are their father's sons."

King Gudmund nodded.

"What of Jorund and Eric? Are they men you should back, their lineage aside?" I asked.

"Eric rules their lands in the north. No doubt, Jorund will take his brother's place there, letting Eric sit on the throne in Uppsala," King Harald told me.

"But are they good rulers?" I asked.

"Depends on your definition of good, Jarl Hervor," Gizer told me. "If you ask the late King Gudlög of Hålogaland, the answer would be no."

Gudmund huffed his breath through his lips. "We all wanted Gudlög dead."

Hofund turned to me. "Jorund and Eric have a good reputation amongst their people. They rule well and do not leave their people to famine and despair. They have been peaceful allies."

"Not to King Gudlög," Gizer said with a chuckle.

The others laughed.

"And King Hugleik?" I asked.

"His sole *brave* act was murdering his father to take his crown," Gizer replied.

King Gudmund reached out for the pitcher, refilling his cup. "So, the question we face today, my friends, is, do we save King Hugleik or let him fail?"

"Hugleik has no chance of success alone?" I asked.

Hofund shook his head. "Unlikely. Jorund and Eric said that the sea kings have been rebuilding their numbers."

I frowned.

King Gudmund stared into his cup. "I was never fond of King Alf, nor of his son. But these days, my mind is fixed on the future. What is best for our sons, our daughters?"

"Forget sons and daughters. What is best for me?" Gizer asked with a laugh.

"No matter what, we must not let Haki and Hagbard get a hold in Uppsala," Hofund said firmly.

King Gudmund nodded. "Harald?" Gudmund asked the king.

"I think," he said, then looked into his cup, "that I am out of ale." He reached for the pitcher.

Gudmund shook his head. "Gizer?"

He nodded slowly, tapping his finger on the table in tandem. "If Uppsala looks ripe for the picking, it endangers us all. Let Haki and Habgard try Hugleik's mettle. If, by the will of the gods, Hugleik wins, there is nothing more to say. He will be angry with us for not helping but too weak to do anything about it. If Hugleik fails, we will chase the sea kings from our lands. I've had many dealings with Prince Jorund and Prince Eric. They are made of the stuff of King Yngvi, whom everyone respected. I would not be sad to see them reclaim their father's throne."

"Yes," King Harald said with a nod. "I am in agreement. We should back Jorund and Eric."

"Then, we do nothing for Hugleik?" Hofund asked.

"Sometimes, the best way to win is to let others fail," Harald said, then drained his cup once more.

"May the gods protect you from anyone ever feeling the same way about you, King Harald," Hofund told him.

Harald laughed. "The gods favor me because I have earned my place, as has Gizer and you and your father and your wife. As for Hugleik..." he said, then shrugged.

Gudmund nodded. "We shall meet together with the princes again tomorrow. For now, we will turn our attention back to the dísir," King Gudmund said, lifting his cup. "To Frigga, Freyja, the Norns, and all the other dísir. Skol," he called.

"Skol," we answered.

When King Gudmund set his cup down, I saw very briefly that his hand was shaking. He slipped it into his lap before anyone else noticed.

"Now," Harald said, rising, "with that matter settled, I have business in the market."

King Gudmund nodded to him.

Inclining his head to us, Harald left.

With a sigh, King Gudmund leaned back into his seat. "I will rest before the ceremony tonight. I'm getting too old to wake up for the dísir," he said, then slowly rose. "Hofund, ensure that Eric and Jorund are comfortable."

Hofund nodded to him. "Yes, Father."

With that, Gudmund excused himself, leaving us with King Gizer.

Gizer swirled his drink in his cup as he thought. "This business with Hugleik does not sit well with you," he told Hofund.

"I question the wisdom of letting a king, who has asked for our help, fall. We are encouraging the enemy," Hofund said.

Gizer grinned then leaned forward on his elbows, his chin on his folded hands. "Who is encouraging Haki and Hagbard?"

"Through our inaction...us," Hofund said with a frustrated shake of the head.

"In the very least, we are not helping," I added.

"You are right there, Jarl Hervor," Gizer said, then sat back. "We are not helping. One day, Grund will be yours. Then, you will be the ones who need to make uncomfortable decisions. Think of it like this... Scandinavia is one large garden. If you let the rot set in one corner, it affects the whole crop. But if you pluck it from the roots? Problem solved. Hugleik must go." He shrugged then rose. "What is right is not always easy. What is easy is not always right."

"You sound like a gothi," Hofund chided him.

"May the gods forbid. I cannot think of a worse use for my talents."

"Talents?" I quipped.

He swaggered over to me, sitting on the table beside me. "I have two. One day, on the battlefield, you will see the first. As for the second... Well, you being wed and all, it's too late to show you the second."

"King Gizer," I said stiffly, forcing the grin from my lips even if I was unsuccessful in removing it from my eyes.

Hofund shook his head, smiling wryly.

Gizer chuckled. "Now, Jarl Hervor, if you ever find yourself in need of a new husband..." he said, then winked at Hofund, who frowned playfully at him. "Very well," Gizer said, a defeated tone in his voice. "I guess I best find somewhere else to press my talents. There is a shield-maiden in your group—green eyes, golden curls..."

"Kára?"

"Kára. Right. Well, it's time I go make Kára's acquaintance. Prince," he said, bowing to Hofund. "Jarl," he added, bowing to me. With that, he left us.

Hofund rose, shaking his head. "Pay him no mind. He is an unapologetic flirt. Generally, he is successful with the ladies—married or not. You must pose an interesting puzzle for him."

"That puzzle has no answer," I said, then rose.

Hofund pulled me close and set a kiss on my lips.

"What was that for?" I whispered.

"For being my puzzle."

"You should expect no less. Nor do I expect no less of you."

Hofund raised an eyebrow.

"I've heard, at least twice, that a man may take more than one wife. I have also heard that everyone expected you to marry Revna."

Hofund sighed heavily. "Assumed by everyone but myself and Revna."

I gave Hofund a questioning look. Did he really think the woman so innocent?

"Don't always assume the best in people," I told Hofund.

"You sound like Yrsa."

"That isn't a bad thing."

"I have known Revna since we were children. Her coyness is all show. Pay her no mind. She will try to take your measure. That is all. Just be yourself. She will learn soon enough."

I debated on whether or not to tell my husband how wrong he was but realized that in doing that, Revna would have won, causing a quarrel between Hofund and me. I wouldn't give her the satisfaction. No matter what Revna thought, felt, or wanted, Hofund felt nothing like that for her. Even if he was deceived, he had no romantic interest in her. I loved my husband enough to trust him.

I grinned at Hofund. "And what will she learn?"

"That no one backs a wolf into a corner and remains unscathed."

"That is the truth. May the dísir watch over her," I said with a wink.

## CHAPTER 22

We passed the day in the hall with merriment and cheer. Blomma made herself scarce, but my warriors from Bolmsö were enjoying the festivities. I filled a horn of ale and circled about the room, listening to the conversations underway. Unlike in Dalr, where my skulking went unnoticed, people wanted to talk to me everywhere I went.

"How do you find the blót, Jarl Hervor?" a voice asked from behind me.

I turned to find Soren there.

*Wonderful.*

"The dísir are well-honored," I replied.

"To what god do you pray, Jarl Hervor?" he asked.

"I honor all the gods," I answered simply. My instincts urged me to tell this man nothing of myself.

Soren nodded. He looked around the hall, his blue eyes sharp as he surveyed the people there. "That must be why they gifted you with dwarven steel, an island, and a prince. You went from being the bastard of Dalr to our future queen. The gods must love you well."

I looked at him. My heart was already beating faster, my hands beginning to shake, but when I saw the smirk on his face, the fury faded.

I smiled. "I honor the gods in all sincerity. Perhaps, if others were more honest in their intentions, the gods would reward them as well. After all, if I can rise from such a low station, it should be easy to ascent from a high one. Unless, of course, the All-Father scorns you because you're a liar and weakling."

Soren looked like I had slapped him. Not saying anything else, he turned and left.

*Loki... You must find it amusing when they try to channel your craftiness.*

"I never waste time on those with more tongue than wisdom."

*He'd best watch that tongue, or I'll wear it for a necklace.*

"And his balls as earrings to match."

*Does he have any?*

I heard a laugh in reply.

Soren sauntered across the room to a group of well-dressed merchants. He clapped two of the men on their shoulders and fell into conversation with them. But out of the corner of his eye, he was looking at me. I had unnerved him. He hadn't expected that. Good.

I turned my attention back to the hall.

King Gizer was telling Kára a story, re-enacting the fierce fighting and making her laugh. Even though Gizer was a shameless flirt, Kára was a good match for the king.

With her mouth, she could out-talk him. With her brains and brawn, she could match pace with him. I was curious to see what came of it.

Yrsa and Rök were gone, off to who knew where. Knowing Yrsa, she was probably climbing the mountain or exploring the waterfall, somewhere far away from this crush of humanity. For a moment, I felt jealous. Grund exceeded my expectations for wealth and the sheer press of people. I could see why Svafa had thrived when she visited Uppsala. She loved to talk and to be in the crowd. No doubt, my mother had shined like a gem in such a place. As for me, it was too much.

"Missing your island?" Bjorn asked as he joined me, refilling my ale horn.

"How did you know?"

"You have a look on your face which tells me you aren't sure whether to be disgusted or delighted."

I laughed. "I need to guard my face more closely. It reveals too much truth."

He tipped his head from side to side. "There is strength in being forthright. At least people know where they stand with you. Some monarchs, such as Gudmund, rely on measured statecraft. And then there are those like Gizer, who do whatever their gut tells them to do at the moment."

"Which is better?"

"Neither. One is not passionate enough. The other is too passionate."

"Is it fitting that a skald should decide how a king should rule?" I asked.

"Of course. Aside from singing songs and telling stories, my other primary job is to pass judgment on everyone else."

I laughed. "Then you should inform Soren he's missed his vocation."

Bjorn grinned. "He doesn't have the voice for it."

"All I hear is croaking."

He chuckled. "Then you have already marked him well," he said, then nodded. "Being a good king is no different than being a good father."

"I had no father save the All-Father."

"What better example is there?"

I tapped my horn against the skald's.

THE DAY PASSED. YRSA REAPPEARED, HER KNEES AND HANDS dirty. From the looks of her and Rök, my earlier guess wasn't far off. As the sun dipped low onto the horizon, Hofund collected us, and everyone headed outside for the blót.

A roaring fire had been lit at the center of the square. The vendors stopped their sales, crating up their goods for the night, and waited for the ceremony to begin. Hofund, Blomma, Yrsa, and I waited at the front of the crowd. Rök sat beside me, his ears twitching.

King Gizer and King Harald waited along with us, the princes not far away.

"What will happen now?" Blomma asked.

"My father and the gothar will lead the prayers to the

dísir. Then, there will be a sacrifice," Hofund said, motioning to a drowsy-eyed doe that was tied to a post nearby. A gythia tended the animal.

"Why is the deer so calm?" Blomma asked.

"They probably fed her an herb to quiet her," Hofund replied.

I scanned the crowd. The crew from Bolmsö was there, as were Hofund's warriors and all the others. Thorolf caught my eye, giving me a brief nod. I responded with half a smile. Soren took note, following his brother's gaze. I looked away.

A horn sounded from the hall. We looked back to see the gothar emerge. King Gudmund followed along behind them. A gothi walked at the front carrying a drum. Several of the veiled priestesses from the Dísarsalr processed with the king. Along with them, male priests in black robes, their faces marked with runes, joined the retinue.

One of the gothar sounded a horn.

The crowd fell silent.

All that could be heard was the sound of flickering torchlight.

A slim priest with kohl under his eyes came forward. "People of Grund, on this holy night, we call upon the Norns, Frigga, Freyja, and Skadi to join us here. May these wise women bless our undertakings. May they bless our endeavors on land and at sea. May your ancestors, your mothers, daughters, sisters, and grandmothers, see you from the beyond. May all the dísir gather to be honored."

King Gudmund stepped forward. "Grund, on this

Dísablót, we honor those who have passed. Speak their names. Call them out so they may be remembered!"

The crowd called out the names of their female ancestors.

"Thyra," Hofund yelled loudly, adding his voice to the others.

I squeezed Blomma's hand, encouraging her.

"Solva," she called.

"Eyfura," I added.

"Olga," Yrsa yelled into the wind.

A soft breeze blew. When the voices died down, King Gudmund spoke once more. "Oh sacred dísir, ancestors, we honor your divine spirits. From the realms of Hel to the golden hall of Valhalla, watch over us. Guide us. And most of all, be honored. You are beloved here. We rejoice on this Dísablót, remembering you, honoring you," he said, then motioned for the doe to be brought forward.

Norna and Ardis led the deer in front of the crowd.

Rök rose.

"Still," I said, motioning for him to sit once more.

Suppressing every urge he had, Rök whined then sat again.

Norna set a bowl under the doe to catch the blood.

Ardis lifted a silver knife high into the air. "Dísir, we honor you this Dísablót. May this blood please you," she said, stroking the doe softly as she whispered into its ear, then slit the animal's throat.

It gave a loud, trumpeting cry then fell.

Norna collected the blood.

When it was done, Ardis stood before King Gudmund.

Dipping her fingers into the bowl filled with the red liquid, she marked the king's face.

She then descended the hall steps and came to the crowd. She approached Hofund and marked him similarly. Turning, she stepped before me. Through the cover of her veil, I saw her dark eyes.

I closed my eyes.

*Sisters of the starlight steeds, I honor you.*

The blood on Ardis's fingers was warm. I could feel her trace her fingers down my face from my brow to my chin. When she was done, I opened my eyes once more.

Ardis knelt before Blomma and similarly marked the child.

Moving on, she then marked Yrsa, ancient Heidrek, Frika, Rolf, Soren, and Thorolf. After blessing them, she moved on to King Gizer, King Harald, and Princes Eric and Jorund.

When she was done, she handed the bowl to Norna. Other gythia came forward, wetting branches with blood. The priestesses then made their way through the crowd, scattering droplets on the assembly as one of the gothi beat a drum.

Ardis nodded to Gudmund.

The king spoke once more. "People of Grund, this night, we honor the dísir. Tonight, leave a plate out for your ancestors. Pour them a drink. Let them know they are honored and remembered."

The horn sounded once more. It rang across the city.

Ardis lifted her hands to the heavens. "Dísir. Ancestors. Sacred mothers. We honor you. Watch over us all, and give us your blessings. You sacred Norns who weave our fates—Urd, Verdandi, Skuld—make a good future for Grund. Skadi, while your tears fell on our shore, we remember your pain here. You suffered for this land, which would one day be Grund. Your tears nourish us still. We honor you. All hail the dísir."

"All hail," we called in reply.

"Let it be done," Ardis said, then lowered her hands.

The gothi sounded his horn once more, letting out three long calls.

King Gudmund turned to Ardis, inclining his head to her.

"Now, good people. Eat, drink, and be well," King Gudmund called, dismissing the crowd.

With a cheer, the crowd relaxed, many of them departing.

"Hervor," Blomma whispered.

I looked down at her. She had a look of amazement on her face. "What is it?"

"Did you see them too?" she asked.

"See who?"

"When Ardis lifted her hands, spirits hovered above her. I saw Skadi."

I looked back toward Ardis, who was speaking to King Gudmund. "I saw nothing."

"Did you...did you hear anything?" she whispered.

"No. Did you?"

She nodded. "Whispers."

Again, the whispers. I knelt, meeting her eyes. "Many

times, Odin whispers to me, but I did not hear him today. What did you hear?"

"I didn't hear Odin. I heard a woman."

"What did she whisper?"

"She said, 'Come to the hof. Come to your sisters.'"

I stared at Blomma. The dísir were calling her.

"We must not ignore such voices," I told Blomma. "Especially on the blót. If the dísir want you to come, you will go. I will talk with Hofund."

Blomma nodded then looked back at Ardis once more. "I'm sorry you didn't see the spirits. They were beautiful. Their dresses floated around them like clouds."

I set my hand on Blomma's cheek. "I'm sure they did."

"Shall we return to the hall?" Hofund asked us, setting his hand on my shoulder.

I nodded then rose.

"Yrsa?" he asked, turning to her.

"No," she replied. "I'll be back in a while. Come on, Rök."

With that, Yrsa left us. We headed back to the hall. Ahead of us, Soren and Frika walked together. Frika worked hard at wiping the sacrificial blood from her arms and face.

"One would think it unwise to displease the dísir on a blót," I told Hofund, motioning with my chin to his aunt.

He shook his head. "She was born with the benefit of never having to struggle for anything. She never hungered. Never labored. She does not know what it means to honor the gods or why. Everything has been handed to her."

"Surely, as the daughter of the king, she saw how the people suffered."

"She did, but she didn't see how their suffering was hers. She learned nothing. My grandfather married her into wealth knowing she would not survive without it."

"And yet, your father married a priestess."

"He did."

"I am sorry I never met your mother."

"Don't worry," Hofund said. "She saw you. And she liked what she saw."

"What about me?" Blomma asked.

Hofund picked her up. "My mother was a priestess at the hof. I'm sure she saw you there this morning when you made your prayers."

Blomma flexed her brow. "Did your mother have very dark hair but a stripe of silver, just here?" Blomma asked, touching her temple.

Hofund stopped. "She did."

Blomma smiled. "Then, yes. You're right. I saw her there this morning."

Hofund turned and looked at me.

While the gods were silent for me in Grund, apparently, they had much to say to Blomma.

*Skadi, Frigga, and Freyja.*

*Watch over my adopted daughter.*

*Keep her safe.*

A soft wind blew, and a feminine voice whispered in reply:

*"As she is yours… so is she ours…"*

## CHAPTER 23

I woke the following morning to find Hofund already gone. Rök, whose feet were muddy—and the coverlets to match—was snoring at the end of the bed. I rose groggily.

There was a knock on the door.

"Jarl Hervor? It's Bodil."

Rising, I went to the door.

Bodil smiled at me. "I see I'm just in time," she said. Under her arm, she was carrying three bolts of fabric: indigo, red, and green. "These came from the market," she said, setting them on the bed. "Such lovely colors. What shall we do with them?"

"Is there someone here who can make a gown?"

"Magna. She has gifted hands. Wait until you see."

I nodded. "The red is for Blomma, the blue for myself. The green is for a friend who is a bit taller and trimmer than me."

"I'll see to it," she said, then went to my trunk. "And what for you for today?"

"Trousers and my jerkin will do."

Bodil frowned. "But the princes and King Harald and King Gizer are still here."

"And?"

"Well, I just thought…"

"Trousers and a jerkin will do."

"Very well," Bodil said, but I could see the disappointment on her face. "May I at least braid your hair? It's rather a mess. And… the others will gossip about me if they think I am not doing my duties to you. Revna always has something to say."

*That she does.* "Very well. Arrange my hair as you think best."

At that, Bodil smiled. "Thank you, jarl."

After I washed up and redressed, I sat down on a stool so Bodil could fix my hair.

"I'm very good at braids. You'll see. I used to braid all my sisters' hair."

"How many sisters do you have?"

"Six."

"Any brothers?"

"Not one. I was thrilled when Magna recommended me to King Gudmund. It is very crowded in my house. And we were all so excited to learn that Hofund got married, especially to someone like you. You'll make a fine queen for Grund."

"I will try."

"Then, I am sure you will succeed. Now, I shall do the braids from the brow and on the sides, is that all right?"

I chuckled. "As you wish."

I sat patiently—well, as patiently as I could stand—as Bodil worked. In her innocence, she had revealed a truth about herself. She and her cousin were not as close as I'd feared. Good. For that knowledge, I was willing to endure a little grooming—excessive though it may be.

When I was finally ready, Bodil stood back and smiled as she looked me over. "There," she said happily. "Very pretty."

"Thank you, Bodil."

"Of course, Jarl Hervor."

"Just Hervor is fine."

The girl's cheeks reddened. "All right, Hervor."

"I'll be off then," I told her.

Bodil gave me a little curtsey.

Was that how Eydis was supposed to behave all those years, demure and ready to serve? No wonder she annoyed Grandfather. I went downstairs, finding Yrsa in the hall.

She eyed my hair. "Is it your wedding day?"

I gave her a look.

Yrsa laughed but said nothing more.

"Where's Hofund?" I asked.

"He went with the princes to the market."

"Blomma?"

"Kára and Sigrun took her to ride her pony."

"Why don't you show me what you've been busy with? I know you're up to something."

Yrsa grinned. "So to speak. Come on," she said, and we went outside.

Yrsa and I left the longhouse and headed toward the hof. Halfway there, we broke from the path and went down another winding road that led away from the village toward the waterfall. Rök raced along ahead of us, his nose to the ground. We came to the river. Turning, Yrsa and I walked upstream toward the waterfall.

"Met a few men fishing yesterday. Stopped to talk a bit. In fact, I've been all over Grund. Talking. Listening. There is a lot to hear outside the hall if a person bothers to listen."

"What did you learn?"

"It's quiet here. The people are not in rebellion against Gudmund, but not everyone has food nor a proper roof over their heads. Grund is a big city. They don't feel seen. Only people who go to the hall are seen."

I frowned. "That's not good."

"No. It isn't." Yrsa squatted down beside the shore. She picked up a rock and skipped it along the water's surface. "Fishing is good, though."

Once more, I was eternally grateful to Yrsa for remembering the important things and steering me down the right path. Honestly, I felt lost here. I knew it would take time to acclimate to Grund, but so far, I felt so out of place.

Yrsa motioned for us to go on. We headed upriver. As we went, I saw a few fishermen checking their traps. As we neared the waterfall, I was taken with the beauty of the place. The tall mountains rose above Grund, the water falling majestically toward the river below.

The waterfall cast a fine mist on us. The waves were fierce at the bottom of the falls. Rök raced around the nearby field, kicking up birds as he went. A large rock stuck out over the water. Yrsa and I carefully crossed the slippery stone for a better look.

"Reminds me of that rock in Dalr where you meet with Freja."

"Me too, but we don't have that in Dalr," Yrsa said, looking up at the waterfall plummeting over the cliff.

"Skadi's Tears," I said.

Yrsa nodded.

We stood there in silence for a long time, just watching the water.

After a while, Yrsa said, "After this business is done with Haki and Hagbard, I'm going back to Bolmsö."

"You won't stay in Grund?"

"No. But you will be needed here. King Gudmund doesn't look well."

"So, I'm not the only one who noticed. What are they saying?"

"Nothing. He just doesn't look well *to me*. You have hard work ahead of you," she said, then turned back and looked toward the village. "But there's your work," she said, motioning to the houses. "Not there," she added, bobbing her chin toward the hall. "Not sure if King Gudmund thinks like that. Nor your prince. They aren't overlooking the obvious on purpose or out of malice.

They were born here. It gets easy to miss the stink of your own house once your nose gets used to it."

"That's a pleasant metaphor."

"Weren't you always the one telling me my cave smelled like bears?" Yrsa said with a laugh. "I never smelled it."

I chuckled. "I understand your meaning."

Yrsa nodded. "And I don't like those cousins of Hofund's. Watch that Thorolf."

"You mean Soren."

"I mean Thorolf."

I was confused. "Why? Of the two, he's far more amiable."

"Exactly."

"Soren is an easy mark, but I think you are mistaken about Thorolf."

Yrsa grinned at me. "You're just like your mother. You forget how pretty you are, especially with those braids. There is more than one kind of trouble."

I raised an eyebrow at her.

"Watch Thorolf."

"All right."

"When are we going after Haki and Hagbard?"

"The kings decided to let Haki and Hagbard attack King Hugleik. They will decide what to do after that outcome is decided."

Yrsa shook her head. "That's a bad precedent."

"You are not the only one who thinks so."

"So, we wait."

"We wait," I agreed, then looked back out at the water. "Good fishing hole down there," I said, pointing.

Yrsa nodded. "Bring your pole next time."

"And here I thought you were out searching for a cave."

"I was."

"What?"

"There are caves behind the waterfall. I can just see them there. Water would probably break your neck to get to them, though. But up there," she said, eyeing the mountainside. "Lots of caves if you ever need a place to hide."

"You don't need a cave if you're going back to Bolmsö."

"I don't, but you might."

I laughed. "Yrsa…"

She grinned. "Now, come on. Enough drinking in the hall and gossiping. Let's get to work."

"Meaning?"

"I left Trygve, Kit, and Öd at the tavern. Told them to wait for me. Time to meet the people of Grund."

I shook my head. "Frika is going to be scandalized."

"You say that like you aren't thrilled to be the one to scandalize her."

I laughed. "You're right. Let's go. Rök," I called, and then whistled to the wolf.

He paused in the tall grass, only the tip of his ears and his tail sticking up.

Yrsa and I both chuckled.

Rök joining us, we walked back to town.

"Yrsa, what do you think of the priestesses at the hof? Blomma seems very interested in them and them in her."

Yrsa shrugged. "Remember what Eydis said about Blomma. If the dísir call her, you should let her go."

"When did you start believing Eydis's prophecies?"

"Always. But don't tell her."

I laughed.

As we made our way down the main thoroughfare, the villagers nodded to me but gave Rök plenty of space. Grund was bustling, the blót drawing people from farmsteads from far away. Everywhere we looked, people milled about.

Yrsa and I entered the tavern to find the others huddled over their mugs of ale. She signaled to the tapster to bring two more.

The man eyed me and the wolf then nodded.

"Well?" Yrsa asked Trygve.

"Found lots of ways to spend the jarl's silver," he told Yrsa with a laugh. "But there are some simple things to attend to: a widow with a broken sheep pen, roofs that need a patch, small things that we can see to."

Yrsa nodded.

"It's very good to take note of such things, but I'm not keen on spending Bolmsö's money here. Doesn't Gudmund have people attending to such matters?" I asked Yrsa.

"No. I asked."

I frowned then looked back to the men. "What else?"

"The roads leading into Grund from the land side are open. No watchtowers or men stationed there of any kind," Trygve told me. "Ports are busy, but there are limited guards."

"The city has its share of miscreants and trouble," Kit told me. "Drunkards. A few thieves. King Gudmund has men in the village to keep an eye on that."

"All the layabouts are at the hall," Öd told me. "In the city, people work."

A girl set my mug of ale in front of me. "Princess," she said, curtseying awkwardly, then wandered off.

"Princess," Yrsa said with a laugh as she sipped her mug. "Trygve is more princess than Hervor."

"Hey," he protested. "Just because Ragal isn't here doesn't mean you have to keep up the tradition."

Yrsa winked at him.

We finished our ale then rose.

"Well, what first?" I asked.

"Widow Jorgenson is closest," Trygve said.

"Sheep pens it is," Kit said.

"And here I thought we'd come to Grund to live richly with the jarl," Trygve lamented.

"Then you've followed the wrong jarl, *princess*," I replied.

The others chuckled.

Widow Jorgsenon met our crew at her door with an equal mix of skepticism and gratitude. It finally took Yrsa to convince the woman we were simply looking to help before she let us get to work.

"But Jarl Hervor," the old woman said, stopping me as the others went on. "This is the work of...of common folk."

I set my hand on her arm. "Can't have your sheep running amuck and disrupting all of Grund."

At that, she chuckled, then let me go.

It felt good to be working once more. Rök kept one eye on the sheep—and they on him—and the other on the commotion on the streets, as the rest of us worked on mending the pen. After we fixed the widow's enclosure, we made our way through the town, offering help to the elderly or needy. In a city so large, it would never be possible to develop a sense of close community as on Bolmsö, but something was better than nothing. As it was, I saw far too many thin children and old men in tattered clothes. Surely, something could be done.

Each house we visited led us to another in need. We had just finished patching the roof of a fisherman's hovel when I stumbled across King Gizer at an auction. While horses and other goods waited to be sold, at that moment, the man at the front was selling thralls.

"Jarl Hervor," he called, spotting me. He looked me over from head to toe. I realized then that I was covered in mud and sweating. He raised an eyebrow at me.

I chuckled then turned to Yrsa. "I'll catch up," I told her.

She inclined her head to King Gizer and went on.

"What are you doing this fine morning? Out for a stroll?" Gizer asked, his eyes glimmering mischievously.

"Just doing a bit of work."

"What kind of work?"

"So far, mostly mending roofs and fences."

"Is that right?"

I shrugged. "Better than sitting in the hall all day getting drunk and fat."

At that, he laughed. "I can see why Hofund married you. Remember, Jarl Hervor, if you ever find yourself in need of a new husband…"

"You'll be the first to know," I said, then turned back to the auction. A hearty man with long, black hair was up for sale. I frowned heavily. "I hate this."

"What?"

"The selling of people."

King Gizer shrugged. "We raid. We return with the spoils, including people. A man like that would be a good worker."

"Then his life is valued no higher than that of a horse or plow. Isn't a human life worth more?"

"Easier to bring back a person from a raid than it is a cow."

"Cattle have no mind. A person is another matter."

Gizer gave me a thoughtful look. "What would you do? How would you change things, Jarl Hervor, when the taking and selling of thralls is a tradition in our land?"

"Well, if it were up to me, I would forbid it. I would encourage people to employ workers instead, pay a wage for the work. Then, the whole community would prosper."

Gizer laughed. "I like your mind, Jarl Hervor."

"Thank you."

Gizer grinned. "The rest of you is not bad to look at either, especially with those lovely braids."

I rolled my eyes at him then gave him a wave, leaving him behind.

IT WAS SOMETIME IN THE AFTERNOON WHEN HOFUND, ALONG with Bjorn, finally found us. I was pounding on a roof when he called up to me.

"Hervor?" he called, a questioning tone in his voice.

I paused for a moment to look down at him.

He grinned at me. "You have straw in your hair."

I laughed then motioned to Trygve to take over my work while I climbed down. Hofund moved forward to steady me as I slipped off the roof and onto a barrel. Taking me by the waist, he helped me down.

"There was a rumor that a warband from Bolmsö was attacking the city with their hammers," Bjorn told me. "Of course, once news reached the hall, Hofund and I decided to investigate."

"And here we find you on a roof," Hofund said.

I grinned at him. "This is the home of Arneed One-Eye," I said. "His sons are all dead. He needed a hand. We provided it."

Hofund looked up at the others who were finishing the repairs.

A moment later, Arneed One-Eye appeared at the door. His wispy hair was as white as snow. The ancient man wore a tattered shirt and breeches, his feet covered in knotted-up rags. His missing eye was closed, the other a rheumy blue.

"Prince Hofund," he said, moving to kneel.

"Please, don't," Hofund said, stopping him. "At your age, it's not always easy to rise again, my friend," Hofund told him gently.

The man patted Hofund's hand. "Your wife and her men have been on my roof. Never thought I'd have a band of berserkers attacking my house to fix it."

Hofund laughed. "If there is one thing I have learned about the people of Bolmsö, there is much heart there—in battle and in peace."

"I thank you. I thank you all. By the All-Father, I am grateful. I would lay in bed and listen to the wind whistle at night. Mighty cold this past winter, it was."

Hofund nodded.

I was relieved to see Hofund was not upset. I had not asked Hofund's or King Gudmund's permission to do this charity. Should I have? I wasn't sure. But Yrsa was right. I had no place lingering in the hall with mead in my hand. I'd felt suffocated and bored. If we weren't going after Haki and Hagbard anytime soon, then I could hardly see myself sauntering around chatting with Soren and Revna all day.

"I am pleased to know you will not be cold any longer," Hofund said, then paused. "How do you get by without your sons?"

"Oh, I do a bit of fishing. It's enough to feed me. And I tie up nets for the others when my hands aren't aching too much," the old man said.

Hofund set his hand on the man's shoulder. "We can do better than that."

"I pray to mighty Thor to look after me. When I was your age, I swung a hammer alongside your great-grandfather Heidrek. Now, we are both old men, and most of my friends are in Valhalla. I lost this eye at your father's first battle. Gudmund was always a fine warrior."

Bjorn grinned at him. "You must have many tales to tell. Do you mind if I visit you sometime? I would like to hear your stories."

"Of course. Maybe you can work them into a song."

"Maybe so."

"Done here, jarl," Trygve called, then slipped off the roof.

Kit and Öd had paused to drink water while Yrsa finished tying up the last hinge on the broken gate holding the man's goat.

"You should be settled now. No more cold wind," I told him, motioning to the roof.

The old man took my hand. "Bless you, princess. May Thor and Frigga watch over you."

I inclined my head to him. The old man left us to go offer thanks and shake hands with the others.

When we were done, all of us headed toward the square.

"You all look like you could use a hot meal and an ale," Hofund said. "Have you been working since morning?"

"Yes. Yrsa is to blame."

Yrsa rolled her eyes at me.

Hofund laughed. "Leave off your work for a moment

to eat and drink," Hofund told us. "I'll join you in your tasks afterward...if you'll have me."

Yrsa bobbed her head as she considered. "I suppose you'll do."

Hofund chuckled then turned to Bjorn. "And you, old friend?"

"Oh, no. I suspect my talents lie elsewhere."

Hofund laughed. "Come on now, Bjorn. A little hard work never hurt anyone. Perhaps it's time we both learned a few new things."

## CHAPTER 24

Back in the hall, we ate and drank as Yrsa went over the names of some of the other families she'd learned needed help.

I watched the thoughtful expression on Hofund's face as he listened. He sat stroking his beard. After a long time, he said, "Yrsa, you have done a great service here."

"It's just a few houses," Yrsa said with a shrug.

"No," Hofund replied. "It is more. I am humbled. You have shown me where this house has failed its people. I will not leave you all to do this work alone. I must speak to my father and our housecarl, Halvar. We must help with these tasks."

"The more hammers, the better," Yrsa said.

I turned to Hofund. "Not all of Grund's people have fared well over the winter. There is much hunger out there," I told him. "Many people asked us for food."

Hofund looked at the opulent spread of food before us. "By Thor," Hofund half-whispered, then looked up at me. He kissed the side of my head then rose. Leaving us, he crossed the room and joined his father. After a moment, Gudmund and Hofund stepped away from the crowd and went to the meeting room at the back.

Bjorn laughed then drank his ale. "Well, Jarl Hervor, you've accomplished something I could never manage."

"What's that?"

"You've given Hofund a purpose here in Grund."

"How do you mean?"

"Hofund was suffocated by this hall. By his cousins. By his presumed future wife. By the expectation to be princely. His only escape was on a ship, so he took it every chance he could. I don't think he ever realized he could remake this world and his role in it until this moment."

My eyes drifted back to the meeting room into which Hofund and Gudmund had disappeared.

"Did we overstep?" I asked Bjorn.

"On the contrary. I suspect Hofund knew that marrying you would change his life. Perhaps he simply underestimated all the ways that could happen," Bjorn told me with a wink.

My eyes drifted back to Yrsa.

She lifted her cup to me.

I returned the gesture.

*Odin.*

*All-Father.*

*Finally, I feel you here.*

"Hervor.

"Daughter

*"Wherever you go, I am with you."*

THAT AFTERNOON, WE CONTINUED OUR WORK, HOFUND AND Bjorn joining us. Bjorn had been honest. He was weak with a hammer, but he kept the families entertained as we went about our work.

"My father was moved by your charity," Hofund told me. "Halvar will oversee a census of the people. We can do better. And we will."

"The credit is Yrsa's. She was the one to remind me that Grund is here, not there," I said, motioning from the town to the hall.

Hofund's gaze went to Yrsa, who was scratching a hog's ear and chirping sweetly at the beast, trying to get it to move so she could mend a gate.

Hofund smiled. "The dísir work in mysterious ways."

AFTER A LONG DAY'S WORK, WE FINALLY RETURNED TO THE hall. At Bodil's insisting—after politely informing me that I smelled like a pigsty while silently despairing at the state of my braids—I cleaned up, dressing in a fresh hangerok, then returned to the hall. That night, King Gudmund feasted King Gizer, King Harald, and Jorund and Eric. The kings and princes would leave soon, and we would all wait for news of King Hugleik's battle with Haki and Hagbard.

"Doesn't make sense to me," Yrsa whispered. "Suppose King Hugleik wins. Don't expect him to be at anyone's call if the need ever arises."

"They do not expect Hugleik to win. They expect him to die. And then, they will remove Haki and Hagbard."

Yrsa frowned. "They underestimate the sea kings."

"I agree."

"Hervor," King Gudmund called. He and King Gizer were busy playing a game of hnefatafl. "Come, daughter-in-law."

I raised and lowered my eyebrows to Yrsa then joined the king.

"What can I do for you, King Gudmund?"

"Lend me your mind. King Gizer has laid a bet on this game, and I can't lose. But right now, I see no way out. Do you play?"

"Not often."

"No matter. I will rely on your sense of strategy."

"You have taken an unfair advantage," King Gizer told Gudmund with a good-natured laugh.

"Not at all," the king replied. "I've simply exchanged champions. Here, Hervor, take my chair, and play for me."

The ornate seat with wooden sides did not accommodate Tyrfing, so I set the blade on the table beside me and settled in.

I surveyed the playing board. Gizer had Gudmund blocked in several corners. At first glance, it appeared there was no way out.

"What a mess you're in," I told King Gudmund.

He laughed. "Why do you think I asked for your help? Hofund has gone off on an errand and left me at Gizer's mercy."

Hofund was truly far better at the game than I was, but I was determined not to let King Gizer win.

I moved the piece away from Gizer.

He laughed. "You will not get away from me so easily, berserker. And that thing is of no use to you on this battle-field," he said, motioning to Tyrfing.

"No matter. My wit is just as much of a match."

"We'll see," Gizer replied, then leaned over the board once more.

Behind me, I heard Soren approach King Gudmund, the two of them falling into a conversation. While I tried to keep my attention on what Gizer was doing, I couldn't help but hear Soren speaking to Gudmund about Hofund.

"Toke said he is gathering some men to do work in the city," Soren said.

"Yes. Repairs and the like," Gudmund said with a tone that told me he was trying to dismiss the conversation.

"No doubt, a wise use of money. It is unfortunate these souls cannot afford to care for their own homes. Don't they work? Drunkards and the like? We should see to it they pay off their debts the next time Hofund sails out. Perhaps Hofund can take them with him to battle," Soren said. "Is the prince planning to go abroad again soon?"

"Eyes on the game, jarl," Gizer told me. "Nothing of value in the prattling of a goat."

I pulled my attention back to the board. "You're right."

Gizer moved his piece, once more putting me in a bad position.

I sighed.

Gizer laughed.

I leaned over the board and studied the moves, thinking ahead. How could I outpace him before he noticed? Finally, I selected a piece and shifted it.

"Is this Tyrfing? The dwarven blade?" Soren asked, pulling both of mine and Gizer's attention away from the board.

I turned to look to find Soren holding Tyrfing by the hilt.

"I haven't seen this famed blade yet? May I?" he asked, but without waiting for a reply, he unsheathed the weapon.

The metal made an angry clang. The air seemed to shiver.

Out of the corner of my eye, I saw Yrsa rise and pull her sword. The warriors from Bolmsö right behind her, they crossed the room in a flash.

I rose, pulling Huginn. "You have made a grave mistake," I told Soren.

He stared at the blade. The metal shimmered brightly, the light of the fire in the room emanating from it like a crystal. The hall fell silent. I didn't dare take my eyes off Soren, but terror had swept over me. How had I been so foolish to let Tyrfing out of my hand for even a moment? Soren had heard the story of the cursed blade the night Bjorn had sung of Arngrim and my father. How could he be so reckless?

"It's a miracle. It truly is dwarven steel," Soren said.

My heart pounded in my chest. How long would it take for Soren to realize that anyone who held Tyrfing was unstoppable? How long before he remembered that the sword made its wielder practically invulnerable?

Apparently, I wasn't the only one thinking the same thing.

Gizer pulled his sword.

"Set the blade on the table and back away," I said, my voice harsh. I pulled Muninn and stepped toward Soren.

"It's such a beauty. It's so rare," Soren whispered.

"Are you deaf, boy? She told you to put it down," King Gizer growled at Soren.

Soren, shaken by the rough tone in King Gizer's voice, looked at us.

The muscle under my eye twitched. My hands wrapped around my axes ached. It took everything in me not to cut Soren down at that moment. I remembered how Arngrim had taken the sword from Sigrlami. All I needed to do was to take his hand.

"Nephew," King Gudmund said, his voice firm. "May Thor forgive your ignorance and blindness. Set the sword down now, or I will step back and let Hervor take it from you."

Soren turned and looked at me.

And then, I saw a flicker in his eyes as realization washed over him. He realized what he had, what he could do.

And with that look, I remembered my father's

pleading that I never take Tyrfing from the barrow. Out of my hands, it could be a weapon used for great ill.

I saw that evil in Soren's eyes.

He was calculating.

"Tyrfing is bound to me and will not betray me," I said in something of a lie. "You will be in a pool of blood on the ground before you even tremble to strike."

My words unnerved him.

"Hand it to me by the hilt. Nice and easy."

Recomposing himself, Soren shook his head then sneered at me. "You're all show," he hissed at me, then tossed the sword onto the table beside him like it was a hot piece of coal. The metal clanged loudly, then bounced across the table and onto the floor on the other side, landing with a terrible clatter.

On the other side of the table, Soren's mother, Frika, jumped backward with a yelp.

"Soren," she growled then winced, reaching for her leg.

*No.*

*All-Father.*

*No.*

Moving quickly, I rushed around the table. Tyrfing had slid from the table, slicing Frika's leg before it fell to the ground. There was a cut in Frika's dress and a splash of red blood on the fabric.

"What have you done?" I yelled at Soren, then turned to King Gudmund. "Quickly. You must call for a healer. Quickly."

King Gudmund stared from Soren to his sister.

I snatched Tyrfing and belted it once more. "King Gudmund, Tyrfing is a poisoned blade. Your sister is cut. A healer. Quickly," I said, looking from the king to Bjorn, who understood.

Bjorn turned. "You there! Fetch Ardis at once. Be fast. Tell her to come quickly."

"I...I feel lightheaded," Frika said, swooning. Thorolf, who stood just behind his mother, caught her. "You great fool," Frika scolded Soren. "What have you done?"

"Frika," King Gudmund said, rushing to her.

"Lay her down," I told Thorolf, kneeling to examine the wound.

Yrsa appeared beside me. Working quickly, the pair of us pushed up the woman's dress to her knee, exposing the cut. There was a gash, no more than two inches wide, on her shin. It was bleeding profusely.

"It's just a small cut," Soren said. "It's just a small cut. What's all the fuss?"

"You empty-headed rat, didn't you hear a thing? Tyrfing is a poisoned blade," Thorolf yelled at his brother, shoving him away.

Yrsa yanked off her belt then tied it around Frika's leg, cutting off the flow of blood. Grabbing a length of my skirt, I cut it off then pressed it against the wound.

"What's happening?" Frika asked, then inhaled deeply in pain, hissing air between her teeth. "By the gods, it hurts. What sorcery is this?"

I pressed hard against the wound, but it wouldn't stop bleeding.

"Jarl?" Kára called through the crowd.

"More bandages," I called to her.

Kára disappeared for a moment only to return with a bundle of cloth. The blood was already pooling under Frika's leg. The wound was bleeding abnormally, as if she'd been cut deep in her neck or belly. The blood gushed from her.

"Hervor," King Gudmund said, his tone aghast.

I worked hard, trying to bandage the wound, but every bandage I applied soaked through immediately.

Sigrun went to Frika, kneeling on the floor beside her. She lifted the woman, propping her up.

"Lady Frika," she said, trying to rouse her. "Lady?"

My eyes darted through the mass of people for Kit. "Find Hofund," I told him.

With a nod, he darted off.

A moment later, I heard the sound of rushing feet.

"What has happened?" a feminine voice called.

I looked up to see Ardis and Norna approaching.

When Ardis saw Frika's wound, she gasped. "So much blood. What has happened?"

"An...an accident," King Gudmund replied.

Ardis knelt beside me.

I moved my hands so she could see. "She was cut by Tyrfing," I told the priestess in a low voice.

"What if we take her leg?" Yrsa asked.

"Her leg?" Gudmund said, aghast.

Moving quickly, Ardis examined Frika, who was now as white as snow and senseless.

The priestess looked at me. Through her veil, I met her questioning eyes.

"It is a cursed blade. Any cut from Tyrfing is lethal."

"Then she will die," the priestess whispered to me in a voice too low for the others to hear.

I nodded.

Ardis set Frika's leg down. She reached into the small bag hanging from her belt and pulled out a tiny vial. She joined Sigrun, motioning for her to hold Frika's head still. Moving carefully, she opened the woman's mouth and poured something inside.

"What was that?" Thorolf asked.

"Something to ease her passing," Ardis replied.

"Passing? What are you talking about? It's just a small cut. Mother," Soren called. "Mother!"

Thorolf turned and punched his brother in the mouth.

Soren stepped back. He held his hands to his lips. "Mother," he whispered.

"Our mother is dying because of your reckless jealousy," Thorolf screamed at his brother. "You have killed our mother!"

King Gudmund went to his sister. Yrsa gave the king a hand, helping him to the ground where he took Frika from Sigrun, collecting her in his arms.

"Sister," he whispered.

"Guddi?" she replied in a soft whisper, her eyes opening just a crack.

"Don't go from this world, my little sister."

"My boys," she whispered to him. "Don't blame Soren. It was an accident. My boys. Watch over my boys."

"I will. By Thor, I promise it," he told her, then kissed her on the head.

Frika smiled at her brother, then grew still.

The entire assembly fell silent.

Then, Thorolf turned on his brother.

"You stupid, sniveling, ambitious little rodent," he said, then punched his brother again, and again, and again.

"Thorolf," Revna said, stepping toward the pair, but Thorolf paid her no mind. Instead, he kept beating his brother, who had now fallen to the ground.

Kit and Hofund appeared a moment later. Taking in the scene, the pair rushed across the room, Hofund pulling Thorolf off his brother, Kit dragging a bleeding Soren away.

"I'll kill him," Thorolf told Hofund. "You hear me, Soren. I'll kill you!"

"Enough," Hofund told him, pushing him back. "Enough. That is enough," Hofund said, commanding the room to silence.

At that, Thorolf relented.

Hofund turned and looked down at his father, who held Frika in his arms.

After a moment, King Gudmund looked up. "She's dead," he told Hofund.

Hofund nodded to his father then turned to me.

I shook my head, disbelief washing over me. I stepped away from the scene. My hands were covered in blood. Yrsa, Sigrun, and Kára also stepped back, allowing the family to gather around.

I turned to find King Gizer beside me.

"The gods work in mysterious ways. Now, they will fear you," he whispered to me.

"I didn't want that. I never wanted that."

"No. But it's what they needed. It's for their own good. Take the advice of your next husband," he said, then headed back to the living quarters away from the horrible sight.

Yrsa set her hand on my shoulder.

"My father was right. I should not have taken Tyrfing from the barrow," I told her.

"It wasn't you. It was him," she said, gesturing to Soren. "For a moment, he thought about killing you. You know that, right?"

I nodded.

I stood still in shock, unsure what to do. Then, a soft hand took mine.

"Come away, Hervor," Blomma told me. "It's better if you aren't here. Besides, your hands are covered in blood. I'll clean you up." Blomma tugged on my hand, pulling me away from the scene. Unsure what to do, I followed her. Without another word, she led me upstairs to my room and made me sit before the fire. She fixed a small pot of water then got to work washing off my hands.

After a while, I slowly started to come back to myself.

"Blomma," I said, giving her a soft smile. "Thank you."

She smiled at me. "Don't feel sad, Hervor. It wasn't your fault."

"It was."

"How?"

"Because my father told me not to take the blade from the barrow, but I took it anyway."

"You're not the one who cut Frika."

"But Soren—"

"Soren didn't do it either. It was the gods," she said, then leaned toward me. "It was Loki. He was whispering to Soren. So don't feel bad. It wasn't your doing."

"How do you know it was Loki?"

"I just know."

"Blomma."

Blomma looked at me. For a brief moment, I saw a flash of silver in her eyes. "I could see him, but Soren could not. He was there, in his horned helmet, whispering. Now, no more questions and no more feeling guilty. It is done as the gods will it," she said, then went and poured me a glass of water. "Drink," she said, handing the cup to me.

"Is there no ale?"

"There is, but you will drink water today."

"Why?"

"Because I said so. Now drink and then sleep. I'll stay with you until Hofund comes."

"Where is Rök?"

"With Yrsa."

"All right."

I drank the water, then lay down. Keeping Tyrfing beside me, I slipped onto the bed. Blomma took Hofund's spot. She wrapped her hand around mine.

"Sleep now, Mother. In the morning, you will feel better."

I closed my eyes. I would not argue with my child, but my heart was filled with despair. I had disliked Frika, but I hadn't wanted her to die. Tears slipped from my eyes.

*Loki.*

*You trickster.*

*What game are you playing now?*

But there was no reply.

## CHAPTER 25

The dream was the same.

I walked toward the Bone Tree. The buildings around me were all on fire. Smoke billowed upward, embers floating into the sky. While the dream was the same, the sense of desperation and fear that usually gripped me was gone. Instead, I felt deep sadness in my chest. A weight like no other settled in on me. Every step I took felt hard. I knew I had to go to the Bone Tree, but I didn't want to.

I stopped.

Looking around, I realized I was alone.

No Hofund.

No Leif.

No Mjord.

There was no one, nothing, except me, the fire, and the tree.

I turned around.

No. I would not go today.

I would not see what darkness awaited at the tree.

I didn't want it.

But when I turned, I found Loki in his guise as the wanderer who came to Dalr standing behind me.

"Where are you going?" he asked, a mischievous grin on his face.

"Away."

"I've never known you to miss a fight, shield-maiden."

I looked back over my shoulder, that same sense of heavy dread washing over me. "Not today," I said, then turned back, but Loki was gone.

In his place, I found a bear.

I paused.

The creature rose up on its back legs, towering over me. It sniffed the wind, its nose working, then lowered itself once more. The creature bowed its head, its eyes on me.

Fear shot through me, and I began to back away.

The bear growled low and mean.

Turning, I rushed toward the tree.

As I ran, I looked behind me, seeing the bear chasing me. The creature's body moved like a shadow, its eyes blazing red. I rushed toward the tree, but just as I reached it, the bear swiped at me.

I dropped to the ground. The bear rose on its back legs then pounced at me. Yet it didn't harm me. Instead, it sank into me. The creature evaporated like smoke, sinking into my chest. The heaviness was so palpable that I woke with a scream.

"Hervor," Hofund said, grabbing my arm.

The room was dark. Rök, who had been sleeping by the brazier, looked up at me.

"It's all right," I whispered. "Just a dream. When did you get here?"

"Some time ago. I found you and Blomma asleep here. I took her back to her room."

"Oh, Hofund," I whispered. "What terrible trouble I have brought to this house."

Hofund stared at me, then shook his head. With his voice firm, he said, "No, Hervor. You must not blame yourself. It was Soren."

"But your aunt is dead. The king..."

"My father is distraught and angry...with Soren. It was all Kit and I could do to keep Thorolf from killing his brother. But no fault lies with you. You are a victim here. Soren took something from you he should not have. It was a betrayal of your trust. He has meddled between you and the gods, as Ardis scolded him. And they have punished him for it."

I remembered Blomma's words but decided not to repeat them. If Loki had truly urged Soren to act, then it was not Soren who was meddling. I didn't know why the trickster had doomed Frika, but I knew Loki well enough to know that he must have had a reason.

"Tyrfing lay safe with my father. Angantyr was right. I should not have taken the blade. If I had not, this would not have happened."

"How many lives have been spared because of that sword? How many good people still live because you wield that blade? Your father may have warned you against removing Tyrfing, but it is the All-Father who guides your hand, Hervor. Of that, I have no doubt. In fact, in such matters, you have humbled me."

"What do you mean?"

"Bjorn and I spent the evening mulling over what you and the warriors from Bolmsö so innocently pointed out to me. There is suffering in Grund. Suffering that my father never sees and I was too busy escaping to notice. Bjorn and I walked the city ourselves. There are people in Grund who need my help. It took you coming here, your actions, to help me see it. Grund might be five times the size of Bolmsö, but that doesn't mean we cannot do something. Alms for the poor. Help for the elderly. And whatever else you've thought of," he said, then set his hand on my chin, giving it a little wiggle.

"Trygve noticed that nothing is protecting Grund's back from an assault by land," I said with a soft smile.

Hofund laughed lightly. "Of course. I was so busy trying to escape the weight of this place, I never thought how to ease that weight off of others. In that, you have taught me to do better."

"It is Yrsa you should thank. She was the one who reminded me that this hall is not Grund."

Hofund smiled gently. "What would we do without Yrsa? She has taught us both."

"Oh, Hofund, but your aunt…"

He nodded. "It is a great tragedy. The gothar will arrange for her funeral rites. We will go at dusk tomorrow to see her on her way. But you must not blame yourself. Hervor, you are all good. Please," he said, then tipped his head toward mine, setting our foreheads together. "Please," he whispered again. "No one blames you."

I said nothing, but I could not shake the nagging feeling inside me. In truth, I had disliked Frika. I had found her snide and haughty. Could I have prevented this somehow? Could I have taken Soren's hand as Arngrim took Sigrlami's, saving Frika in the process? Could I have done anything differently?

*"Hervor.*

*"Don't be stupid.*

*"I moved the boy's hand, not you."*

I exhaled slowly. *Why?* I asked.

But there was no reply.

"Come, lie back down," Hofund said, pulling me into his arms. "You worked hard today. No doubt, your body is aching." Hofund pushed the hair away from my face. "All will be well," he said tiredly. "In the end, this darkness will pass."

We lay together in silence.

Hofund's breath became shallow. He sighed sleepily then whispered, "We will know the deepest of night. This darkness is merely the dusk before midnight comes."

I stilled. "Hofund?"

He exhaled slowly and deeply.

He was already asleep.

The murmurings of a vision.

*Odin.*

*All-Father.*

*Hofund speaks dark things. Guide me. Protect those I love. Let me do your will.*

In the darkness came a whispered reply.

*"Hervor.*

*"Daughter.*

*"I made you to do my will."*

# CHAPTER 26

The next morning, I rose slowly to find Hofund still asleep. Still feeling miserable, I washed my face and redressed, pulling my long blonde locks into a simple braid. Rök, taking advantage of my leaving, slipped into my warm spot on the bed behind Hofund then went back to sleep. Sliding Tyrfing onto my belt, I went next door to check on Blomma and Yrsa. I could hear Yrsa snoring before I even opened the door. Peering inside, I saw Blomma was also asleep. Leaving them behind, I headed to the hall, hoping to find King Gudmund.

I was surprised to find the hall was quiet. There were guards at the doors, and the thralls moved about quietly, but there was no sign of the king. The only person awake was Thorolf, who was slumped on the floor near the fire.

Uncertainty clenched my heart, but I went to him all the same.

"Thorolf?" I called gently.

He looked up at me.

From his disheveled clothing to the swimming look in his eyes, I realized then that he'd never left the hall. He'd been there all night, drinking.

"Hervor," he said, his voice slurring slightly.

Pity moved me.

Taking the half-full horn from his hand, I set it aside. "Let me see you home," I said, offering my hand.

"My mother always said that, one day, Hofund would leave Grund and not return. She said he was too bold, too reckless to be king, always throwing himself headlong into a battle. 'Stay here,' she told Soren and me. 'Stay here and learn to fight the battles here.' Soren learned to talk with a serpent's tongue. And me? Well, I would stand on the dock and wave goodbye to Hofund every time he sailed away, feeling Thor's disappointed gaze upon me. And for what? For what? My brother has murdered my mother. And me? I am no man. I am less than a man."

I stared down at him. "A child crawls before it begins to walk. So take your first step and stand," I said, my hand still extended.

Thorolf looked up at me. After a long moment, he took my hand.

Taller and heavier than me, he was hard to help to his feet. And, given he was coursing with more alcohol than blood, he was unsteady. He stumbled toward me. I caught him and gently righted him. When I met his eye, he had a look in his gaze that caught me off guard.

"And look...look what Hofund found out there," he said, then moved to touch my face.

"You are lost to drink and sadness. Silence your tongue before you say something you regret," I said, then put his arm over my shoulder, my other arm around his waist, and led him from the hall.

"One does not need to be sad or drunk to acknowledge a beautiful woman," Thorolf told me.

"But a less drunk version of yourself would tighten that tongue. Come on." We headed outside.

It was that thin, grey hour before dawn. Fog covered the streets of Grund. A few people were up and moving, but otherwise, it was quiet.

"You must go home and sleep. They will hold the rites for your mother tonight."

"Yes," Thorolf said. "My mother...my mother, whom Soren killed. I am sorry, Hervor. I'm sorry that you have come to this place. I'm sorry that my brother took your sword. You must watch him. He will not let the sting of blame fall on himself."

"Then, he's right."

"How can he be right? It was his hand that moved, not yours."

I said nothing more.

"No. It was not you. You are too good, too beautiful. And they say you are strong, a fierce warrior. I am envious of everything Hofund has."

"There is no need. Make a life for yourself that pleases you. Stop listening to others, and have the life you wish."

Thorolf didn't reply.

Not far from Gudmund's hall was another grand house the size of our great hall in Dalr. This was where Thorolf lived with his own family. In the mist, we made our way. Thorolf, big as he was, was a heavy burden to bear. He stumbled as he walked, tripping when we crossed a slanted stone. He tripped, nearly falling. Lucky for him, I was able to catch him in time.

But in so doing, I found my face pressed against his.

"Hervor," he whispered. Setting his hand on my cheek, he moved to kiss me.

I stepped back, letting him fall.

Anger boiled in my veins. By the gods, what was he thinking?

Sitting on his arse, Thorolf sighed heavily. "I'm drunk. I'm sorry, Hervor."

I said nothing. Leaving him where he was, I went to the door of his house and knocked. A burly guard appeared.

"Thorolf needs help getting the rest of the way home. I'm afraid he was too much for me," I told the man, pointing up the lane.

The servant peered through the mist. "I see. Thank you for bringing him this far, princess."

I nodded, then the two of us headed back to Thorolf.

"Drunk, Thorolf?" the man asked, offering him a hand. "Better get you inside. Your father is already in a state."

Despite my better judgment, I offered mine as well.

I met Thorolf's gaze, then nodded to him, encouraging him to take my hand. Working together, the pair of us pulled Thorolf up.

Once he was on his feet, I settled him in with his servant.

"I'll see him the rest of the way, princess. Thank you."

I nodded.

"Hervor," Thorolf said, an apology in his voice.

"Get some rest," I replied.

He nodded, then they turned and headed to their home.

Shaking my head, I made my way back through the fog to the hall. What a family. But I could hardly complain. After all, Jarl Bjartmar had tried to kill Hofund. At least no one here had tried to murder me.

*Yet.*

WHEN I GOT BACK TO THE HALL, IT WAS STILL SILENT, BUT King Gudmund was now awake and seated at the table. One of the thralls had brought him something warm to drink. He was nursing his cup as the servants worked busily preparing something for the king to eat.

"King Gudmund," I said, approaching him.

"Hervor," he said with a nod and weak smile. "You're awake early. Out already?"

"I saw Thorolf home."

King Gudmund sighed heavily, then nodded. "He's a good boy, Hervor. Not like his brother. He always reminded me a bit of my late brother, Thorgood."

"You had a brother?"

King Gudmund nodded. "My elder brother. He died

very young, long before our father passed. My god, he was a brute of a man, just like Thorolf. Good fighter. I looked up to him like he was Thor himself, but Odin took him to Valhalla young. So it goes sometimes."

"Then I am doubly sorry for your loss," I said, setting my hand on his arm.

"Ah, Hervor. I am ashamed of Soren. I do not know what to say to you. And with Gizer, Harald, and the princes here..."

"I am the one who is sorry. It was my sword that—"

"That Soren took against your will and without your permission. The gardener is not to blame when the cook serves spoiled vegetables."

I nodded, his words finally settling into my heart. "Then you should take your own advice. The other kings cannot fault you for the actions of a rotten nephew."

"Gizer and Harald are my closest allies. I trust them before all others, but it is never good to let people see your weakness. Not even those you trust."

"No?"

"How do you think I kept this for so long?" he asked, tapping the circlet on his head. Gudmund patted my shoulder. "You will learn, Hervor. You will learn. In time, you will be queen here. From the moment Hofund set his eyes on you, I knew you would come to Grund, no matter what Jarl Bjartmar said. Silenced his tongue on that matter, didn't you? I can think of no better woman to rule at my son's side. He needed a partner, not a pet, as I had with Thyra. But I will tell you something," he said, meeting my eyes. "Do not be afraid to show them what you are."

I nodded to him.

"King Gudmund," a servant said, setting bowls of food before the king. They handed me a plate as well.

"Come, Hervor. It will be a long, miserable day. The least we can do is eat well," the king said, then set a massive slab of currant-and-nut cake on my platter.

"As you command, King Gudmund," I said with a wry smile, then dug in, the pair of us eating silently together in the empty hall.

## CHAPTER 27

A strange hush had fallen over Grund. The joy of the Dísablót had deflated, leaving us with the silence that often follows death. The usual band of merrymakers and layabouts had abandoned the hall for their own homes, leaving only those close to the king behind. I was glad. While I had pitied Thorolf, I had not appreciated his drunken efforts at a kiss. Now I understood what Yrsa had meant by trouble. If my brief dalliance with Asger had taught me anything, it had taught me that I had no business with flirtations. Svafa and Angantyr were robbed of the love of a lifetime. I had never even dreamed I could love like that. And then, Hofund had appeared, changing everything. I had stumbled in my brief consideration of Asger, but I would not be swayed again.

Hofund joined us in the throne room later that morning, Blomma along with him.

"Blomma," King Gudmund called to her, motioning for her to come to him.

Smiling shyly, she went to the king.

"What do you have here?" he asked her, seeing her small hand was clenching something. She opened it to reveal one of Hofund's carved reindeer. "A stag?"

She shook her head. "A reindeer."

"Ah, a reindeer."

"Like those belonging to Jarl Mjord."

King Gudmund nodded thoughtfully then turned to me. "Hofund tells me the jarl—the Reindeer *King*—fought well in Dalr."

"He has proven himself a strong ally. But I suspect he strongly prefers the quiet of his mountain jarldom to more tumultuous waters."

"I cannot blame him. When I was young, it was all fighting. When I grew old, it became all talk. But there is more to life than talk. My son has told me of the good works you have started in Grund—you and your people. I instructed Hofund and Halvar to take men and silver and expand on your work."

"Thank you, King Gudmund."

He nodded slowly, then rose. "I will go now to the hof and see to the preparations for my sister."

"Shall I come with you?" Hofund asked.

Gudmund shook his head. "Stay here, my son. It is a lonely walk to say goodbye."

I frowned, my heart aching for the king. I reminded myself that I was not to blame for the millionth time, but still, guilt plucked at the strings of my heart.

THE DAY PASSED IN QUIET. WE DECIDED IT WAS BEST TO LEAVE off our work for the day in honor of Frika's memory. Even Yrsa kept to the hall, where people talked and drank in quiet contemplation.

King Harald and the princes made themselves scarce, heading to the docks to peruse what ships were for sale. I strongly suspected they were uncertain if they should stay or go, but they stayed all the same.

Late in the day, I found myself alone with King Gizer.

I sat down beside the king, who was nursing an ale as he looked into the fire. He turned his attention to me, giving me a smile.

"You look pensive," he told me.

"I was about to say the same to you."

He grinned. "I'm plotting. You?"

I shrugged.

"As I told you yesterday... What happened does nothing but bolster you. At worst, they might try to murder you."

"Is that supposed to comfort me?"

He laughed. "You will be queen, Hervor. Of course, someone will try to murder you. Trust me. They frequently try to murder me," he said with a laugh.

I chuckled. "Who tried to murder you?"

"I used to have cousins."

"Used to?"

"Exactly," he said.

At that, I clicked my cup against that of the king. "Skol."

"Skol."

LATER THAT EVENING, THE GYTHIA NORNA ARRIVED TO collect the king and the rest of the family for the funeral rites.

"Your Majesty," she told him. "We are ready for you."

Gudmund nodded to her.

We had all redressed for the ceremony. I wore a black gown but kept my axes and sword on my side. Holding Blomma's hand, Hofund and I followed behind King Gudmund as we stepped from the hall. When the doors opened, a horn sounded. The sound punctuated the darkness, the tune echoing across the mountains. The horn called low and long, again and again.

Norna motioned to the gothar who waited. Leading the procession, they drummed as they guided us through the town. A mass of people waited on a hill above the village. I saw their torches flickering.

I looked back. King Gizer walked along behind me. He met my eye, giving me a nod.

In the crowd behind him were King Harald, Jorund, and Eric. Yrsa and the warriors from Bolmsö were not far behind them.

I set my hand on Rök's head. The wolf, sensing my anxiety, was never far from me these past days. As we passed through the village, many called to King Gudmund.

"Peace, my king."

"Prayers, great Gudmund."

"She is with the All-Father, my king."

Gently calling their condolences to their leader, I felt love for Gudmund for the first time. Grund was so big, and Gudmund seemed so removed from his people, but they still honored him. They were not close to him as those on Bolmsö had been with Arngrim, but they loved him from afar.

The hill upon which the pyre was set was very steep. I was surprised to see Rolf, Thorolf, and Soren waiting at the end of the path. When we arrived, Norna motioned for them to join us. Soren kept his eyes to the ground.

I avoided Thorolf's gaze. I hoped the drink had addled his mind enough that he did not remember the encounter between us. If the gods were kind, they would make him forget the whole thing. A man was often lustful when he was lost to drink. And Thorolf was a broken person. The best I could do for him was to forget the whole affair and help him find his way forward. Maybe if I aided him in finding the path the gods wished him to follow, it could heal those broken parts in him and make him a better man. As for the near kiss…it was nothing, and I would treat it as such, a mistake better forgotten.

We followed Norna to the pyre, winding up the side of the mountain. At the top, a great bonfire had been readied.

Frika lay in a beautiful, white gown. Her long hair was undone and decorated with flowers. Her hands were folded across her chest, a small silver hammer in her grasp. She was adorned with heaps of jewels, rings on every finger, and an elaborate necklace. The black stones thereon glimmered in the firelight. Ardis stood at the woman's feet, a torch in her hand.

The robed gothi and the veiled gythia stood in a circle. Norna led us to a space just behind Ardis. In the field below, many villagers waited, their torches lifted into the night. I heard the sound of crying coming from the crowd. It surprised me. Frika had struck me as someone who probably had not even noticed the existence of the small people of Grund, yet they wept for her. Why?

Once we were all gathered, one of the gothar sounded a horn once more, quieting the crowd and calling the gods.

Everything became still and silent.

The torch flames flickering in the darkness was the only sound.

Ardis motioned to one of the gothi. I recognized the man. He was the priest who had spoken alongside Gudmund at the evening rite for the Dísablót.

The man drew a hammer from his belt. I had not noticed it before, but an anvil stood at the head of the pyre. He struck the anvil, making a resounding ringing sound. He beat the anvil three times. So doing, he hallowed the space.

"Great Thor," Ardis said, lifting her hands to the sky.

"We come to you tonight to remember Frika, child of the house of Grund, and to send her on her great journey to the beyond. May the dísir who rule this time accept this woman's spirit. Let Frika join with you, Frigga, Freyja, and Skadi. May she feast alongside her ancestors, her mother, her grandmothers, and all the mothers and sisters of Grund. May the dead dwell together and watch over the living. May Frika be remembered for her good deeds," Ardis said, motioning for Gudmund to come forward.

"Sister," Gudmund called. "I honor you and wish you safe passage to the otherworld. I will always remember you as my sweet little sister, following me everywhere I went, always ready to talk, and talk, and talk," he said with a laugh. "How I look forward to hearing your sweet voice again. I shall see you again one day, my sister. Until then, may the gods be with you."

Gudmund then turned to Rolf, Frika's husband.

The man's eyes were tinged red. He stepped forward. "Frika, my wife and mother of my two sons, you had every quality a man could ask for. You will be sorely missed. Feast and be with the gods. I will see you again."

Rolf turned to Soren.

There was a moment where Soren paused. His eyes went to Ardis, who motioned for him to speak.

Looking painfully uncomfortable, he said, "Mother," in a broken voice, but nothing more. He turned to Thorolf.

Gudmund frowned, making no attempt at hiding his frustration with Soren's lack of words.

Thorolf stepped forward. "Mother," he called, his

voice loud and clear. "I honor you who gave me life. You nourished me, taught me to talk, to walk, and to reason. I do not know why the gods have called you home so soon, but I swear by Thor I will make good the life you gave me. As you struggled and fought to bring me to this world, so shall I struggle and fight to make myself a better man. In your honor." He turned to Hofund.

Hofund stepped forward. "Aunt," he called. "You always had a word of wisdom for me, a piece of advice to share. I have remembered your words, locked them in my heart. Rest now. Drink and feast with our ancestors. You have set forth on a new journey. One day, we will join you. Until then, dance and be merry with the dísir. By Thor, we shall see you one day again."

At that, Ardis raised her hands to the sky.

"Cattle die. And kinsmen die. So will the self die. But a person lives on forever in their deeds. Frika, we send you onward now." She motioned for the gothar to step to the pyre. They set it aflame.

The dry twigs and leaves quickly blazed. We stood in silence, watching as the fire engulfed the pyre and the woman lying thereon.

I looked down at Blomma, who was staring at the sight. I gave her hand a gentle squeeze.

Blomma looked up at me. There was no fear in her eyes. She gave me a slight, reassuring smile then turned back once more, watching respectfully. Her other hand was pressed against her chest. Therein, I saw she was holding one of the small, carved reindeer. She stared at the pyre, the flames reflected in her eyes. And once more, for just a brief moment, I saw a flicker of silver.

I turned back.

Exhaling slowly, I set my other hand on Rök's head.

I closed my eyes. *Frika, forgive me.*

Overhead, I heard the call of a raven. Then another.

I looked up.

Far above the fire, a pair of ravens circled, rising on the heat of the flames.

*Odin.*

*All-Father.*

The ravens trilled once more, then spiraled away, back into the starry sky.

I looked around at the others.

None of them were looking skyward, not even Ardis. Had no one else seen the All-Father's ravens?

I looked into the sky once more. A dense feeling filled my chest. No. They had not seen. They honored the gods in this place, but their love for Thor and the dísir was omnipresent.

But somewhere in the starry sky overhead, ravens called.

I was not alone here.

As always, the All-Father watched over me.

"*Hervor.*

"*Daughter.*

"*My will shall come to pass through you.*"

I looked back at the pyre.

Across the flames, I saw a woman standing with the gothar. She wore strange furs and a cap, her long, black hair blowing in the breeze. Her eyes sparkling silver, she met my gaze. She was the same woman I'd seen in my dreams all those months ago.

"*Hervor.*

"*Remember what I told you.*

"*Do not forget.*"

And then, she disappeared.

## CHAPTER 28

That night, King Gudmund held a feast in Frika's honor. Rolf, Thorolf, and Soren sat with the king. Turid, Revna's mother, was red-eyed and half-hysterical with grief. Revna and her father did nothing to stop Turid's emotional theatrics, even though both Prince Jorund and Prince Eric looked exasperated by the scene. King Harald sat with his own men. Both the princes and King Harald had announced they planned to leave in the morning. I also kept my distance. Hofund, sensing my discomfort, stayed by my side. We sat with Yrsa and the warriors of Bolmsö.

King Gizer, having refilled his ale horn, pushed in beside Kára.

To my surprise, she gave him a flirtatious smile.

"Tell me, Jarl Hervor," Gizer began—though his eyes were on Kára—"are all the women on Bolmsö so beautiful?"

"What is their beauty compared to their ferocity?" Öd answered for me.

Gizer turned to him and laughed. "Skol, boy. Skol," he said, clicking his ale horn against Öd's.

Sigrun shook her head.

Kára, however, was grinning mischievously at Gizer.

"When will you come to see me in Götaland?" Gizer asked Kára.

"I go where the jarl goes," she said with a grin.

"Is that so?" he replied, then turned to me. "When will you come to Götaland, Jarl Hervor?"

"If we are to go anywhere, it will be Uppsala."

At that, Gizer nodded thoughtfully. "You are right there," he said, then turned to Hofund. "Any word?"

Hofund shook his head.

Gizer sighed heavily. "I will leave the day after tomorrow. One way or another, we will all find ourselves in Uppsala soon enough. Of course, that also means I need to find a way to pass the rest of my time in Grund," he said, then gave Kára a knowing look.

Kára laughed.

I gave Yrsa a sidelong glance.

She rolled her eyes.

"What is Götaland like?" Blomma asked Gizer.

Grinning, Gizer turned to her. "My lands are vast, and like Bolmsö, my hall is on an island in Götaland called Gotland. Isn't that funny how they are named so similarly? But it is a magical place. As you sail down the coast, the vættir whisper to my enemies and strike fear in their hearts, making them turn back or crash their ships. Only the true of heart will find my city hidden amongst the ash and oak. My hall sits in the heart of an ancient forest. Freyr and a legion of warrior elves watch over my village from the trees. If they don't like you, they will shoot you with their arrows or send their golden eagles to pluck out your eyes."

"Ash, oak, *and* stones," Blomma said.

Gizer tipped his chin in surprise then grinned at her. "And stones. Yes, you're right. Deep in the forest sits a circle of runestones carved by the All-Father himself."

"It is a good place," Blomma said with a thoughtful nod. "The gods watch over you there."

At that, Gizer laughed. "Yes. It is. Your foster daughter is wise," he told Hofund and me.

Hofund stroked Blomma's long, black tresses. "She is a gift from the gods," he said, then kissed her on the head.

Blomma smiled up at him.

The night wore on. Deep in the evening, King Gudmund motioned for Hofund to join him, Soren, and Rolf.

Blomma, who had been leaning against me, yawned tiredly.

"Come, let's find Magna and see you to bed," I told her.

She nodded sleepily.

Taking her hand, I led Blomma away from the hall to her private chamber.

"Hervor," Blomma said sleepily.

"Hmm?"

"King Gizer's forest is a healing place. There, the trees

whisper to people. It is a good place for people with broken hearts and minds."

I was puzzled by her words. "Does Gizer have a broken heart or mind?"

"No. Not him. Just...just remember that it is a good place for people like that," she said with a yawn.

I kissed her hand. Like Eydis, Blomma was riddling but didn't know why. I would not press her. Through Blomma, the gods were speaking.

"All right. I will remember."

Magna was busy banking up the fire when we arrived.

"Ah, there you are, sweet girl," she told Blomma, rising. "I was just about to come for you. These are long, tiresome days."

"Blomma has had her fill for the night, I think."

"I will see to her, princess. Come, blossom. Let's get you ready for bed."

I gave Blomma a hug. "Sleep well."

Blomma kissed my cheek then went to Magna.

I left the pair behind and returned to the hall. When I did so, I found the place nearly empty. Yrsa and Sigrun sat by one of the central fires, drinking and talking, Rök sleeping on his back beside Yrsa. The men of Bolmsö had gone...as had Kára and Gizer. I could not begrudge the shield-maiden. The king had an allure to him. While he was not made for me nor I for him, I could see how he and Kára must have got along well. They probably kept one another laughing all night long—when they weren't otherwise occupied. I heard Hofund's, Gudmund's, Soren's, and Rolf's voices coming from Gudmund's meeting chamber. I had no wish to be near Soren again. King Harald and the princes were also missing. I moved to join Yrsa and Sigrun but spotted Thorolf sitting alone by another of the fires, nursing his ale.

I sighed, and against my better judgment, grabbed a horn and sat down beside him.

We sat in silence, side-by-side, both of us sipping our drinks.

"When you leave for Uppsala, I will come with you," Thorolf said finally.

I nodded slowly. "Good."

Again, there was a lull of silence between us.

"Hervor..." Thorolf finally said, turning to me.

I met his gaze.

"I wanted to apolog—"

I lifted my hand. "Say nothing."

"But, I was—"

"In grief and lost to drink and reason. I understand. If I did not, you'd have a black eye and bloodied lip. There is nothing to say. We shall carry forth as friends."

Thorolf searched my face. He nodded slowly then smiled appreciatively at me. "Then, skol, cousin."

"Skol," I said, clicking my horn against his.

The pair of us sat in silence for a long time. Finally, I heard Hofund's voice in the hall once more. I looked back to see him and the others.

"My father," Thorolf said with a shake of his head. "He's worried about our connection to this house, his wealth, and Soren's future. As if Gudmund would simply stop supporting us now that my mother is gone."

I reflected on his words. Thorolf was wrong. It wasn't Gudmund that Rolf was worried about, it was Hofund. When the great king passed, what would happen to Soren? He was no friend to Hofund or me, and Rolf was smart enough to realize that—albeit too late.

Rolf and Soren nodded to the king, then to Hofund, then turned and left the hall without giving Thorolf a second glance.

Thorolf watched them go. His gaze hardened. He turned to me, a serious expression on his face. "My brother is no warrior, but he is cunning and cruel. He will not forget what happened, and he blames you for it. He will seek revenge upon you."

"Why are you telling me this?"

Thorolf gave me a knowing look. "I would not have anything happen to you."

I frowned, ignoring the insinuation. "If he thinks he can kill me, he is sorely mistaken."

Thorolf's gaze followed his brother. "In your drink, your sleep, or by the hand of someone you trust, that's his way. He is not brave enough to cross a blade with you. Be on your guard. He has sworn to avenge our mother."

I stared at him. "Have you told Hofund this? Gudmund?"

Thorolf shook his head. "I have told you."

I sat back and drank once more. After a moment, I tapped my horn against Thorolf's but said nothing more.

Behind me, the sound of light laughter caught my attention.

I looked over my shoulder to find Hofund and Revna

talking. Revna's hand gently stroked my husband's arm. She was smiling and whispering to him.

To my surprise, Hofund was grinning.

Furious jealousy flickered to life in me, surprising even me. I turned away as the low rumble of rage shook me.

Thorolf followed my gaze. "My brother is a menace, but you have other enemies in Grund," he said, then turned back to the fire.

Rising, I set my hand on his shoulder. "Goodnight, Thorolf."

"Goodnight, Hervor."

Taking a deep breath and composing myself, I joined Revna and Hofund.

"So, I will take my leave of you for the night. Be well," Revna said, then turned, finding me there. "Ah, Hervor. I was just bidding Hofund farewell. Goodnight."

"And you," I said stiffly.

She nodded to me, then turned and joined her parents, who waited for her by the door.

I tried to quiet the jealousy inside me, but it nagged at me. "What was she on about?" I asked Hofund, with more annoyance in my voice than I intended.

He shook his head. "Trying to lighten the dark spirit of the place."

"Frika is dead. Grief is not out of place here, nor should it be quickly swept aside. Some still feel their losses most stingingly," I said, looking over my shoulder at Thorolf who was, from what I could see, alone in his pain.

Hofund followed my gaze. The lingering smile on his face, generated by the irksome Revna, faltered. A flash of shame crossed his features. I was glad to see it.

"You are right," Hofund said. He turned back, meeting my gaze. He set his hand on my cheek. "My wife," he said. "You are always here to remind me of what is good." Giving me a quick kiss on the forehead, he left me, joining Thorolf.

I eyed the hall. I was done with this place for the day.

I gave a low, soft whistle.

Rök woke from a dead sleep, flipping over to look for me. When he finally caught sight of me, he tilted his head.

I motioned for him to come to me.

Yrsa turned and met my gaze.

I nodded to her.

She returned the gesture.

Rök rushed across the room. "Come on, you," I said, scratching his ear. "Let's go to bed. Apparently, someone might try to kill me. Seems to me, it would be good if you stayed close," I told him, then left the hall.

I sighed. I suddenly wished I was back on Bolmsö beating Asmund's face in. Grund was turning out to be far more complicated than I had ever expected.

## CHAPTER 29

In the days that followed, we bid farewell to King Harald, Prince Jorund, and Prince Eric. The day Gizer left, we joined him on the pier to say good-bye. It was misty that morning, a light rain falling. My hair was damp, the dewdrops clinging to the strands of my blonde locks.

"I think I will hear from you soon," Gizer told us.

"News will come one way or the other," King Gudmund replied.

"Until then, may Thor keep you," he told the king.

"And you."

King Gizer turned to me. "Keep your axes sharp, shield-maiden."

"Always."

Gizer set his hand on Hofund's shoulder. "In blood and honor," he said.

"In blood and honor," Hofund replied, slapping Gizer on the back.

Gizer turned to Kára, motioning for her to step aside with him. He whispered something in her ear, making her laugh loudly, then set a surprisingly passionate kiss on her lips.

Hofund and I exchanged a glance.

King Gudmund chuckled.

When they separated, Kára turned and looked at me. A mock-innocent grin on her face, she shrugged.

Gizer and his men departed, leaving us alone once more. The blót was done and Frika had been sent to the gods. Now, there was only the lull of silence between the battles.

King Gudmund sighed. "This mist is making my bones ache. Come, let's go back to the hall and find something warm to drink."

"I'm sorry, Father. I have something to show Hervor. Do you mind?"

Gudmund shook his head. "No, of course not."

"I'll come with you, King Gudmund," Kára told him.

"Good, good," he told her, taking her arm. "Come with me, shield-maiden. I'll fill your ear with all manner of warnings about King Gizer."

Kára laughed. "I can't wait to hear them. But I wonder, who will warn him about me?"

At that, King Gudmund laughed.

Hofund motioned for me to come with him, and the two of us went into the village.

"What do you think of Kára and Gizer?" I asked Hofund.

Hofund smirked. "Gizer finds a beautiful woman in

every town he visits. I hope Kára will not have her heart broken."

I shook my head. "I'm more worried about Gizer."

Hofund laughed. "Gizer is one of the first men, besides my father, I ever looked up to, respected. He is sincere and silly in turns. But I would trust him with my life."

We headed into town, passing the workshops of blacksmiths and tanners, alehouses, and homes. As we went, the people eyed us with curiosity, inclining their heads as we passed, one wary eye on Rök.

"I have something for you," Hofund told me.

"Indeed?"

Hofund smiled lightly. "To win my bride, I brought her a warband. But since we returned to Grund, I have been continually reminded of something else. Not only did I win myself a bride, I won Grund a queen. So, this is a gift for the future queen of Grund."

Hofund stopped before a large building that was in desperate need of repair. The roof was missing timbers, as were the walls.

"What is this place?" I asked.

"It was used for the livestock fairs back in my grandfather's time, but the market has moved since then. It's been sitting, rotting. We will repair it. You can use this place to offer alms to the people of Grund…food, supplies, a warm place to sleep for those without. I will see to it you have men to work the place and the money to keep it going. If it pleases you, princess."

I laughed. "Princess. Now, that is a title I have not

gotten used to. It was not so long ago that I was a father-less bastard."

Hofund took my hand. "You have always been someone destined for great things, including being my wife," he said with a chuckle.

I jabbed him playfully in the ribs.

Hofund laughed.

I took his hand. "Thank you."

Hofund pulled me close, kissing the side of my damp head. "No. Thank you," he said, then motioned to the building. "Come on. Let's go see how many rats we need to chase out."

WAITING FOR NEWS OF UPPSALA AND HAKI AND HAGBARD grew excruciating. As time pressed on, Yrsa grew more irritable. The only upside was that the repairs on the almshouse were finished quickly as Yrsa threw her back into the work and nagged those tasked with completing the repairs with a sharp tongue.

Knowing better than to get in her way, I kept to my own task of meeting the people of Grund and doing what good I could.

Late one afternoon, after having fallen into a pigpen—in the rain—I found myself falling into step alongside Revna, who was making her way to the hall.

At first, she did not recognize me, but when Rök appeared by my side, she gave me a second glance. "Her-vor," she said, unable to hide the surprise in her voice.

"Revna."

"I didn't know you under all that...mud," she said, then inhaled sharply, trying to avoid the scent.

"Mud and pig shite," I said with a laugh. "Bodil is going to kill me."

She stared at me.

"I fell."

"I see."

"I'm going to the hall."

"Me as well. Father and mother grew tiresome. I'm hoping Bjorn will have some entertainment for us tonight," Revna said wistfully.

I nodded but said nothing more. I didn't understand women like Revna and Asta. Their lives seemed so empty to me.

"How is Hofund? I have not seen him much of late," Revna asked.

"We are all busy." Hofund was working with his men, seeing that two new ships were outfitted and ready when news came from Uppsala.

"Oh, I have heard about your almshouse. It is a nice thought, but don't you worry it will encourage laziness? I mean, if the king provides for his people, what incentive do they have to farm, hunt, or fight for their own means?"

"No one chooses to be hungry. I would rather feed a dozen old men and have one be a liar than let the others starve."

"Fair enough," she said with a heavy sigh. "It is such a bleak time now that the blót has passed. Frika's death sent everyone into a funk. Have you seen Soren at the hall lately?"

"You would know better. You're there far more often than me."

"The death of his mother weighs on him."

"Then, he is a loving son."

"Yes," she said lightly. "Such a tragic accident. But let's speak on it no more. I don't wish to cause you any pain remembering what trouble your sword caused. I often see your daughter in the company of the gythia Norna. What is the child's name again?"

"Blomma."

"Blomma. Such a pretty name. Did you name her?"

"No."

"Then...her father?"

"I don't know. She is my adopted daughter."

"Oh. I see. Her parents are deceased?"

"Yes."

"You are brave to adopt a young child before you have your own children. Don't you fear your children will be jealous of her or her of them?"

I suddenly wished I was still facedown in the pig shit. "I have no such fears."

"No, you wouldn't," she said as we approached the door to the hall. "Ah, here we are. And just before the rain begins again," she said, looking up toward the sky. Thunder rolled across the horizon as the clouds darkened. Lightning cracked. "Well, the only good thing about the rain is that it will blow Hofund back to the hall."

I met her gaze.

"I'm sure you'll want to freshen up," she said, eyeing me from head to foot once more. With a light smile, she turned and breezed into the hall, her ebony-colored hair shimmering like the wings of a raven in the firelight, her plum-colored gown fluttering behind her.

Frowning, I slipped into the hall. Avoiding the crowd, I headed to the back then upstairs to the family quarters. There, I found Bodil banking up the brazier.

"Hervor," she said in surprise. "By the gods, you smell terrible."

I laughed. "No doubt. Would you mind helping me with a bath?"

"I'll see to it straight away."

"Bodil... that indigo-colored fabric... Did Magna ever make a gown out of it?"

"She did. Didn't you see it? It's in your chest. It's the most exquisite thing."

"I'll wear it tonight."

Bodil let out a little happy shriek, accompanied by a small hop, and she pressed her hands together. "Oh, I can't wait to see you in it."

I sat down on a stool near the fireplace and pulled off my muck-covered boots. I ruffled Rök's ear. "Nothing worse than a bitch in heat," I told Rök. "Though I'm not sure you'd agree. Just what happened with you and that black she-wolf of yours, huh? Naughty boy. Well...in all things, we shall see. Bitch or not, there is only one alpha in this hall."

BODIL DISAPPEARED TO FETCH SOME HOT WATER. WHEN SHE returned, we got to work, Bodil helping me comb the mud out of my hair. "Blomma is back from the hof. Magna is dressing her for dinner. It's raining so fiercely out there. Hofund and the others just returned. Even Soren and his father have come. Soren looks as waspish as ever."

"He and Revna can sting one another."

Bodil laughed. "Revna may be my cousin, but she is nothing like my sisters and me. She's all show. And she's made a job out of trying to marry your husband."

"So I have heard. And Hofund?" I asked tepidly. I hated that I felt jealous, but I could not squelch it. "Did he ever seem to want to…"

"He and Revna have been friends for many years, but I don't think Hofund ever saw her as she saw him. You mustn't worry yourself. Some whispered that Hofund would take a second wife, but that's not his nature. Revna knows she has lost. If she cannot have Hofund, she will move on."

"To whom?"

"Oh, I'll let you sort that out," Bodil said with a laugh.

Once my hair was washed, Bodil took it upon herself to fix my braids. Then, she helped me dress in the gown. The dress shimmered beautifully in the firelight. Magna had embroidered the collar with wolves in a silver-colored thread. As Bodil tied the laces, I wiggled uncomfortably.

"Hmm," Bodil mused. "Let me loosen it a bit," she said, then adjusted the gown. "There you go."

I exhaled deeply. "The food in Grund is making me soft. My armor isn't even this tight."

Bodil chuckled. "For now," she said, then added, "All right, princess. You're ready. Freyja is shining her light on you. How beautiful you look. If they ever needed a reason to be jealous of you, they'll find one tonight."

"It's not Freyja's doing but yours. Thank you, Bodil."

She gave me a smile. "Thank you, Hervor."

And with that, I returned to the hall.

I WISHED THAT EYDIS WAS WITH ME. NO ONE COMPLAINED more loudly than Eydis that I never dressed like I should. My life was about *doing* not *seeming*. And the more Bjartmar forced me to be that kind of woman, the more my spirit resisted. But, maybe, I resisted too much. There was power in feminine wiles. I could see that. From time to time, a person could wield such weapons equally effectively. After all, I was Svafa's daughter and Eyfura's granddaughter. Perhaps I was letting one of the best weapons go unwielded.

Rök and I left my chamber just in time to meet with Magna and Blomma.

Blomma smiled at me. "You look beautiful!"

I bent to kiss the girl. "As do you, my little flower."

Magna looked me over from head to toe. She nodded happily. "I'm glad to see it fits."

I set my hand on her arm. "It's beautiful. Thank you so much."

Taking Blomma's hand, we headed downstairs and into the great hall. There, the usual crew had gathered. Fires burned brightly, warding off the damp, spring air. My eyes searched out Hofund, who was sitting by the fire with Bjorn.

Rök left us, going to Yrsa.

Blomma and I went to Hofund and Bjorn.

As we crossed the room, I felt eyes on me. The chatty crowd hushed for a moment, and then the whispers started. I didn't meet any of their gazes.

Bjorn spotted me first, catching sight of us out of the corner of his eye. He paused mid-sentence, causing Hofund to turn and look.

Hofund rose. "Hervor," he said, extending his hand to me. "Now, *that* is a blue dress."

"Do you like it? My husband purchased this fabric for me."

"Smart man."

"I confess, I was covered in mud—and worse—an hour ago. It is Bodil's seidhr you're seeing."

"Then she is a very talented gythia," Hofund replied. He stepped forward and touched my cheek. "You look lovely."

"Thank you."

Hofund set a soft kiss on my lips.

I didn't know where Revna was, but I could feel her eyes burning into me.

Good.

When Hofund finally let me go, he touched my chin gently then turned to Blomma. "And here is my little blossom. What have you been doing all day? Rolling in the mud with Hervor?"

Blomma shook her head. "Ardis took me into the caves at the hof."

Hofund arched an eyebrow. "Did she?"

"Did you know the cave network in the mountain is very deep?"

"I did not."

Blomma pursed her lips and let out a "hmmm." After a moment she added, "Perhaps I shouldn't say more. Maybe it is a secret."

Hofund gave her a wink.

"Jarl Hervor," Bjorn said. "You've inspired a new song: The warrior maid in blue…"

I laughed. "Who knew a wardrobe change could provide such devotion?"

"Depends on the wardrobe and who is wearing it."

Not long after that, the king appeared. We all joined him at the table.

Even King Gudmund looked twice as I approached. "By the gods, Hervor, you look lovely tonight. You are positively glowing."

"Thank you, King Gudmund."

"What handsome children the pair of you will make," King Gudmund told Hofund and me, then lifted his ale horn. "Grund," he called, gathering all of their attention.

I looked down the table to see everyone's eyes on the king. When my gaze fell on Yrsa, she gave me a knowing smirk.

"Grund, besides our good fellows from Bolmsö, the

rest of us we were not able to celebrate the wedding of Hervor and Hofund, but let's toast their marriage and the future of Grund tonight. To Hofund and Hervor."

"To Hofund and Hervor," the assembly called in reply.

Hofund lifted his horn and motioned to the rest of the table.

I followed suit. When I did so, I met Revna's eye.

The expression therein was precisely what I had hoped. She was jealous. And furious. But then, she did something unexpected. She smiled at me, inclining her head ever so slightly, acknowledging defeat in this battle.

I lifted my horn to her, then turned back. When I did, Thorolf caught my gaze.

He was staring at me with such intensity that it caught me off guard.

I smiled lightly at him, then turned back to Hofund.

Hofund clicked his horn against mine. "To the future," he said.

I nodded. "To the future."

THE EVENING PASSED PEACEFULLY. BJORN SANG AND TOLD wondrous tales while we all sat by the fire. Yrsa pulled Blomma onto her lap as we listened to the skald.

"Any news from Uppsala?" she whispered to me.

I shook my head. "Not yet."

"I hate all this damned waiting."

I nodded. "As do I, but it is as the All-Father wills. We can't rush the will of the gods."

"Or King Gudmund."

I chuckled. "Well, he is king."

"You are looking the part of future queen tonight. Too bad Eydis can't see you."

"I can hear her from afar."

"Any particular reason for the scrubbing up?"

"I grew weary of someone's haughtiness."

"You need to find her a husband, so she gets her eyes off Hofund."

"Who has their eyes on Hofund?" Blomma asked, a sharp tone in her voice.

"Nevermind that," Yrsa told her.

"There are mushrooms that can make a person blind," Blomma said, causing both Yrsa and me to look at her. "I saw them at the hof today." She shrugged. "I'm just saying."

"Some matters require a more delicate hand," I told Blomma.

"All right," Blomma said, then turned her attention back to Bjorn.

Both Yrsa and I smothered a laugh.

"Any suggestions for a husband for her?" I whispered to Yrsa.

She bobbed her chin at Thorolf. "Kill two problems at once."

"She won't take the younger brother. His reach is too low, even if he's much better looking."

Yrsa chuckled then considered. "Hmm. Well, there are always Blomma's mushrooms."

We both laughed.

The night passed on, and soon, I grew very tired. Magna had already taken Blomma to bed. Finally, all of the aches from the day's labor cropped up, nagging at me.

"Come," Hofund told me. "You look like you're about to fall asleep in your seat. Let me take my beautiful wife to bed."

I nodded then turned to Yrsa.

She yawned tiredly then stretched out. "The ale is good tonight. I'll linger a bit longer."

I set my hand on her shoulder. "Goodnight, Yrsa."

"Goodnight, Hervor."

With that, Hofund and I left the hall.

As we did so, I marveled. Between Rök and Tyrfing, I had managed to subdue much of the conspiring against me in that hall. But in the end, it had taken a blue dress and a head full of pretty braids to silence the one person who still hoped to take something precious from me.

As we turned and left the hall, I looked back over my shoulder.

My gaze met Revna's.

I smiled lightly, then looked away. My husband loved me. And while I found the use of such weapons distasteful, I had allure enough to win any man I wanted. The old Hervor would not have seen that or even wanted to admit it, but it was wise to accept the gifts given to you and use them when you must. Revna would never have Hofund. Tonight, I made sure she understood that.

*"So, Hervor has finally learned how to play the game... Well done, shield-maiden."*

## CHAPTER 30

I t was past Goi blót when the news finally came from Uppsala. Yrsa and I had been eating our morning meal when a messenger arrived.

"That's one of Jorund's men," Yrsa said, eyeing the messenger. The man spoke to Halvar who quickly sent runners to fetch Hofund and the king. Halvar turned and motioned to me.

"Come with me," I told Yrsa, and the two of us approached.

"Jarl Hervor, this is Magnus. He's come from Prince Jorund," Halvar told me.

"Welcome to Grund. I'm Jarl Hervor, wife of Prince Hofund," I told the messenger. "This is my foster-mother, Yrsa."

The man inclined his head to us. "Thank you for the welcome."

"Come," I said, motioning for him to take a seat by the fire.

Taking a pitcher of ale, I poured the man a cup. "I trust your journey was well," I told him.

He nodded. "May Njord be praised."

"And Jorund and Eric?"

"Both well, jarl."

Hofund appeared a moment later.

The messenger rose. "Prince Hofund."

"Please," Hofund said, motioning for the man to sit. "It is a rainy morning. Catch your warmth."

"Thank you, prince," the man said then rubbed his hands before the flames. "I was in the court of King Gizer. Jorund and Eric are there."

"News of Uppsala?" Hofund asked.

He nodded.

King Gudmund appeared a moment later, looking like he'd just rolled out of bed. I eyed him warily. His face looked puffed and red, as did his neck and hands as he fumbled with his clothes.

"King Gudmund," the messenger said, bowing.

The king nodded to him. "You are welcome in Grund. What news?"

"King Hugleik is dead. Haki and Hagbard have taken the city. Jorund and Eric ask that you and your jarls meet at King Gizer's hall by the new moon."

King Gudmund nodded slowly. "Very well," he said. "We will make our preparations. Please, take your rest. When you are ready, Halvar will see that your ship is outfitted for the return."

"Thank you, King Gudmund."

early today, Blomma. Let's leave Hervor to her business, and you and I shall find something good to eat," he said, offering her his hand.

"All right," she told him with a smile.

I set a quick kiss on her head then headed toward the kitchens to see to the provisions. I mulled over King Gudmund's words for a moment. Why hadn't he thought I would go with Hofund and the others? Did Gudmund feel unsafe in Grund? Surely not. Maybe he just didn't want to be alone. Leaving the thought aside, I made my way into the kitchen. As soon as I entered, the smell of cooking meat and baking bread reminded me that I hadn't finished my breakfast. My stomach growled so loudly that it startled a kitchen boy working there.

"Jarl Hervor," he said sweetly, a smile on his face. "I think you're hungry."

I laughed. "I think so. Work first. Eat second."

The boy handed me a small round of bread. "Or both at once."

I tousled his hair. "Both at once it is."

# CHAPTER 31

The call to war swept across Grund. The warriors prepared to head out as ships were rigged, supplies readied, and plans made. The news that Uppsala had fallen to marauding raiders stunned the capital. If Uppsala could fall, so could Grund. That fact seemed to shake a stark sense of reality into people who seemed otherwise nonplussed by the grim realities of our world.

I was making my way through the hall when Revna called my name. "Hervor?"

I paused, swallowed my irritation, and then turned to her. To my great misfortune, I found both Revna and Soren there. Wonderful.

"Is it true?" she asked, her brown eyes wide. "King Hugleik is dead?"

I nodded. "It is."

"So much for my father's new venture in Uppsala," Soren said sourly.

"And what venture was that?" I asked.

Soren stiffened. "Furs," he answered, as if surprised that I'd even inquire.

"Was it these same marauders who tried to take Dalr?" Revna asked.

"Yes."

"Sad you were not able to end them in Dalr," Soren said.

"Yes. It is. Perhaps you'd like to join us in the effort this time?"

Soren stuttered, unable to form an answer.

"That's what I thought. If you'll excuse me, there is much to be done."

"Of course," Revna said.

I headed out of the hall. As I made my way through Grund, I saw signs of war. Everywhere I looked, I saw warriors mending their armor, sharpening their weapons, and preparing for the launch. As I passed the leather-worker, I was surprised to see Thorolf there. The man was fitting him with a new jerkin.

Curious, I joined them.

"Hervor," Thorolf said, a mildly abashed expression on his face.

"Jarl," the leatherworker said, inclining his head to me.

"What's this, then?" I asked.

"The leather on my old jerkin cracked. I wanted to make sure I was properly dressed for Uppsala."

"Good," I replied then eyed the jerkin he was wearing. It was a very handsome piece with silver trim and pounded designs, good for impressing the hall, but not made to keep someone alive. "Now, take that off, and fit yourself with that instead," I said, pointing to a simple leather piece made of thick material and lined for the cold.

"But it's so..." Thorolf began.

"Sturdy," I answered for him. "And well made. It will keep you alive, not looking like a peacock."

The craftsman laughed. "I told him the same."

"Then he should have listened to you. That one," I said, pointing.

At that, Thorolf nodded then motioned for the man to help him remove the pretty jerkin.

I gave him a small wave then left, making my way to the docks. There, I found Yrsa and my band from Bolmsö preparing to debark.

"Leaving without me?" I asked them jokingly.

"Thought we might kidnap you, jarl," Kára told us. "But I suppose we trust Yrsa to keep us in one piece until we see you again."

Yrsa simply shook her head.

"Have everything you need?" I asked her.

She nodded. "Hofund sent these men along with us. We'll head to Eric first, then on to Leif in Dalr."

I looked over the ship. Everything seemed to be in order.

"Be safe," I told them.

Öd nodded to me. "We'll see you very soon, jarl."

Sigrun whistled, calling Hábrók. A moment later, the bird appeared in the sky overhead. I waited with them until their ship was ready to debark. Yrsa joined me one last time before boarding.

"Watch yourself," she told me.

"And you. May the All-Father keep you safe."

She patted my shoulder then boarded the ship.

As they prepared to debark, Rök whined.

"Don't worry," I told him, stroking his ear. "We'll be with them again soon."

The ship unmoored from the dock and began turning back out to sea. Yrsa gave me one last wave. My heart felt heavy as I watched them go. I stayed on the dock until their ship was out of sight. Admittedly, I felt as torn as Rök. No sooner had I earned my place as jarl in Bolmsö than I'd left. It felt wrong to be here alone with only Hofund and Blomma. No Eydis. No Yrsa. No Lief. Now, I had only the life I'd chosen for myself. Thank Odin I had picked a good man, and the gods had seen fit to grant me with a daughter like Blomma. Otherwise, I'd feel very alone. For someone who always thought of herself as a cast-off, I was beginning to see that I had never really been alone. I'd always had family around me, such as they were. And now, I had a family of my own. And one day... I set my hand on my stomach. One day, there would be more of us. That, and I really needed to stop eating so much. My trousers were growing tight, and my stomach was pouchy where it hadn't been before. Which reminded me...had I eaten? Surely, there was something left in the hall.

"Come on, Rök," I told the wolf. "Let's see what we can find to eat."

I RETURNED TO THE HALL, FINDING HOFUND AND KING Gudmund in the meeting room. The pair was looking over a map laid out on the table.

"Up the river," King Gudmund was saying. "That's the only way to take the ships in."

Hofund frowned. "They will be ready for that."

I joined them, eyeing over the map. Uppsala was not on the seaside. The only way to access the city was by river or over land.

"If they are smart, they will have riders at the mouth of the river," Gudmund said, pointing. "Any approach will be announced."

Hofund considered. "The longer Haki and Hagbard don't know we're coming, the better for us."

"What if we land here?" I asked, pointing to a section of the map slightly northeast of Uppsala. "How is the terrain there? Could we land our ships here, make our way by foot, and attack the city from the rear?"

King Gudmund nodded. "Not an easy crossing. A lot of wetlands to the east of the city. But perhaps to the north..." King Gudmnd said, then sighed and rolled up the map, handing it to Hofund. "I wish I was coming with you. When will you sail?"

"Tomorrow morning. Yrsa left for Hárclett and Dalr. Magnus has sailed for Halmstad. We will go directly to Gotland."

King Gudmund nodded. "Thorolf is strutting about the hall dressed for battle, making sure everyone knows he is going. I guess with Frika gone, he has no skirts to hide under."

Hofund frowned. "I will do my best to bring him back alive."

"Remind him to sharpen his sword," Gudmund said.

Hofund huffed a laugh.

I frowned but said nothing.

"We shall sacrifice to Thor tonight," King Gudmund said, rapping his knuckles on the table. "May the thunder god watch over you all. In blood and honor."

"In blood and honor," Hofund replied.

The king turned to me. "At least I will have Blomma to keep me company. What a curious child she is, the questions she asks. You never know what she's going to say. The gods have touched that child."

"Let's hope their purpose is a good one," I replied.

"And let's hope she has many more siblings to come," Gudmund told his son, then winked at me. Taking my arm, he said, "Come along, Hervor. It is nearly midday meal, and I still haven't eaten. Hofund hears the drums of war, but all I can hear is the rumbling of my belly. The warhorn sounds for me no more, but there is always the dinner table."

"May I live so long to be afflicted with such problems," I replied with a chuckle, then we headed to the hall.

## CHAPTER 32

H ofund ate quickly then set off for the docks
once more. King Gudmund and I lingered
awhile over our plates for longer than we
should have. I checked for Blomma only to discover that
she and Magna had already left for the hof.

On my way out of the hall, I spotted Thorolf chatting
with some merchants.

Gudmund was right. Thorolf was posturing proudly.
Aggravated, I called to him. "Thorolf?"

He nodded to the men then joined me. "Hervor? What
is it?"

"Get your shield and come with me."

He looked at me, a confused expression on his face,
but did as I asked. We headed outside, Rök trotting along
beside us, excited to be on an adventure.

We headed to the river. There was flat ground there,
and the place was out of sight from passersby.

"You were right about the jerkin," Thorolf told me. "It is thick leather."

"It is. So, tell me, do you fight better with sword or axe?"

"I...axe."

"And with two axes or axe and shield?"

"I think... Maybe axe and shield."

I nodded, hearing the uncertainty in his voice.

"Where are we going?" Thorolf asked.

"You'll see."

I waved to a fisherman as we passed by, not stopping until I found a secluded spot. "This will work," I said, then tossed my shield to the ground. Pulling Muninn, I turned to Thorolf. "A man your size will be a target. Everyone on the field will think you a fierce fighter and a good prize. The biggest men will try to take you down. Haki and Hagbard's warriors are cutthroats. They are hard to fight, even for the most seasoned warrior. Hagbard took Leif's eye, and Leif is one of the best fighters I know. Now," I said, then readied my stance. "Come at me."

"Hervor? But—"

"We have one day to make sure you know what you should have spent a lifetime learning, and from what I can see, no one here is going to be bothered to teach you anything. May Thor protect you, because if you don't learn quickly, you will soon be dead."

Thorolf stared at me. I watched the realization of what I was saying play on his features.

"But you—"

"You are twice my size, and not so long back, I put you on your ass. Now, come at me. Let's see how fast you can learn."

"All right," he said tepidly. Lifting his axe, he charged at me. When he did so, he left his belly exposed. Anticipating his move, I leaned in with my left shoulder and bashed him in the stomach, pushing him sideways and to the ground. He fell, his axe and shield tumbling from his hands.

He sat on the ground for a moment, a dazed look on his face.

I offered him my hand. "You're dead. No one will fight fair. This is not a fancy show of weapons nor bout played for fun during a blót. Your opponent will do anything to kill you. Now, get up."

After a moment, Thorolf took my hand, then rose.

"Yes. Yes, you're right. I just...I don't want to hurt you."

"You think you can?" I asked him with a laugh. "Now, if you're going to use that shield, then use it. Keep it in front of you, like this," I said, modeling what he should do. "Hold the grip firm, keep it close to your body, protecting your soft middle. But you can also use it to block. Shield yourself from arrows. In the shield wall," I said, modeling the moves. "While it keeps you safe, you can also use it as a weapon."

"The shield? How?"

I grabbed my shield, then held it in front of me. "Attack me," I told him.

Keeping his shield before him, protecting his body as I had instructed, he swung his axe one more.

When he did so, I blocked his blow with the axe while giving him a healthy bash on the face with the boss of my shield.

Thorolf staggered back a step. Surprised, he slipped his axe into his belt then touched his nose, which was bleeding. "You broke my nose!"

"No, just injured it," I told him. And, as I had planned, I'd also made him angry. "Now, stop playing nice and fight," I said, then advanced on him.

Then, the dance began. As we moved, I saw that he had been honest; he'd been hesitant to fight me, unwilling to risk harming me. Now that he realized I wasn't going to go easy on him, he stopped holding back. Still, it was clear he'd never fought in a real battle before. He had a lot to learn. Fast. Otherwise, he'd be dead in the first wave.

As Yrsa had done for me, I spent the afternoon teaching Thorolf what I knew, giving him several painful reminders that no matter how big he was, how strongly built, he needed to train his body how to move. He had to think quickly. And he had to plan for the unexpected.

"Let Thor guide you," I told him. "Let the god speak to you. Let your hands move with confidence. Even if you die, as long as you die well, you will go to Valhalla. There is nothing to fear. Use your size. Use your strength. You are bigger and stronger than other men. But don't let it make you slow," I said as he attacked me once more. I swiped my leg out, tripping him. Again, Thorolf fell on his arse.

Thorolf heaved a heavy sigh. "Who taught you to fight like this?"

"Yrsa. And...experience," I said, holding out my hand to help him up once more.

Thorolf took my hand, but to my surprise, he pulled me down. I landed on my back with a huff. A moment later, I felt Thorolf's steel on my neck.

"You're not the only one who can play tricks."

I grinned at him. "Very good. You *almost* learned something today."

"Almost?"

At that, I tapped the dagger I was holding against his side. "And that is why I have a blade on my belt and in my boot. Just in case anyone gets clever."

Thorolf laughed but held my gaze.

Again, I saw a look in his eyes that made me uncomfortable. I wriggled away from him and rose, pulling my water skin. I took a drink then handed the skin to him.

He took a drink, then we stood in silence for a long moment, both of us catching our breath. Thorolf wiped his mouth with the back of his hand then handed the skin back to me. "Thank you for helping me. My uncle thinks me a lost cause. Hofund is too busy to teach me what he believes I should have already learned. He is right to think like that. But it was never my choice to stay behind."

"Perhaps not. Now you must make up for the time you have lost by making better choices. You are not your father or your brother. A better future waits for you if you choose to take it."

"The gods brought you here to save me from myself, Hervor."

"I am here today to save myself from having to protect you in Uppsala," I said with a laugh. "You will do well if you remember what we practiced. Sacrifice to Thor tonight, a sacrifice of your own choosing and of your own expense. Show the god you are ready for him. He will come."

"How can you be so sure?"

"Because there is one thing in this world in which we can always have faith—the gods."

Thorolf nodded. I slipped Muninn back into my belt then fastened my shield on my back once more.

"You only fight with your axes? Never with Tyrfing?"

"When you see Tyrfing on the field, then you will know it's time."

"Time for what?"

"To fight like you mean it or die," I said. Turning, I whistled to Rök, who had spent most of the afternoon chasing voles around the field. "I will go to the hof now."

Thorolf nodded. "Hervor...thank you."

I inclined my head, then turned and headed toward the shrine, leaving Thorolf behind.

*Odin.*

*All-Father.*

*I hope I have done right here.*

*"Hervor. My Valkyrie. May our will be done through you."*

## CHAPTER 33

After collecting Blomma from the hof, we walked back to the hall.

"Should I continue to go to the hof while you're gone?" Blomma asked me.

"As long as you feel safe."

"I think King Gudmund will be lonely in the hall."

"You can keep him company. But I want you to stay clear of Soren. You do not have to speak to him. And even Revna…tread carefully when you are near her."

"Soren whispers about you and Hofund to the others. He never sees me, but I hear him. He tries to tell the others that Hofund is never here, that he has no love for Grund and will be a bad king. He tells the others that is your fault his mother died. But that is a lie. He was the one who touched Tyrfing when he should not have done so."

"Soren hopes he can convince the others to make him king instead of Hofund."

Blomma laughed. "I hear the others' whispers too. Many think Soren is foolish."

"So he is."

"Many…but not all."

I nodded. "If someone thinks Soren can advance their wealth and standing, they will support him. But you do not have to fear such things. Soren will never win Grund from Hofund. But stay clear of him all the same."

Blomma nodded. "It doesn't matter what he wants anyway," she said, stopping to pick a blade of long grass, which she swished before her like a sword.

I lifted an eyebrow at her. "And why is that?"

She shrugged then skipped along. "It will be as the gods will. And the gods don't like people like Soren."

"Is that so?"

She nodded.

"How do you know?"

She shrugged. "I just know. Come on," she said then pulled me along. "We don't want to be late for the sacrifice."

As with Eydis, I considered Blomma's words carefully. The child had already had prophetic visions. Did she see something for Soren? Leaving the issue of the adder-tongued Soren for now, I went to the hall. Tonight was for Thor. And tomorrow, we would be back at sea. Neither place held any room for Soren.

That night, King Gudmund stood before our ships, a hammer in his hand. The entire assembly of Grund had gathered to watch.

"Mighty Thor," Gudmund called. "Grund sails tomorrow in your name. Our warriors from Grund sail to defend the sacred site of Uppsala, to protect the holy land of Freyr and the great hall, tree, and shrine. Thor, we carry your hammer to war. Strike your anvil. Fill our hearts with fire. Let the sparks fall inside these warriors. Let them return home victorious. We fight in your name! In blood and honor."

"In blood and honor," the crowd called.

Gudmund motioned for Hofund to come forward.

Hofund lifted his twin axes. "Thor, I lead the warriors of Grund in your name. We honor you, mighty thunder lord. Tonight, we offer these sacrifices in your name." He motioned to the elder gothi who'd spoken at the blót. The man struck a small silver hammer against a round of metal. A sharp sound rang across the water.

The other gothar who waited sliced the throats of the goats they had brought with them. Once the blood was collected, they handed one bowl to Hofund, another to Gudmund.

Hofund and Gudmund went from ship to ship, splashing the blood onto the ornate prows. The serpents, waterhorses, rams, stags, and other fierce faces that adorned our ships were soon dressed in blood.

"May Thor be praised," King Gudmund called. "And may Njord protect these ships as they travel on dangerous waters to free our ancient city. Protect our warriors, mighty Thor. We honor your name. All hail Thor!"

"All hail Thor!" we answered in reply.

I looked down at Blomma. Her eyes were wide in fascination as she looked at the boats. I lifted her small hand and set a kiss on her fingers. She looked up at me. Her gaze was very far away. It took a few moments for her to come back to me. After a moment, she shook her head as though to clear her thoughts, then gave me a light smile.

When the ceremony was done, King Gudmund motioned to Hofund.

"Please, everyone, join us in the square for ale and food," Hofund called.

At that, the crowd cheered.

Hofund joined Blomma and me. He lifted Blomma, setting her on his shoulders.

I turned, waiting for Gudmund.

"Do you think Thor heard us?" Hofund asked Blomma.

"Of course," she replied. "He is always watching you, Hofund. I see him in the sky. He peers down at you to make sure you're doing what you should. And he listens to you through your hammers."

"Through my hammers?"

"Yes. That is how he hears all who follow him. Are your hammers ringing? Are they wet with blood? Or do they sit at home and become covered with dust? He hears your prayers—from your lips and your hands—through the metal. That is why he likes you to wear the amulet of

Mjolnir. Hammers sing to him night and day, if he chooses to listen."

Gudmund laughed. "What a fabulous imagination you have, Blomma."

Blomma looked down at him, a surprised and somewhat offended look on her face. "I am not imagining it. It is so."

"And how do you know?" King Gudmund asked her.

"Because Loki told me."

"Ah," Gudmund said. "Now, you must be wary of Loki. He is a liar."

Blomma nodded. "I know. That's why you have to be smarter than him, so he cannot trap you in a lie," she said matter-of-factly.

Gudmund looked at me. "I don't know what to make of her at times. Is she telling the truth?"

"My dear friend, Eydis, who married my cousin Leif, also heard the voice of the trickster god. For some reason, Loki is fond of our little group. I'm not surprised he speaks to Blomma."

"Hmm," Gudmund considered. "Hofund's mother, Thyra, was the same. Sometimes, she would stare off into the distance. When she came back, she would talk in riddles. But I learned, over time, that if you paid attention, there was truth to her words. Frigga and Freyja whispered to her. As for me...I am stuck with the mundane world."

"Mundane? You are king. Look at all you have accomplished," I said, motioning to Grund.

Gudmund nodded slowly. "The warrior's paradise. That is what they have always called Grund. When I rode with my men, the ground would shake. They would say it was like the Wild Hunt had come. I was always more fond of horses than ships whereas Hofund has an affinity for the sea. I am proud of him. He is a fine son, and he has married a good woman. I will leave this paradise to him...and to you."

"Don't be so anxious to leave us anything."

He laughed. "I am in no rush to join my comrades in Valhalla."

I patted his hand. "Very good."

"Now, come on, let's see what they have to eat."

I chuckled. "That, I can agree to. My stomach has been rumbling for the last two hours."

"No doubt, my dear. No doubt."

THE CELEBRATION WAS A RAUCOUS EVENT, THE WARRIORS OF Grund crowding the hall in preparation for departure tomorrow. Their presence minimized that of the layabouts who seemed uncomfortable of the show of might in the hall. They still slunk their way around, drinking and talking, but their impotence next to Grund's warriors was obvious. A brute of a warrior accidently backed into Soren, causing Soren to spill his drink on his fine clothes. The man, who was laughing heartily, never even noticed. Soren looked like a flustered rooster.

Hofund and Thorolf stood together drinking, Thorolf looking decidedly more confident that he had earlier that morning. Perhaps the dark rings under his eyes from that bash in the nose and his puffy lip had bolstered his confidence. If so, I was glad.

It was strange to be without Yrsa and my crew from Bolmsö. Rök sat alert, but still, beside me. At the same time, for the very first time, the king's hall felt comfortable. It was a place for warriors. In the hall that night, I saw the potential of this place. There was joy here rather than smirking scheming. Perhaps Hofund and I could bring a much-needed change.

"Look at them," a soft voice said, coming up behind me. "They are all ready to fight."

Revna. I suppressed a sigh. "Good," I replied. "No use in taking them with us if they weren't."

"Thorolf told me that you're the one who blackened his eyes."

I paused, feeling the spider spin her web around me. Any answer would bring me trouble. I said nothing.

Revna continued, adding, "It's good that someone has finally taken an interest in him. He has moped about this hall like a lost puppy all his life. Pathetic, in a way."

My temper flared, but I tried to restrain it. "At least he is brave enough to change. Only those who are too weak to even try are truly disdainful," I replied, my eyes flicking to Soren.

"Not all battles take place on the bloody field."

I laughed lightly then turned to her. "Only the ones worth fighting. Good night, Revna," I replied tartly then left her standing alone.

I patted Rök on the head. "Next time she sneaks up on me like that, feel free to bite her."

I made my way through the crowd, clapping arms and patting the shoulders of the warriors gathered there. Many had fought with us in Bolmsö, Dalr, and Silfrheim. I worked my way through the crowd, reveling along with them. The night drew on, and finally, I found my way to Bjorn. The skald's eyes were tinged red with drink. He was leaning against a pillar, presumably to keep himself upright.

"What do you think of this gathering?" he asked me, his voice overly loud.

I laughed. "I like it very well. In fact, I like it much better than the usual well-dressed rabble that swarm this place."

Bjorn nodded. "I agree. I very much agree. I will sail with you tomorrow. Did you know that?"

I raised an eyebrow at him. "I did not."

"I fight well enough not to get killed. As long as I wear this," he said, motioning to the medallion of a skald on his chest, "and give the rest of you space, I should make it out alive."

I laughed. "Why risk yourself?"

"For Uppsala. For that great temple. For the enormous tree. For all the things I never saw before!"

I laughed. "Those are good reasons."

Bjorn set his hand on my shoulder and looked me deeply in the eyes. "And I want to see you use that sword, not see Soren fumble about with it. I want to see that dwarven blade work its magic so I can sing of your golden hair spinning like a scythe, cutting down the sea kings."

"I'll do my best not to disappoint."

"And Rök," he continued, his words beginning to slur. He pointed toward the wolf, his ale sloshing from his horn. "I want to see…is he really a man? Tell me the truth. Is he a god? A landvættir or shifter?"

"Well, I guess you'll find out," I said with a chuckle.

"I shall sing of it. I will call it *The Saga of Hervor*. You will see. I shall start at the beginning with Sigrlami, then tell of Tyrfing and how the blade came to you. I shall make you famous, shield-maiden."

"Very good. But first, and most importantly, you must stay alive. If you do that, you can sing of me as much as you like."

Bjorn laughed. "Yes. It's a deal."

I patted him on the shoulder then left him. The night was already ebbing onward, and I was feeling tired. I scanned the room, looking for Hofund. He was talking with his father. I joined them.

"Ah, and here is your pretty wife," Gudmund said.

"Pretty but weary," I said.

Hofund nodded. "It has been a long day."

"Hofund was just telling me it was you who bloodied Thorolf up," Gudmund said with a laugh.

I turned to Hofund who had a bemused expression on his face. "He told me."

"You might be the first person to ever knock him on his arse," Gudmund told me.

"It was far too easy to do. Hopefully, the next person finds it a little more difficult."

Gudmund nodded. "You've done well, Hervor. My

sister's boys. Perhaps we can make something out of one of them yet."

Hofund grunted but said nothing more. "I'll see Hervor to bed then return," he told his father.

Gudmund nodded to him.

"Good night," I told the king, setting my hand on his shoulder.

"Good night, my dear."

Hofund and I left the others. In the family section of the hall, the noise receded. Magna had taken Blomma to bed hours before.

"Why did you help Thorolf?" Hofund asked me. There was a tone in his voice I didn't recognize. Was it annoyance? Jealousy? I wasn't sure.

"I felt pity for him."

"Why?"

*Why, indeed?*

We paused outside the door of our chamber.

"I spent my life in Jarl Bjartmar's hall trying desperately to escape who he wanted me to be. The jarl pressed an image on me. One I hated. One that drowned the real me. Yrsa threw me a line. If not for her, I'd be just like Asta. I don't know. Maybe I saw some of myself in Thorolf."

Hofund kissed me on the forehead. "You are too good."

I wrapped my arms around him.

"Sleep tonight, my love. We will wake before the sun tomorrow," Hofund told me.

"Don't stay up too late."

He chuckled. "I need to go roll Bjorn to bed. I'll join you shortly afterward."

"Very well."

"Goodnight, Bolmsö."

"Goodnight, Grund."

I went into the chamber. Feeling ridiculously exhausted, I pulled off my boots then lay down on the bed, Rök jumping onto the bed beside me. I put my arm around the wolf then pulled him close. "And to think, Bjorn thinks you're secretly a god. If you are, I'm going to be very mad at you for lying to me all this time."

In reply, Rök sighed heavily then passed a ridiculous amount of smelly gas.

"For the love of all that's sacred," I swore, sticking my nose into my pillow. "Some god you are," I said with a laugh then promptly fell asleep.

## CHAPTER 34

We woke early the next morning. A dense bank of fog covered the streets of Grund. A hush had fallen over the place as we gathered at the docks to launch. Gudmund looked stoic as he watched us prepare to depart. Blomma held his hand, watching the bustle with interest. Warriors hurried to and fro, boarding their ships.

Rök ran wild among the people, excited to be on an adventure once more.

We were nearly ready to go when Bjorn finally appeared.

"Good morning," I told him.

He winced. "Not so loud."

I laughed lightly. "What a son of Thor! Thor drank from Útgarða-Loki's horn, the end of which was in the ocean, draining the ocean and creating the tides."

"Who is the skald this morning?" Bjorn said with a laugh, then winced again. "I think I'll board the ship."

I nodded then patted him on the shoulder.

Hofund was going from ship to ship, making sure all were settled. With everything in order, he motioned for one of the men to sound the horn.

It was time to leave.

"Hervor," a voice said from behind me.

I turned to see Thorolf there.

"Well met, cousin. Sail with us," I said, pointing to the lead ship.

He inclined his head to me, then went to the boat.

Behind us, the villagers called their goodbyes.

Hofund motioned to me. Together, we joined the king.

"Ready, then?" Gudmund asked Hofund.

He nodded to his father then knelt to meet Blomma's gaze. He reached into his pocket and pulled out a small, carved wooden ship. He handed it to her. "Keep us with you," he said, "and pray for us as we cross the bobbing waves," he added, making the tiny ship dance on imaginary water.

Blomma took the little ship from his hand then wrapped her arms around Hofund's neck.

"I will see you soon," he told her.

"Yes," she replied, squeezing him tight. "Soon."

After a time, she let him go.

I leaned down, kissed her on the forehead, and then met her eyes. We held one another's gaze for a long time, then she hugged me as well. "Be safe," I whispered to her.

"You too."

I set my hand on her head, stroking her long hair one last time, then turned to the king.

"With blood and honor," Gudmund told his son.

"With blood and honor," Hofund replied.

"May the Norns watch over you, shield-maiden," Gudmund told me.

I inclined my head to him. "Thank you."

With that, Hofund and I boarded the ship. Rök found a spot between the men and sat, his muzzle resting on the side of the boat, looking out at the water. Once we were aboard, the ships began to maneuver out of port. I went to the front of the boat just behind the prow on which was carved a winged maiden, her sword hoisted in front of her.

I turned back one last time to look at Blomma.

I lifted my hand to wave farewell to her.

She returned the gesture.

Princess of Grund. Blomma's life had taken as many unexpected turns as my own. The wind blew gently, blowing the girl's skirts and long black hair. At that moment, I saw her in double: as the child she was, and as a young woman of striking beauty, her hand raised, a tall staff before her, her silvery eyes shining.

I blinked, clearing the image away. The gods had a special fate planned for Blomma. What that was, I was not sure just yet.

With a sigh, I looked back out at the water. As for me, it was time for war once more. Finally, Haki and Hagbard would pay for the injustices inflicted on my blood: on Mother, on Yrsa, on Leif. For the innocent lives of Gobi and Bo. Soon, I would have those sea kings' blood on my sword.

## CHAPTER 35

Our ships jogged across the sea, spray blowing up on us as we went. The journey to King Gizer's holdings would take several days. Night and day passed on the waves, but the wind was good. The red-and-white striped sails of King Gudmund's boats billowed fat-bellied, pulling us through the water.

I was glad Bjorn had joined our ship. As we rolled across the waves, he entertained us with tales of heroes, sea monsters, and the gods. Bjorn, however, was probably regretting his choice. In between telling tales, he spent much of his time vomiting. The rolling sea and his stomach did not agree with one another.

Aside from that, the warriors joked and laughed with one another.

"Thorolf is quiet," Hofund said, eyeing his cousin. "I don't remember you this quiet, cousin."

"He's trying to decide if he can swim back," one of the men said.

The others laughed.

Thorolf laughed lightly. "Unless Rök will let me ride him to shore, I think my fate is set," he said then smiled good-naturedly. "Perhaps I did not sail with you before, but I am glad to be here with you now, cousin."

"It is good you have come," Hofund told him.

Thorolf gave Hofund a thankful glance.

I was glad to see some thaw between the cousins. In a way, I could not blame Hofund. I had no use for small men either. But things would be different now. If Thorolf lived.

WITH THANKS TO THE GODS, THE WEATHER HELD FOR US. ON the morning of the fourth day, we finally spotted land.

"Gotland," Hofund told me. Pulling his horn, he called to the other ships.

Rök put his nose into the air and sniffed busily.

"You see, we are near land," I told him, gesturing into the distance.

A wind blew across the ocean, and with it, I caught the faint smell of trees and earth.

Rök's ears perked up.

I gave him a pat, then wrapped my arms around his neck. "Another island, just like Bolmsö. We will meet with King Gizer. And, hopefully, Yrsa and Leif."

Rök turned and looked at me, recognizing the names.

I gave his head a scratch. "You will see," I told him.

Our ships sailed toward the island. Soon, I was able to

see many of the small farms along the coast. And then, in the distance, I saw the port. My eyes took in the scene. Standing, I eyed over the boats gathered there. But it wasn't until we drew near that I spied three ships with green-and-white sails with a large tree emblem.

So many boats had gathered. Amongst the others, I also spotted Jarl Eric's and Jarl Egil's colors, King Harald's, and many others, including Princes Jorund and Eric. The size of the fleet that had gathered was impressive.

I turned and looked at Hofund who was grinning.

"Something tells me Haki and Hagbard will soon regret their choices," Bjorn said with a laugh.

"When Yrsa finally catches hold of Haki, he will have more than regret to contend with," I replied.

Hofund laughed lightly. "May the gods let it be so."

As we neared Gotland, a horn sounded from the city.

Hofund called to the others, and soon we began to make port.

Rök, impatient to have it over with, jumped from the side of the boat and swam to shore.

"Now's your chance," one of the men called to Thorolf who laughed in reply.

The ships made port. The village was deeper in the forest-covered island. As Gizer had told Blomma, tall stands of ancient oaks and ash covered the place. But there was no sign of elves. I could just make out the peaked roofs of the buildings. Smoke drifted upward from between the branches of the trees. As we tied up the ships, a delegation of people arrived from the village. At the front, I spotted King Gizer who was laughing heartily, Leif at his side. Yrsa and Kára walked just behind them.

Rök, who had also spotted them, rushed toward Yrsa.

A number of people at the dock paused, unsure what to make of the sudden appearance of the wolf in their midst. Unable to contain himself, Rök jumped up on Yrsa, licking her face. He then danced around Kára and Leif in turn before running down the dock to rejoin us.

"I heard thunder rumbling in the distance," Gizer called to us. "Lightning struck over the sea, and the ships of Grund appeared."

Hofund laughed. "We are the sons and daughters of Thor. Did you expect any less?"

The others tied up the ship while Hofund and I debarked.

"By the gods, well met," Gizer told Hofund, pulling him into an embrace.

I turned to Yrsa, Leif, and Kára, hugging each in turn. I set my hand on Leif's cheek. The scar there had healed, fading to a deep fissure across his face. Still, he wore an eyepatch, covering his broken eye.

"Cousin," I said. "It is good to see you."

"Every time I see you, your army is larger," Leif told me with a laugh. "By the time we are old men and women, you will be the queen of all of Scandinavia."

"May we both live that long," I told Leif who chuckled.

I turned to Yrsa. "All went well?"

She nodded.

I set my hand on her arm, feeling relief to be near her once more.

"Jarl," Kára said, inclining her head to me.

"The others?" I asked her.

"All well. At the hall."

I nodded then turned back to Lief. "How are the little ones?"

Leif smiled. "Arngrimir is standing on his own. He yells at us when we walk away from him. He can't stand that he cannot follow us. He will no doubt crawl very soon. Eylin is not far behind him, but she is more moderate in her moods. Our 'Grimir is the one with all the fire."

"Taking after his namesake, I see."

Leif smiled then looked over the crew behind us. "By the gods, is that Thorolf?"

Hofund smirked. "So it is."

Leif laughed. "Thorolf! Are you lost, brother? This was a launch to go to war, not a sumbel."

Thorolf smiled abashedly then joined us. He clapped Leif on the shoulder. "It's good to see you, Leif," he told him.

"At first, I thought my good eye was deceiving me, yet here you are. And look at you, bloodied up already. How did you manage that?"

Thorolf laughed then turned to me. "Hervor."

Leif looked at me then laughed. "Well, that explains it. It is good to see you," he told Thorolf then looked to Bjorn. "Ah, even the skald is here. By the gods, man. You look white."

"They sea and I do not agree," Bjorn told Leif.

"Ah, I see you have brought my future wife," Gizer told Hofund then turned to me. "Don't fear, my friend, I shall give you proper burial rites before I take your bride."

Chuckling, Hofund shook his head.

"Well met," I told King Gizer, embracing him —briefly.

Gizer laughed. "Come, let's go the hall. There is someone there who wants to meet you, Hervor, and I have left Harald to deal with some quarrelsome jarls."

My curiosity piqued, I turned and followed along behind him.

"How is Eydis?" I asked Leif.

He laughed. "Busy. Remaking Dalr as she sees fit."

"Your mother? Any news of your sibling?"

Leif shook his head. "No sibling yet, but she is due any time now. She barely let Egil leave. He looks almost relieved to be here. Things are amicable between us. I'm glad. It is Hakon and Halger who are furious with me for leaving them behind," he said with a laugh. "They tried to stow away with the supplies. I admire their fire. In the very least, they aren't cowards like Calder. Speaking of," he said, looking over his shoulder. "Thorolf?" He shook his head. "Of all the people in Grund, I never imagined you would befriend *him*."

"You know me. Glutton for castoffs."

"Hmm," Leif mused. "Well, of the two brothers, I'm glad you picked this one to take under your wing."

"The way things are going, the other is going to end

up under my blade. There was an incident in Grund," I whispered. "Ask me later."

Leif nodded.

We headed into the village. A path curved between the trees, across small bridges, past waterwheels powered by the fast-moving currents, then around knolls and houses made of both stone and wood. Some of the small, stone buildings with earth roofs covered in lichen and ferns looked ancient. In a way, the place reminded me of Bolmsö. The forest here felt old, as if the village had grown up alongside mankind. Deep in the forest, sitting on a hill, was Gizer's hall. The trees around the hall had been cleared. Beams of sunlight shimmered down through the evergreen boughs and leaves to the peaked roof. The square before the hall was bustling with warriors. In the crowd, I spotted the red-and-black shields of Bolmsö. I waved to Trygve, Sigrun, Kit, and Öd. Also in the crowd, I spotted the warriors of Dalr, including Frode, Ivar, and Bridger.

I turned back to Yrsa. "Ragal?"

"He sent men from Halmstad, but he had to stay behind."

I nodded. Halmstad and Bolmsö had suffered a long, difficult year. It was better that Ragal stayed where he was.

We walked into the hall.

There, I spotted King Harald, as well as Jarl Egil and Jarl Eric. Bryn was there as well.

"Grund is here," Gizer called to the crowd who cheered in reply then turned to us. "Drink. Rest. There is time for arguing over the details later," Gizer told us. Then, with his arms open wide to embrace him, he made his way toward King Harald.

We joined Eric, Bryn, and Egil.

"Hofund, Hervor," Eric said, inclining his head to us.

"I'm pleased to see you all," I told them then turned to Bryn. "Don't tell me your father is here?"

She laughed. "He is on his mountain with his reindeer, but he sends you his good tidings. No, I am here with my husband," she said, turning to Eric who smiled abashedly.

"Leif told us the good news. Congratulations to the both of you," I said, hugging Bryn and Eric in turn.

I turned to Egil. "I'm glad to see you," I told him.

He nodded to me.

"How is my aunt?"

"Ripe as a berry and growling like a bear. I think I'll have a new son or daughter by the time this is done," he told me.

"May Freyja and Frigga watch over her," I said.

"So, we shall take war to Uppsala," Eric said, looking at the mass of people gathered in the hall.

"We seem to follow Haki and Hagbard everywhere they go," Leif replied.

"For the last time," Yrsa said.

"Has there been any news?" Hofund asked.

Egil motioned to the back of the hall. "Some. There is a warrior here who was with Hugleik. He survived the fall of Uppsala and has been speaking with King Harald."

"A warrior? Who?" I asked.

"Hervor?" King Gizer called. I turned to see him

approaching with a bald-headed warrior who was about Yrsa's age. He was a fierce-looking man with tattoos on his head, his features weathered by age and battle.

"Him," Egil said in a low tone.

I stepped forward to meet the pair.

"Hervor, may I introduce Orvar-Odd, warrior of Uppsala."

## CHAPTER 36

Orvar-Odd. The hero had fought on Samso alongside Hjalmar, who had killed my father. This man had my uncles' blood on his hands. But it was also Orvar-Odd who had seen the sons of Arngrim buried with honor. It was he who had left Tyrfing in the mound with my father.

I paused. My family had met this man and his companion on the battlefield and died. Yet, it was my uncle Hjorvard's unwillingness to let go of the Princess Ingeborg, who loved Hjalmar, that had brought about their demise.

Reining in my feelings, I inclined my head to him. "I know your name and some of our shared history. I honor you for seeing my father and uncles honorably laid to rest on Samso."

In Bjorn's song, he had sung that Orvar-Odd was equipped with magical arrows and a shirt woven by the elves, which protected him in battle. Even now, he had a quiver strung on his back.

The warrior smiled lightly at me. "By the gods, you look just like your mother. I am pleased to meet you, Hervor. I was in Uppsala when you were born. I remember you, a tiny thing in your mother's arms. And now, there are rumors all across this land that you are the most fierce shield-maiden in all of Scandinavia. But they failed to remark that you also have Svafa's beauty."

I paused. I was not one for flattery, and remarks upon my beauty did little to impress me, but the idea that this man had played such an important role in the shaping of my life was not lost on me.

"May I present my husband, Prince Hofund of Grund," I said, turning to Hofund.

"Prince," Orvar-Odd said, inclining his head to Hofund.

"I am pleased to meet you," Hofund told him. "I have heard of you. Is it true that you have traveled to the Mediterranean?"

"After Hervor's mother declined to marry me, I had to find a way to distract myself from the disappointment. I journeyed from here to those blue waters just to forget her," Orvar-Odd said with a laugh, but there was a lingering hint of pain in his voice.

Stunned, I stilled. Then, I remembered...in Svafa's mad ramblings, she had mentioned the name of Orvar-Odd. The name had meant nothing to me, so I had dismissed it. Apparently, my mother had known this hero far better than I ever guessed.

I looked at Yrsa who shrugged, the expression on her face revealing that she was just as surprised as I was.

"You must tell me your story," Bjorn told Orvar-Odd. "I have heard you were with Prince Oleg in Novgorod as well. If you would indulge me, I would love to sing your song."

Orvar-Odd nodded to the skald.

Gizer chuckled. "And here I thought she might try to take your head for the death of her uncles," he told Orvar-Odd with a laugh. "Seems some time in Grund has taken the feral out of my future wife. Pity." Gizer patted Orvar-Odd on the shoulder. With a laugh, he turned and left us, calling to another party.

Orvar-Odd chuckled awkwardly then motioned to me. "May we have a private word?"

I nodded to him.

Hofund met my gaze. Therein, I saw his offer to come along. I smiled gently at him, gave his hand a squeeze, then let him go. Orvar-Odd and I worked our way through the crowded hall, then went back outside.

"What an army we have amassed," he said, motioning to the crowd. "Surely, Uppsala will be free once more." Orvar-Odd nodded thoughtfully. "I remember when your father and uncles strode into the great hall of Uppsala. Bright as gods and fierce as wolves. They awed those in attendance. Those who had heard of their exploits feared them. It was clear to any who saw them that they were favored by the gods. I was intrigued, of course, and annoyed by their appearance."

"Annoyed?"

He laughed lightly. "I had nearly worked up the courage to ask Svafa to marry me when your father stole her out from under me. Even Prince Alf lost his hope for a bride that day."

"Then, Svafa did not deny you if you never had the courage to ask."

"There, you are wrong, Jarl Hervor," he said, his smile fading. "I returned to Uppsala after the disaster on Samso. I was there when Ingeborg's heart broke and the princess died. Svafa, too, suffered. Your mother was so bereaved that she nearly drowned. I saved Svafa—and you—from the icy water. Did you know that? Afterward, I stayed by Svafa's side. When you were born, I went to your mother. I offered my hand in marriage, promised to take her to my hall, treat her well, and raise you as my own daughter. But the gods had already taken Svafa's memories. There had been a fondness between your mother and me. I think... I think if she had been herself, we might be standing here as foster-father and daughter."

I stared at him. This renowned man, who had fought and killed my uncles, had also loved my mother. He had offered to raise me, care for me. But the gods had forbidden it, taking Svafa's memories, and with them, a different life.

I inhaled deeply then said, "Just over a year ago, a wanderer came to Dalr. He arrived in the middle of a freak winter storm. That night, he wove a tale of the great hall of Uppsala, recanting many events that happened there, and the interference of the gods. Until that day, I had never known my father's name nor what befell Svafa in Uppsala. When the stranger finished weaving his story, Svafa's memories returned. All these years, my mother was lost. She seemed like a mad woman. But..." I said, taking his hand, "she did speak your name. She remembered you had asked her something, and she had not properly answered you. It would distress her greatly until she forgot once more."

Orvar-Odd gave me a broken smile. To my surprise, tears welled in his eyes. "When Hjalmar died, I was cast adrift in the world. I had hoped to comfort Svafa, that maybe we could comfort one another, but the gods did not decree it. I am glad to hear that, even in her sorrow, she remembered me. How is she now?"

"She is well. Her mind returned to her. She is on Bolmsö. I think she is wounded by the loss of time, but she is healing."

"Such a bright thing. Never in this wide world have I heard a voice like Svafa's. Nor shall I again, I fear."

"You should go to Bolmsö. If I know my mother, she would be glad to see you."

"Who am I to step on that ancient isle with blood on my hands?"

"What did Bolmsö take from you? My uncle Hjorvard is to blame for it all. Not you. Not Angantyr. Not Hjalmar. And we must remember, they all sit together now in Valhalla toasting one another."

Orvar-Odd nodded, his eyes going to the sword on my hip. "The rumors are true. You have recovered Tyrfing."

I nodded. "Yes, from the mound on Samso."

"When my work was done and the dead were properly interred, a wall of blue flame erupted at the entrance to the tomb. The gods protected the dead. I never thought to see that sword again."

"It took some doing to retrieve it."

"I'm sure. It is a cursed thing, taking a brother from me and a father from you, but I hope, in your hands, it brings peace and justice to our land."

"That is a blessing I gladly take from my would-be foster-father."

Orvar-Odd reached out and touched my chin gently. "How like your mother…except those eyes. I would know those eyes anywhere."

I smiled at him.

"Hervor?" a voice called from the door.

I turned to find Leif there.

"Gizer is calling the kings and jarls," he told me.

I turned to Orvar-Odd. "Time to see how to bring about that peace and justice."

"And, as ever, it starts with the sword. Let's learn what the Norns have woven for us next."

**CHAPTER 37**

When Orvar-Odd and I returned to the hall, we found King Gizer banging his horn on the table. "Well met, well met, well met. I am glad to have you all in this hall. Eat and drink, my friends. Soon, we shall sail to the ancient hall of Freyr and offer the blood of Haki and Hagbard to the gods!"

At that, the crowd cheered loudly.

Gizer caught Hofund's eye and motioned to him to come to the back, doing the same with King Harald, Prince Jorund, and Prince Eric.

Leif nodded to Orvar-Odd and me, and the three of us joined the others.

The kings and jarls adjourned to the meeting chamber at the back of the hall. As Gudmund had done, Gizer laid out a map on the table before us.

"Now, my brothers and sister, we must plan. How will we flush the bastards out? What is our plan?"

"We need no plan. With this force, we will make a

direct assault on the city," Prince Eric said. "With Grund's men, we have all the numbers we need. We will make our way to Lake Märlaren then take the city in force."

"And be crushed in the swamps of Fyris Wolds as Hugleik was," Orvar-Odd said.

Prince Eric frowned at the hero. "And yet, here you are."

Orvar-Odd raised an eyebrow at him. "And yet, here *you* are."

The hero's meaning was plain. Had this force come to Hugleik's aid when it was needed, not now, the king would not be dead.

Prince Eric blew air through his lips but said nothing more. How could he? Orvar-Odd was right. It had been the decision of the kings to let Hugleik fall. Now, we were left cleaning up the mess.

"Haki and Hagbard hold the city. There is no easy way to approach by the main port," King Harald said in an effort to interject calm into the tension.

"We have the men," Prince Jorund replied. "And we are not Hugleik."

"No, we are not, but Haki and Hagbard are dug in. They need only retreat into the city to deflect us. I assume you'd rather not burn down Uppsala to get to them," King Harald said.

Prince Jorund frowned.

"If we approach from the river, it would draw them out," Egil noted.

"Perhaps, but so doing, we will lose any element of

surprise," I said. "Right now, they have no idea how big of a force we have amassed."

"Why do we need surprise? We have the men," Prince Eric told me dismissively.

"Do we?" Leif interjected. "How do you know? Do not underestimate these sea kings. You can see what it cost me when I did so," Leif said, motioning to his eye.

"The jarl of Dalr has a point," Gizer said. "There are rumors that Hagbard has a strong alliance with kings to the south. They may have already been reinforced."

Orvar-Odd nodded. "I, too, have heard such rumors."

"Which is why it would be beneficial to maneuver carefully and hide our numbers," I added.

King Harald looked at me. "Do you have an idea, Jarl Hervor?"

"A piece of one. What if we split our forces? Can we pinch Haki and Hagbard's army between us? How can we lure them out then spring a trap?"

Gizer stroked his beard then considered.

King Harald pointed to the map. "A road leads from the city here," he said, pointing to the east, "into a dense forest."

"A tributary river from the lake winds not far from that forest. If some boats land here," Orvar-Odd said, touching the map, "then journey by foot, they would remain largely unseen."

"And to the west?" Hofund asked.

"Fyris Wolds where Hugleik fell. All marsh," Orvar-Odd said.

"I hunted that area many times. Good duck hunting, but not good footing for a fight," King Harald added.

"To the north of the city?" Jarl Eric asked.

"The mounds of Freyr," Orvar-Odd said. "The land is dry."

"A three-pronged attack?" I asked. "One group could attack from the port. That will draw them out. Then we spring the surprise from the east with another force sweeping in. We could protect the rear with a third force from the north. They will either be pinched in the middle or have to retreat to the Wolds where they will fall—as did Hugleik." My gaze went from Jorund to his brother Eric. This gambit was all for their sake. It was for them to decide.

Jorund met my gaze for a long moment as he considered. Eventually, Jorund nodded. "It is a good plan, Jarl Hervor. If we sail up to the city, Haki and Hagbard will throw all his strength at us at once, not expecting the trap." He tapped his fingers on the map.

"I will lead my men around the city and take the position to the north," King Harald said. "I know a way to get us there unseen, but it will take two days to cross by land."

Jorund nodded.

Gizer laughed. "Oh, now we're having fun."

I looked up at Hofund, who nodded to me. "Hervor and I can sail with the princes, leading the advance up the river."

Jorund turned to Gizer. "Will you bring your jarls in from the east?"

"I will."

"Good," King Harald said. "My men and I will sail in the morning. At dawn on the third day, we will all attack. Jorund, Eric, Hervor, and Hofund must draw them out. When they are on the field, Gizer and I will come in."

"Agreed," Gizer said.

King Harald turned to Hofund and me.

We both nodded.

Gizer laughed. "Well, with that settled, let's drink. To Freyr. May he help us win back his great hall. And to the return of the true Yngling line on the throne of Uppsala," Gizer said, lifting his horn, nodding to Jorund and Eric.

"Skol," we all called, lifting our horns.

I turned to Hofund, tapping my cup against his.

And may the All-Father watch our backs.

THE REST OF THE NIGHT PASSED WITH LAUGHER, MUSIC, AND rowdy drinking. I worked my way across the room to join Yrsa and the others. Leif and the men of Dalr gathered there as well.

"Have you ever seen such a fierce force?" Leif asked.

"Gizer will be out of ale by morning," Kára said with a laugh.

"Leif was telling us we are sailing with Jorund and Eric," Trygve said.

I nodded. "We'll approach the city from the river."

"Put us right in the mix, did you?" Yrsa asked.

"What, I thought you'd want the most direct route to Haki."

Yrsa winked at me.

"By the gods, you can barely pack another body in here," Bryn said from behind me, she and Jarl Eric joining us.

"Well, we shall be at sea soon enough," Leif replied.

"I am glad to go," Öd said. "We shall free the great temple of Freyr."

I lifted my horn. "Then, may Freyr guide us! For Freyr."

The others lifted theirs in cheer. "For Freyr."

## CHAPTER 38

King Harald and his men sailed out the following morning at first light. Their journey north of the city, and the crossing by land, would take longer. I prayed that Odin watched over them. If the sea kings got word of Harald's advance, all would be in tatters.

With Harald gone, the rest of us waited. We had to time the raid carefully, crossing the sea by day and sailing upriver and across the lake at night, reaching the city at first light.

The eve before our launch, King Gizer gathered us all into the great hall for one last feast. Gizer's skald treated us to a rather rowdy rendition of the tale of a maiden who fell in love with a duck—who was, of course, Loki in disguise. When it was time for Bjorn to sing, he recanted the tale of the giant who built fortifications around Asgard only to be tricked out of his payment—again, by Loki.

I made my way through the room, sitting down with my crew from Bolmsö to listen to Bjorn sing. Shortly after that, Thorolf joined me.

"Hervor," he said, settling in beside me.

I smiled at him.

"I missed so much staying back in Grund," he said, gesturing to the room. "It makes me ashamed of the man I was."

"The man you were is dead. Now your job is to keep the man you have chosen to become alive. Haki and Hagbard's men hold nothing back. Not all of us will survive."

"That's encouraging."

"I speak plainly."

"So I've noticed," he said with a chuckle. "Your sword...is it true what they say, that the person who wields Tyrfing cannot be defeated?"

"Yes and no. As long as I have the sword, I cannot die. But Arngrim took the sword from Sigrlami by cutting off Sigrlami's hand. The hero Hjalmar disarmed my father and cut him with his own sword, killing him. If someone takes my arm, and my sword along with it, there isn't much I can do."

Thorolf laughed lightly. "Then be careful to make sure that doesn't happen. I like you with both arms."

I chuckled. "So do I."

A lull fell between us, and in that, I felt Thorolf struggling. He was on the precipice of saying something he shouldn't when I turned to him, clicking my cup against his. "Skol, cousin," I said, then left him, crossing the room to join Hofund once more.

Hofund had just turned from his men, who were headed outside, when I joined him. "Hervor," he said with a smile. "I'm weary of talking. Let's rest for a few hours," he told me. "The ships are ready. Now, we just need to make sure we are."

I nodded. "I agree. On every count."

Turning, Hofund and I went to the chambers in the back. I caught Yrsa's eye, motioning to her that we were retiring. She nodded in acknowledgment then went back to nursing her ale horn. Rök, lying on his back, slept at her feet.

Hofund and I had been given one of the few private rooms in the king's hall. Feeling weary, I made my way with Hofund. We entered the small chamber Gizer had given us. One of the thralls had already lit the fire. The room smelled of rich pine and leather. Furs hung on the walls, as well as the horns of stags, decorating the small chamber. I was sorry I didn't have more time to explore Gizer's village. The place had an ancient feel to it, much like Bolmsö, and I felt far more comfortable here than in Grund.

Once again, I reminded myself that one day, I would be queen. When that happened, Grund would be mine to remake as I saw fit—just as Eydis was doing in Dalr.

Hofund sat down on the bed with a heavy sigh.

"What was that?" I asked with a laugh.

"I miss the quiet of your island, Jarl Hervor."

"Stop reading my mind, gothi. I was just thinking

something similar," I said, then joined him. I bent over to unlace my boots then groaned. By the gods, I needed to stop eating so much everywhere I went. The laces on my trousers were getting too tight.

Hofund lay back, pulling me with him.

We lay in the dark and quiet. We could still make out the sounds coming from the hall. Bjorn's voice rang clear. Just under that, I heard muffled talk and cheers.

Hofund exhaled heavily then buried his face in my hair. "I will be glad to sail in the morning. Too much sitting. Too much talking. I am ready to fight."

"Thor is beating his hammer, calling us to war."

"Can you hear him?"

I stilled. "No, but the All-Father is with me."

"Then may the gods watch over us both."

Hofund slipped his hand under my shirt, pulling me close to him. He gently stroked my skin, but then, he paused.

"Hervor…" he began, an odd sound in his voice.

"Hmm?"

There was a long pause before he said, "Nothing. Just a fancy of imagination. Good night, my love."

"Good night."

THE FOLLOWING MORNING, THE WAR HORN SOUNDED LONG and low over the forest city. Hofund and I had risen early and were preparing our ships when the call finally came for the others to join us. Everywhere I looked, I saw boats.

I was glad to see Egil and the men of Silfrheim in the crowd. The fact that they were there showed me that we had made the right decision to return Egil to his place. He wanted to be part of our world, not destroy it.

"Hervor," a voice said from behind me. I turned to find Thorolf there.

"Well met," I told him.

"What can I do?" he asked.

"Stow those ropes then get ready to row," I replied with a grin.

He nodded. "I talked to some of the men of Dalr last night. They had much to say about these sea kings."

"I'm sure they did, considering what Haki and Hagbard tried to take from them." And, no doubt, Thorolf also finally heard enough stories to give him a sharp slap of reality. We were going to war. There was a distinct possibility he could die. A man his age and size was now nursing the nervousness of a boy. I lifted the amulet of Mjolnir hanging on his chest. "Thor watches over the blood of Grund. Soak the field with blood in his name," I said, then slapped his shoulder. Hard.

At that, he nodded, giving me a grateful look, then turned to gather up the ropes.

Leif joined me, stretching and yawning loudly.

"Just awake, Jarl Leif? What happened? Did you get so accustomed to that big bed in Dalr with your pretty wife beside you that you forgot how to do hard work?"

Leif laughed. "Hardly. I have barely had one night of good sleep since Eydis returned. You know how she is. She kicks and talks all night long and steals the coverlets.

Between her and my little ones, I am half starved for sleep."

I laughed. "I'm sure."

Leif motioned with his chin to Thorolf. "Don't get too sentimental, cousin. We may burn his body by the end of the day."

I frowned at Leif. "Don't wish ill on an ally."

"I don't. Just being realistic."

"Then be realistic about those crates that need to be loaded," I said, pointing.

He laughed. "Yes, Jarl Hervor."

I looked back toward the forest. Rök was finishing off the last of his breakfast, which consisted of a pulpy carcass—I didn't want to know what he'd found. I whistled to him.

He looked up, his head and ears shifting around until he caught sight of me.

I motioned for him to come.

Gobbling down the last bites, he rushed down the bank to join us.

Sigrun joined me, chuckling at Rök.

"Where is Hábrók?" I asked Sigrun.

"Left her with Blomma," she told me. "She promised to watch over her for me."

"It was kind of you to entrust her," I said.

Sigrun tipped her head to the side then shrugged. "She is one of us," she said, then turned and got into the boat.

Rök splashed through the water then ran down the dock, pausing to shake off the wetness on some unsuspecting warriors, before joining us once more.

"Get in, you menace," I told him.

Rök hopped into the boat, causing it to sway.

"Rök," Kára chided him. "Sit down before you have all of us as wet as you."

The horn called once more. Gizer and his men appeared. He was talking to his jarls, his men boarding their ships. Gizer's ships' black sails, the white eagle thereon, fluttered in the breeze. The sails on all the boats cast their colors on the surface of the water. It was almost as if the Bifrost was within the water itself. The waves shifted and moved, making the colors bob with it. My mind felt lulled by the sight.

*"Hervor.*

*"Daughter.*

*"All things come to pass, as is my will. Remember this."*

Someone set their hand on my shoulder, startling me. Yrsa.

"Sleeping standing up?" she asked with a wry grin.

"No...it's nothing."

"Good. Let's go."

I nodded.

One last time.

One last battle.

Overhead, I heard the call of a raven. And then another.

I looked up, seeing Muninn and Huginn circling in the air over our boats.

*Odin.*

*I carry my shield in your name.*

*I am your shield-maiden.*

*Your sword.*

*Your axe.*

*For you, I sail to free great Uppsala.*

Overhead, the ravens cried once more, then set off over the sea.

The All-Father was ready.

And so was I.

## CHAPTER 39

The sails on the ships billowed in the breeze. I could hear the pounding of drums as we glided across the water. The fierce faces on the mast-heads scowled angrily into the distance. And overhead, Muninn and Huginn soared, as if the All-Father himself led us to war.

"Your people speak generously of you," Bjorn said, settling in beside me. "They told me that when you go to war, Odin himself comes to watch." He pointed to the ravens. "I thought they were exaggerating."

I looked up at the birds. "I am no gythia, but I do as the All-Father wills. I set my life into his hands."

"Then it is no wonder he loves you so well. Few freely accept their destiny."

I laughed. "I have spent most of my life fighting to be free. Yet that, too, was Odin's will. Even as we fight to do what we wish, we are still doing the will of the gods. In the end, we all meet the fate the Norns promise for us, whether we want it or not, whether we believe the gods brought us there or we ended up at our end through our own will."

Bjorn nodded. "You reason well, jarl. As for me, I will assume it was Loki who inspired my mad desire to get on this boat. Already, my stomach is rocking. Gizer's gythia gave me a tonic," he said, pulling out a small bottle. "She told me it will ease my stomach." He took a sip. "Let's hope she's right."

"Loki is too often blamed for other people's bad decisions," I said with a laugh. "Of all the gods, besides the All-Father, Loki is the wisest. He could not create such mischief without being full of wit."

Bjorn laughed. "For good or ill."

"For good or ill," I agreed with a nod.

*"Finally, shield-maiden, someone has made sense of me."*

I smirked.

Patting Bjorn on the shoulder, I left him and slid onto the bench beside Yrsa, who was sitting quietly, sharpening her dagger. When she was done, she handed the whetstone to me. Wordlessly, I did the same. The expression on her face was pensive. We sat quietly together, looking out at the sea. After I sharpened my own daggers, I gave her back the stone, which she stowed.

With a sigh, I set my head on her shoulder.

Yrsa huffed a light laugh but said nothing.

Soon.

We would be there soon.

WE CREPT OUR WAY UP THE COAST, THEN BEGAN THE JOURNEY inland, up the rivers, across the flats, to Lake Märlaren. As we went, we passed small fishing villages and settlements, many of which had recently been burned. The people who had survived or escaped capture came to the water's edge and watched us pass, their eyes haunted.

"It is King Gizer," a boy called, his voice carried on the wind. "King Gizer! Avenge us, king!"

I looked away, anger making my blood boil. Everywhere the sea kings went, they brought heartache and pain.

Not today. Not anymore.

I sat back, willing my anger to be silent.

Soon.

We would be there soon.

Once, my mother had traveled this path, meeting her destiny in great Uppsala. In Uppsala, Angantyr and Svafa had found love. But my uncle Hjorvard's desire to win the love of Princess Ingeborg, and the fame that would come with her hand, had doomed them all.

*Odin.*

*All-Father.*

*If I must die, let it be for something worth dying for. Let it be in service of the gods, the betterment of our world, for the ones I love. Norns, do not weave me a selfish fate. Use me to leave this world a better place.*

A soft wind blew across the lake.

*"Be careful what you wish for, shield-maiden."*

Loki.

It was very late in the afternoon when we reached

Lake Märlaren. The sun was setting, casting pink and yellow hues on the water.

"Hofund," Gizer called to us. "Jorund."

Hofund and I rose.

Gizer pointed his sword to the river that trailed off to the northeast. Gizer would leave us here. The king then called to his men. Sounding his horn, they began rowing away from us.

Hofund toyed with the amulet of Mjolnir as he watched them sail away. He had a faraway look in his eyes. I had seen that look many times, on Eydis's face and on Blomma's. Whatever Hofund was seeing, I hoped it was good.

I waited at his side, casting a look behind me. Leif stood at the prow of his ship. He had a determined look on his features. Like Yrsa, his heart was set on vengeance. Haki and Hagbard had made this personal for us all. Soon, the sea kings would find that we would not roll over as easily as Hugleik.

Hofund finally turned back. The faraway look was gone. Instead, I saw a flicker of light, a brief flash of something that looked like lightning. Hofund took my hand, pressing our clenched palms against his heart, then nodded to me.

I returned the gaze then took my place on the bench in front of Yrsa.

Without another word, we began the final leg of our journey to Uppsala.

## CHAPTER 40

We traveled upriver under the twinkling starlight. Everything was silent except the sound of our oars gently stroking in the water and the soft voices of spring frogs. No one spoke. We needed to make our way to the city undetected, if at all possible. Everything counted on us arriving by dawn.

The sky faded from deep black to soft grey. The stars retreated with the coming of the sun. Mist rose off the river. From within the long grasses, marsh birds called then flew away, startled by the sudden appearance of our massive force. There was a sweet, earthy scent in the air. In better times, the journey to Uppsala would have been amicable. But not today. As we went, I began to see signs we were nearing the city. The number of small docks along the river, little houses or farmsteads, and more grew readily apparent.

When we passed a small pier, a young maiden stood with a bucket in her hand, watching us wide-eyed.

Kára, with a bright smile on her face, waved to the girl.

She stared but didn't move.

Even after the last ship had passed her, she remained on the dock.

It was nearing first light when the limbs of the great tree of Uppsala were finally visible on the skyline.

Along with that first glimpse of the city, we also heard the first sounds of war. A horn sounded from deep within Uppsala and then another and then another.

"We need to land before we get pinned down by archers," Hofund said.

"It will be wet," Yrsa cautioned. "Land too early, and we'll be slaughtered in the mud."

Hofund nodded to her then surveyed the landscape. He frowned as he eyed over the marsh.

"There," Yrsa said, pointing to a shoal from which fishermen had started fleeing. A rocky bar stuck out into the water. Between it and the city, the land was far drier. "Wet, but the mud won't pull us under."

Hofund nodded then rushed to the front of the ship. "Jorund!"

Jorund turned back.

Hofund gestured to the shoal.

Understanding, Jorund began barking orders to the others, and all of our boats started turning.

"Watch your footing," Yrsa told us. "Hustle toward the city and dry ground."

Thorolf stared at Yrsa. The expression on his face told

me he was truly seeing her for the first time. And, perhaps, he realized that unlike the hall, the *games* played here had far more severe consequences.

I went to my warriors from Bolmsö.

"Look at you," I said, taking each of them by the shoulders, meeting their eyes, and giving them a hard shake. "Odin's warriors. His shield. His axe. His sword. His spear. His pack of wolves. Fierce as Fenrir. Howl at the moon. Swallow the sun. For Odin."

"For Odin!" my pack called in reply.

My gaze met Yrsa's.

She nodded to me.

The prow of the ship made a scraping sound as it reached the pebble shore.

I turned back to Hofund.

He bobbed his chin toward the city. In the distance, we could make out the peaked roofs of the great temple and hall. At the docks, Haki's and Hagbard's ships sat silent. But before the entrance to the great city, I saw a flash of color—shields. An army was amassing to meet us. Their numbers were twice ours.

Frowning, I eyed the forest for Gizer. There was no sign of him. But then, I heard. Muninn and Huginn called as they flew in circles above the forest. Gizer and his men were close.

"Look," I told Hofund, gesturing to the birds.

He nodded. "We will hold them off until the others come."

I nodded.

"Grund. With thunder in your hearts. In blood and honor," Hofund called to the others, who cheered in reply. With that, we exited the boats.

Rök jumped into the water, splashing his way toward the shoreline. When we reached the shoal, I pulled my shield and axe. Looking behind me, I scanned the crowd, spotting Bryn's bright red hair. She, Eric, and the men of Hárclett rushed to the shore. I was sorry her father had not come. We could surely use a practitioner of seidr right about now.

Across the grassy plain between us and the city, I saw Haki and Hagbard on their horses, leading their men. Hagbard's long, golden hair fluttered in the breeze.

Rök growled low and mean.

"Mind yourself," I told him. "Stay close to me."

"Gather," Jorund called to us.

Waving to our warriors, we fell in line with Prince Jorund's and Prince Eric's men. Orvar-Odd, who had sailed with Jorund, stood alongside them. He turned back to look at us. When he did so, he caught my eye. He smiled at me.

I returned the gesture.

All these months in Grund, I had felt lost, feeling my way through uncertain terrain. Now, my world had gathered around me once more. My warriors of Bolmsö just behind me, we made our way across the field. Leif fell in beside me, his freshly painted green-and-white shield in front of him. Yrsa appeared on my other side.

Grinning, she winked at me.

One more time.

For Odin.

For vengeance.

Hagbard and Haki and their men rushed across the swampy land to meet us. Their warriors formed a line, the two sea kings on horseback at the front. Men with spears, swords, and axes waited for us. These were the same bastards we'd fought at Dalr and Silfrheim and whatever men from Uppsala they had forced into submission. Their numbers were greater now, their hold better. We had been wrong to let them escape Dalr. At the front of the army, I spotted a warrior I didn't know, but his clothing, weapons, and shield marked him out. He, too, was on horseback.

We lined up behind Jorund's men.

"Who is that with Haki and Hagbard?" Leif asked.

"Starkard," Orvar-Odd answered. "Murderous giant. I will have his head before this day is done."

Across the grassy field, I heard Hagbard call, "Archers!"

"Form up," Jorund yelled to us. "Shield wall!"

The thunk of wood upon wood rang in my ears as I fell into line between Yrsa and Leif, Hofund just behind me. Our shields above and in front of us, we braced ourselves for the first volley, which came seconds after that.

I heard the whizzing of arrows as they streaked across the sky and then fell, landing on our shields with cracks. An arrow penetrated the edge of Leif's shield between the two of us. We both looked from the jagged tip, inches from our faces, to one another.

Leif met my eye.

"Attack," Haki screamed.

"Behind me. Now," Jorund yelled at us. "Wedge."

We lined up, forming our warriors into a V-shape.

"Hold," Jorund called. "Hold!"

We waited, watching as the other army came hurtling toward us.

Rök twitched nervously at my side.

"Wait," I whispered to him.

"Archers, up," Jorund called.

In the wedge behind us, warriors lifted the archers who were standing on their shields. The archers shot over our heads at the oncoming army.

Taken by surprise, one of the arrows caught Hagbard in the shoulder. He slowed his horse to a stop to remove the arrow. The rest of the army, not expecting the archers, paused.

"Now! For Freyr! For Uppsala," Jorund screamed.

We rushed forward.

Muninn in one hand, my shield in the other, I rushed across the wet ground toward the advancing army. When our wedge hit them, it was like hitting a wall made of wood and steel. Out of the corner of my eye, I saw Orvar-Odd rush Starkard's horse, cutting the legs of the beast out from under the warrior. The horse toppled over, taking Starkard with him. Jorund and Eric advanced on Hagbard, leaving Haki in our sight.

But *only* in our line of sight.

A mass of men, at least five deep, was between us.

The first warrior who stepped before me wielded a spear. He jabbed quickly, left then right. I moved fast, deflecting the stabs, then rushed him, slamming him in the face with the boss of my shield. He dropped his spear, which was useless in close quarters unless properly wielded, then tried to pull the long dagger from his belt. But he was too slow. With a heave, Muninn chopped him in the neck, downing him.

With a scream, a shield-maiden, her face painted blue, her fire-red hair pulled back in braids, lunged at me. She wielded two swords, spinning them wildly around her. A fierce thing, I fought hard against her. Blocking strike upon strike. I swiped at her with my axe, but she jumped backward, evading the blows.

I whistled.

In a flash, Rök appeared from the fray.

The girl turned for just a moment, taking in the long teeth headed her way, then paused.

It was enough time.

Heaving my axe, I attacked her.

She met the blow, but was too late to stop Rök, who lunged at her throat, throwing her to the ground as he held her neck between his teeth. The moment she hit the mud, I heaved my axe and bashed her head.

*Sleep well, sister.*

*May the Valkyries take you home.*

I turned. My heart was thundering in my chest. I could hear the deafening sound of it beating in my ears. That strange rage took over me. And then, everything became a blur of red.

Tossing my shield aside, I pulled Huginn.

Face after face appeared before me. My body began to move automatically. My arms swung. I ducked and turned, deflecting advances. My hands and clothes grew slick with blood.

But there were so many of them.

I looked behind me, seeing the others in the heat of battle. Kit and Öd were not too far from me, Yrsa near them. They fought bravely. And there, among Grund's men, Thorolf screamed then advanced on another man. I paused for a moment to watch, seeing my own moves in his swings. Using his height to his advantage, he deflected a blow and then struck his opponent with his hammer. Blood squirted from the man's ears, eyes, and nose. He fell lifeless to the ground.

Thorolf turned. He caught my eye for just a moment, giving me a nod, then fought once more.

A fierce warrior advanced on me. From his age and scars, I could see he was a seasoned fighter. But that mean thing that lived within me had awoken. Snarling, I turned on him.

The man paused, taken aback by whatever he saw in my face. Knowing he had underestimated his opponent, he lifted his shield.

But it was too late.

The blood of Bolmsö was awake. And in my heart, the wolf was howling. Twirling my axes, I charged.

The shrill of a war horn caught my attention, pulling me from the trance into which I had fallen. Shaken by the sound, my vision cleared. The warrior I had engaged lay at my feet, his face a bloody pulp. I tuned my ears to the sound of the horn. Across the field, I saw Gizer and his men. Their swords raised, their shields before them, they launched their attack.

I spun around, looking for Haki or Hagbard.

Hagbard was far afield, Jorund and Eric making their way toward him, but Haki was still close. Haki had lost his horse, but given his height, I could make him out above the crowd. I saw the expression on his face change. Before, he had looked confident. Now…

"You men," he screamed, directing some of his warriors to form up. "Shield wall. There. Now," he said, pointing. He waved to the men around him. "Gather. Gather," he called, forming the others in a U-shape around him. On the other side of the field, Hagbard was too busy fighting to hear Haki's call. Had Hagbard even seen Gizer's advance?

Yrsa appeared beside me. She was covered in mud and blood.

"About time," she said, looking toward Gizer.

"Now, where is Harald?" I asked, then looked toward the city. I could make out the limbs of the great tree and see the peaks of the temple and great hall, but there was no sign that Harald's army was advancing from the north.

I scanned around for just a moment, looking for Hofund. He and Kára were fighting back-to-back just down the field from me, Leif not far from them. Deeper in the field, I spotted Bryn's red hair, Jarl Eric not far from her. Trygve and Sigrun rushed to join Yrsa and me.

"Come on," Yrsa said. "We must break Haki's line. We need to help Gizer," she told me then pulled the horn from the back of her belt, sounding it.

The men around us who weren't engaged turned.

"Form up," she called.

I looked over my shoulder, spotting Thorolf. He joined our forces.

He was still alive.

Thank the gods.

Yrsa and I gathered our warriors behind us. A moment later, Orvar-Odd appeared at my side. To my surprise, there was a head on the front of his shield: Starkard. Attached to the warrior's shield by a dagger through the eye, Starkard's agape mouth was a horrifying sight. Orvar-Odd was covered in blood.

"Told you," he said with a laugh when he saw me looking.

I shook my head.

"I want the same," Yrsa replied, her eyes on Haki.

"Then let's get that bauble for you, shield-maiden," Orvar-Odd said.

Yrsa lifted her sword and let out a scream, the rest of us joining her. And then, we advanced.

Haki's men fought with renewed vigor, like men who knew their lives were on the line.